MURDER A LA MOCHA

MURDER A LA MOCHA

Sandra Balzo

This first world edition published 2018
in Great Britain and 2019 in the USA by
SEVERN HOUSE PUBLISHERS LTD of
Eardley House, 4 Uxbridge Street, London W8 7SY
Trade paperback edition first published
in Great Britain and the USA 2019 by
SEVERN HOUSE PUBLISHERS LTD

British Library Cataloguing in Publication Data
A CIP catalogue record for this title is available from the British Library.

ISBN-13: 978-0-7278-8824-2 (cased)
ISBN-13: 978-1-84751-958-0 (trade paper)
ISBN-13: 978-1-4483-0168-3 (e-book)

All Severn House titles are printed on acid-free paper.

Severn House Publishers support the Forest Stewardship Council™ [FSC™],
the leading international forest certification organisation.
All our titles that are printed on FSC certified paper carry the FSC logo.

Typeset by Palimpsest Book Production Ltd.,
Falkirk, Stirlingshire, Scotland.
Printed and bound in Great Britain by
TJ International, Padstow, Cornwall.

For Spike and Terra,
who make life brand new again

ONE

'But how are you going to get back? I have your car and . . . hey!' I punched my brakes and hit the horn simultaneously to avoid the pickup truck that was swerving toward me.

The driver wrenched the truck back into his own lane with one hand, while raising the other in apology for not noticing the Toyota Corolla I was driving in the lane next to him.

Since simultaneous seemed the order of things, I nodded my acceptance of his apology while muttering, 'Idiot.'

'Who?' Sheriff Jake Pavlik's voice asked from the dashboard speaker.

'The truck driver next to me. Honest to God, it's like I'm invisible in this thing. Not that the rain helps.' I checked to make sure my headlights were on and turned up the windshield wipers a notch.

'Invisible in what thing?'

'Your Corolla. I mean, my Escape is fairly cookie-cutter, but I've been cut off half a dozen times by people who don't seem to see me. You have a cloak of invisibility on this thing?'

'I wish you'd stop calling my car a thing. All I want from my Toyota is dependability. For fun, I have the Harley. Besides,' he continued, 'there are so many on the road that they don't attract attention.'

'Which I'm sure is lovely if you're on the job, stalking criminals. But not being seen by other drivers doesn't seem to be a good thing.'

A Volvo zipped past on the right and cut back in a little too close for comfort. I slowed my roll. 'Maybe it's the color. This gray is just too nondescript—'

'Silver.'

Which is really just metallic gray, when you think about it. But we had more important things to worry about. Pavlik's mom had fallen ill at our dinner in Chicago – something

I hoped had nothing to do with our announcing our engagement at that same dinner.

Pavlik and I had driven the ninety miles south from Brookhills, Wisconsin, on Wednesday to spend Thursday with his parents in Chicago and had planned to drive back after our dinner together tonight. It would have been nice to stay another night, but duty called at my coffeehouse on Friday morning with our barista Amy away and just me and my partner, Sarah Kingston, to cover . . .

OK, that's all a lie. Or the start of a lie.

Truth was that Amy had offered to come in and cover for me. I'd turned her down. Meeting Pavlik's folks for the first time was a big step, and even though we didn't stay with them, I thought it best to keep the visit short and, hopefully, sweet. And if it wasn't, I had an excuse for us to leave early. Sophomoric? Maybe. But the introduction to my now ex-in-laws hadn't gone well twenty-some years ago, and I didn't have any higher hopes for meeting my new beau's folks. But I did have an escape plan.

Which I hadn't needed. As it turned out, Peggy and Len Pavlik were perfectly nice people, and I would have been pleased to stay another night as they suggested and have breakfast at their Lakeshore Drive condo before heading back to Brookhills.

But now Amy really was unavailable and here I was at nearly one in the morning driving myself home in the rain, leaving Peggy in the emergency room and Pavlik car-less in the Windy City. All when I really should be there with him. 'Are you and your dad going to stay at the hospital tonight?'

'Until the docs can tell us what's going on, at least. Dad is a wreck.'

I imagined so. From what I could tell, Peggy and Len Pavlik had the kind of relationship that's the stuff of romance novels and country songs. The happy ones. The two had arrived at the restaurant giggling and holding hands. After nearly fifty years of marriage.

In a heartbreaking echo, Len had taken Peggy's hand again as the paramedics wheeled her unconscious out of the restaurant on a gurney. 'Do they think it was a heart attack?'

'Nobody is saying. But Mom said she felt nauseated, remember?'

I did. And then Peggy slipped to the ground as she was getting up from her chair to go to the restroom. 'Nausea can be one of the signs of a heart attack for women. We're different.'

'You decidedly are.' I could hear the smile in his voice. Along with the worry.

'Listen, you go be with your mom and dad. I'll be home in less than half an hour and hopefully Sarah is long gone so I won't have to listen to her complaining.'

'Until you get into work tomorrow morning.'

'I'll have coffee to sustain me. She wasn't thrilled to stay with Frank in the first place and then she had trouble getting online.'

Frank is not my son. Frank is my son's Old English sheepdog. When Eric left for college, Frank and I had eyed each other uneasily and – if I may speak for the both of us – hoped for the best. Now, three years and countless gallons of drool and cubic yards of dog hair later, Frank and I had come to terms. In fact, we were buds.

'I thought you said you were going to ask that Little Mermaid relative of hers. The dog-sitter?'

The 'Little Mermaid relative' was Sarah's niece. 'Her name is Ariel. Ariel Kingston.'

'You'd think I could remember that. Tracey made me watch the movie a hundred times when she was little.'

'Which is probably why you've blocked it. Anyway, I tried Ariel, but she was already booked. Courtney volunteered, but Sarah wouldn't let her stay alone overnight, even at my house.'

Sarah had adopted Courtney Harper and her brother Sam when their mother Patricia – Sarah's best friend and my first business partner in Uncommon Grounds – had died. Ariel was grooming (forgive the pun) Courtney as a dog-sitter-in-waiting.

'Can't say I blame her. Courtney's maybe twelve? And petite. If Frank jumps on to the bed with her when she's sleeping like he does with us, he'll crush her.'

'She's fifteen, though I see your point. Not that Frank

necessarily sleeps with just anybody.' God help us if he tried it with Sarah. 'He likes you.'

'He worshipped me,' Pavlik said, 'until I moved in with you.'

'He's maybe a teensy bit jealous.' Pavlik had come to my place to recover from a gunshot wound in March and now it was July and he hadn't left. To my surprise, I found I liked sharing my abode. Frank was less enthusiastic.

'Frank's not a teensy anything. But it's normal for him to want to mark his territory.'

'That territory being me?' There had been that unfortunate incident with my shoe. I'd assumed it was just inattentive peeing, but—

'Or your bed.'

To my knowledge there had been no lifting-of-leg on my Tempur-Pedic, but it was true that somewhere around midnight each night Frank would launch himself on to it, and us, to shoehorn his hairy self between Pavlik and me. By morning we'd be clinging to opposite edges of the mattress while the sheepdog would be sprawled out, snoring away.

'I suppose it's just pack mentality,' the sheriff was saying. 'He is a dog, after all. Eventually, he'll realize I'm alpha.'

I was about to change lanes and hesitated. 'Wait, *you're* alpha?'

'Bad connection. I said that I'm *an* alpha. Along with you, of course.' The smile was back in his voice.

'Nice recovery.' I moved into the lane at the last second to merge on to the Interstate 894 southern loop around Milwaukee toward Brookhills.

'Thank you. I'll leave you to your inattentive drivers, for now. Be safe.'

'I will. Let me know about your mom, OK?'

'I'll call you as soon as we know something. Or probably text, so I don't wake you up once you get home and to bed.'

'Wake me,' I said.

'If there's something significant, I will.'

'Promise. And we'll also talk about when I should come back to get you.'

'I promise. But I might as well just take the train home

rather than have you come all the way back to get me. You can pick me up at the Milwaukee train station, or I can take the commuter spur out to Brookhills.'

Uncommon Grounds was at the west suburban end of that commuter spur. 'I'm happy to—'

'Hang on.' Muffled conversation and then Pavlik was back. 'Doctor's here so I have to go now, but text me and let me know you got home safe?'

'I will. Love you.' It still felt strange to say.

'Did that hurt?' The man knew me.

'A little,' I admitted. 'But I'm working at getting used to it.'

I'd just punched the 'end call' button on the steering wheel when another call rang through. 'Sarah?'

'I'm leaving.' More snap than greeting.

'I thought you'd left hours ago. I told you I'd be late and there was no reason to stay. Frank will be fine.'

'Frank's barely conscious. Courtney had the bright idea to take him to the new dog park today and he's exhausted. Has the fat hairball ever even seen another dog before?'

'He's not fat,' I protested. 'Just kind of . . . puffy. And of course he's seen another dog. I mean, in passing.' Like the other dog was being walked past the front window while Frank watched from the couch. 'Why?'

'Because he seems to think anything smaller than him is a squirrel.'

I cringed. 'He chased them?'

'Sat on them.'

Better than eating them, in my opinion. 'You're right that he's not used to playing with other dogs. Especially in an open environment like a dog park.'

'You're telling me. A guy from the park had to pull his big butt off a Pekingese. I don't think Frank even knew the thing was there.'

Oh dear. 'Was he or she hurt?'

'Eyes were bugging out and it looked like a flattened dust mop, but Doug said that's how she always looks.'

'Nice.' Sheesh.

'I know,' she said, misunderstanding the tenor of my 'nice.'

'She tried to take a chunk out of Frank's leg, once she got out from under. I'm not sure he noticed that either.'

'The owner isn't going to call the police, I hope?'

'Nah. No blood was spilled.'

Sometimes Sarah's bar for acceptable behavior was so low that you could stumble over it. 'Was he banished for life?'

'From the dog park? Doug let him off with a warning this time; said Frank would learn. I told him, "Not with me, he won't."'

I decided to leave the subject where it lay. Sat. Stayed. 'Well, thank you again for dog-sitting. I'm just approaching the Brookhills exit, so you go home. Frank will be fine until I get there.' I went to press the 'end call' button.

'You don't think I stayed for him, do you?'

I sat back. 'I have no idea why you stayed.'

'When we got back and Courtney left, Frank and I ate dinner and watched a movie.'

'And fell asleep,' I guessed. 'Did you just wake up?'

'One of us woke up. Like I said, the incredible mound of hair and drool is still snoring away. When I saw what time it was, I wondered where the hell you were. You couldn't have called?'

Her tone was meant to be grudging, but I knew there was real concern there. 'I thought you'd be gone, so I was going to tell you tomorrow. Pavlik's mom was taken ill at dinner.'

'He told her you're getting married?'

There's a reason Sarah and I are friends. I'm just not sure what it is. 'No, I mean rushed-to-the-hospital sick.'

'Sorry,' Sarah muttered.

It was about as hard to get a 'sorry' from my partner as it was a 'please' or 'thank you,' so I appreciated it. 'I know.'

'Is Pavlik with you?'

And therefore listening. 'He stayed down there – at least until they know more.'

'Was it a heart attack or stroke?'

'We still don't know. Pavlik is going to call as soon as the doctors can tell them something. You go home now, unless at this point it's easier to just stay.'

I loved my partner, but I was really hoping she'd say no.

'No.' What I assumed were her car keys – already out of her purse – jangled. 'Your cable package sucks, by the way.'

'I just have basic, because I watch mostly movies on DVD or Blu-ray,' I said. 'I have Netflix, though. Did you watch that?'

'It kept asking for your password and I didn't have it. I was relegated to watching network TV.'

Wah, wah, wah. 'You should have texted me. I would have told you there's a folder in my top desk drawer marked "Passwords." Netflix is alphabetized as a sub-category under "Television."'

'Miss Obsessive Compulsive. I didn't want to go pawing through your desk. Especially once I saw what was in your bottom left drawer. What do you alphabetize that little beauty under?'

I felt my face flame. 'You got all the way to bottom left drawer and you don't consider that pawing?'

She ignored that. 'At your desk, Maggy? Really? You don't have a nightstand?'

Actually no, I didn't. 'It's USB.'

'What?'

I cleared my throat. 'It just has a USB charger. And I really don't use it—'

'USB?' Sarah repeated. 'Why would that be? Big market in horny office workers?'

'I . . . well, I don't know. Maybe because it's universal?'

'For travel? Could be, I suppose. God forbid you plug the thing into the wrong voltage and blow off something.'

If I could take both hands off the wheel, I'd put them over my face. 'Can we please change the subject?'

'Fine. Your Wi-Fi sucks, too. Did I tell you that?'

'Yes, in fact, you did.'

'And I couldn't even get into my own Netflix account on my phone because Sam and Courtney were signed in on four devices, which is the most you can use simultaneously on one account.'

'Well, that's not the fault of my Wi—'

But patience and reason went out the window when Sarah was ornery, which was most of the time. 'Four screens? How can two kids watch four screens?'

'Maybe they had friends over,' I said, pulling on to the Brookhills exit ramp.

'More than likely. But why bother if you're each going to be sitting there doing your own thing?'

I felt the need to defend the younger generation. 'But think about it: women used to get together in sewing circles a hundred and fifty years ago and you could have said the same thing about them. Why travel miles only to sit in the same room and sew?'

'Because they were isolated somewhere on the prairie. They were desperate for company besides cows, goats, pigs and their husbands and kids.'

'And presumably they did talk, as they sewed. If . . . damn!' I slammed on my brakes.

'What?'

'Sorry,' I said, squinting off into the dark. 'Something just darted across the exit ramp in front of me.'

'Probably a possum. They're nocturnal.'

'It did have a tail, but it looked thicker than a possum's.' I pulled up to the end of the ramp and stopped at the sign.

'So you saw a rat. And you will see *me* tomorrow.' A woman of few words had apparently said her fill.

'Rats don't have bushy tails,' I said to a dead line. Raccoons did, kind of, but this thing had moved more like a puppy or maybe a cat . . .

There it was again, crossing the grass median from the sidewalk into the parking lot of one of the industrial buildings. The area surrounding the off-ramp was light industrial, all but deserted after hours and on weekends. I pulled the car around the corner and into the lot, trying to keep the small creature in sight, but it passed through the pool of light from the security lamp at the front of the building and disappeared into the shadow of the awning over the entrance.

I had the sense it was frightened, maybe approaching the door in hopes that some human there would let it into the warmth and the light. A raccoon wouldn't do that, right?

Knowing I wouldn't be able to sleep tonight if I'd left some poor lost puppy or kitten out in the chilly, wet night, I pulled the car to a stop in front of the building and reached for the

long black flashlight Pavlik kept in the door pocket. Getting
out, I was grateful the rain had let up. I checked the back seat.
No bite-proof gloves, but I did see a blanket.

Gathering it up and tucking it under one arm, I held the
flashlight at arm's length and approached the deserted building.
Away from the security lamp in the parking lot, everything
was pitch-black, but I thought I could see a huddled mass in
the corner by the door and directed my light that way. Dark
fur, with two eyes reflecting the light.

Pavlik would say this was stupid. So would Sarah. And
anybody else with sense. 'Hey there,' I called. 'You OK?'

As if it was going to answer me. Whatever it was.

But then it did. A whimper that sounded canine to my ears,
though that wouldn't necessarily rule out something like an
urban coyote or wolf pup. I moved closer, hoping there wasn't
a mom around bent on defending her young.

As I eased nearer, the thing darted sideways out of the
corner and flattened itself up against the door. Tiny, furry and
matted, with a ferret-like nose sticking out. 'What *are* you?'

This time I got a bark.

'A dog?' And a terrified one, its eyes cartoon-wide before
they closed against the brightness of the flashlight.

I switched off the light and considered my options as my
eyes adjusted to what little light was filtering into the covered
entranceway. I was afraid the little thing would bolt if I got
too close. Leaving the blanket on the ground, I returned to the
car and retrieved the grease-stained bag I had stuffed in the
cupholder next to my now-empty to-go cup. The bag was from
the pretzel place at the Lake Forest Oasis, one of the travel
plazas on Interstate 94 between Chicago and Milwaukee. I'd
finished most of the soft pretzel sticks but had kept the last
one for Frank. The things were covered with salt and butter.
I'd never checked the calorie count, but I had to believe that
something so good had to be very bad. For both people and
dogs.

Which meant a hungry little pooch shouldn't be able to
resist it.

Dangling the pretzel in its butter-stained bag, I approached
what I'd now determined (hoped, prayed) was a puppy. A tiny

puppy, something I didn't have much experience with, since Frank seemingly had emerged fully formed. He was bigger when Eric had adopted him at two months than this pup was at . . . whatever age it was. I didn't have a leash but, given its size, I planned to coax it to me with the pretzel and then wrap it in the blanket.

The silhouette of the pup slid sideways again as I approached. It was back in the corner, so I stopped, too, and shook the treat bag, something that always brought Frank running. The pup's head tilted in classic curious-dog pose. Encouraged, I squatted down to seem less intimidating. 'Puppy want a pretzel?'

Now I had his attention. I crept closer, crooning as I went. 'That's a good pup, yes, you are. Aren't you a sweet baby? Where's your mama, baby, huh? Huh?'

The poor thing was shaking violently, and as I got closer, I realized that it was not a puppy at all. It was something much, much worse.

A chihuahua.

TWO

All right, all right, settle down. I don't have anything against chihuahuas, except I have to check the spelling every time I use the word. Which could and will get onerous.

But I don't hate even that. Or even the chihuahuas themselves. They hate me.

I was about five when I had my introduction to the first adorable eight-pound bag of furry fury. We were on vacation and stopped to visit the best man and maid of honor from my parents' wedding oh-so-many years ago. I was a 'menopause baby,' as my mother used to say (it sounded better than accident), and by the time I came along, Bud and Elaine had moved away from Wisconsin to Alabama. I'd never met them, and here I was, a neurotic little kid in the first place, and we were staying overnight at these strangers' house and, horror of horrors, I was expected to sleep in their basement rec room with their daughter and a neighborhood girl, who were having a sleepover.

The two girls were a few years older than I was and largely ignored me. But I was excited to see that they had a dog. I loved dogs. Dogs loved me. I went to pet it, and as my hand went out, the daughter screamed, 'No! ChaCha is my dog!'

As if to confirm, ChaCha chomped down, razor sharp teeth imbedded in my thumbnail. He didn't let go until my parents, tipping to the fact that the nonstop screaming below was *not* 'the girls just having fun,' had dislodged him, disinfected the wound and bandaged me up. Bud and Elaine banished the dog ('bad ChaCha!') to the yard to my huge relief and sent us back downstairs to play. That's when insult was added to the injury, with the girls blaming me for ChaCha's exile and snubbing me as only two eight-year-old Mean Girls-in-waiting could manage to do.

I sniffled a bit, but eventually fell asleep semi-secure in the knowledge we'd be leaving first thing the next morning. And morning admittedly came before I knew it. Like about one a.m., when I opened my eyes and froze. Somebody had let ChaCha back in. Not only that, but his nose was no more than two inches from my face. I could have convinced myself that he'd taken a liking to me, if he hadn't opened one eye and let out a low, throaty growl.

I squeezed my own eyes closed and lay motionless for the next six hours until ChaCha finally succumbed to the call of nature and kibbles, and got up on his tiny little legs and toddled upstairs.

I hadn't told anybody that day – not Bud and Elaine, not my parents, and certainly not the Mean Girls – but ever since, I've been cowed by and growled at by every chihuahua I've met. Yes, I know: it's my own fault. They smell fear. And nothing is going to cover that up.

Except maybe, in this case, this little guy's own fear.

He was shaking so badly that he could barely stand. And his terror made me forget mine. 'Come here, baby. Are you hungry? Come get this.'

Hesitantly, he walked toward me. A step, and a vibration that threatened to take him down, then another. He was a long-haired chihuahua maybe mixed with something else. I held out the breadstick and he darted toward me, a sudden movement that frightened me. Seeing that, he backed up, too.

I cleared my throat. 'You don't bite me, I won't bite you.'

He looked at me and then the breadstick.

'Deal?' I set the breadstick on the concrete.

Deal, apparently. The dog pounced on the breadstick as if he hadn't eaten in days, which maybe he hadn't. I took the opportunity of the distraction to throw the blanket around him and bundle him and the breadstick to me.

Ugh. We both might smell like fear, but he also smelled the way Frank did when he found something particularly putrid to roll in. 'You stink – you know that?'

He didn't bother to answer, busy with the breadstick – one paw on each side of it like a raccoon.

'You have a collar.' I rotated the red nylon collar on his neck and it jangled. 'And looky here. A tag.'

I'd left the flashlight in the car when I'd retrieved the pretzel but could just make out *Mocha* in the dim light. The other side was too worn to read anything, if there was anything there to read.

'So, Mocha, what are we going to do with you?' I asked, getting to my feet with him. 'Maybe you have a chip the Brookhills Humane Society can scan, but they're closed.' I could call the police, but the City of Brookhills police department wasn't staffed at night and the call would just bounce to the county sheriff's department.

Pavlik being the sheriff. And in Chicago, of course.

And although it would be light fare compared with the bodies I usually called in, I really didn't want to bother his deputies with a stray dog. They had more important things to do on a Thursday night – or now, early on a Friday morning – than pick up stray dogs.

That, apparently, was *my* job. 'OK, it's been a long day and I'm beat. Let's go home and see what Frank makes of you.'

The ranch house I'd bought after my divorce from Ted is one of the smaller properties in Brookhills and located on the far north end of Poplar Creek Drive. A little run-down, the frame structure is nothing like my sprawling pre-divorce house, but it was paid for and it was all mine. Or now, all mine, Frank's and Pavlik's. Before the sheriff had come to stay, I couldn't even call the place a work-in-progress. More a work-to-be-imagined. Sometime way off in the future. If I had time.

The second week Pavlik had been there, he'd replaced the lime-green toilet, and I think he'd have done it earlier if it hadn't been for that pesky bullet wound. Next up was painting the blue stucco walls in the living room – blue, in his opinion, being an unnatural color for stucco. Now he was contemplating a kitchen remodel. I wasn't sure if all this was in preparation for selling or for his totally moving in.

The 'Should we live in your house, my house, or buy a new "our" house?' discussion was ongoing. Pavlik's house was closer to the sheriff's department and a Cape Cod style. Mine was nearer to Uncommon Grounds and had no style at all.

But I like quirky, as evidenced by both my sheepdog and my choice of business partner in Sarah.

The house was dark as I pulled into the driveway, except for the lamp in the living room. Sarah's car was gone. The stray was curled up on Pavlik's gray wool blanket on the passenger seat next to me, and when he saw me looking at him, he lifted his head and wagged his tail, sending the stench of *eau de* toilet my way.

It figured that the only chihuahua that didn't bite me on sight smelled like a sewer rat. A dead sewer rat. I clamped my hand over my nose. 'Eeew. What did you do, poop yourself and roll in it? And assorted road kill for good measure? You can't go into the house like that.'

Poor thing's bowels probably let loose in terror as he tried to cross the highway. I might be developing a soft spot for the stray, but I couldn't take him into the house in this state. Bad enough that I'd have to fumigate Pavlik's car. And maybe burn the blanket. Or vice versa.

I turned off the ignition and considered. Frank's volleyball-sized head was silhouetted in the living-room window. He'd be waiting at the door when I got out of the car and I didn't want him exposed to . . . Mocha, that was it. Bad enough I had a pint-size stinker on my hands. No way I wanted the stench in the giant economy size.

'We're going to have a bath,' I told the chihuahua.

He looked at me warily. I supposed it was the same way Frank did when I broached the subject, if only I could see his eyes under his floppy fur bangs.

I pulled down the visor and pushed the garage door remote to open it. The garage was detached from the house and set at the back of the lot. I routinely parked on the driveway apron in front of the garage, and as the door lifted, the reason why was obvious. 'I've got to clean out this garage, so I can park in it.' What a novel idea.

But mere cleaning wasn't going to do it, unless I bit the bullet and threw out the boxes and furniture that crammed the one-and-half-car garage. There certainly was no place in the house for the contents of the garage, and now that Pavlik and I were a real couple, there was no place for it in my life, either.

You see, the garage was filled with the detritus of my first marriage – my only marriage up to this point – to Ted, Eric's father. My dentist ex had divorced me to marry his hygienist, Rachel, something I long ago had forgiven . . . No, that's not true either. I didn't forgive Ted for cheating on me with a woman some ten years younger. I didn't forgive him for packing up and leaving me one day after Eric had left us for college. I'd just realized that maybe it had all worked out for the best. I was happy. I had Frank, the coffeehouse and Pavlik. And Ted had gotten what he wanted, only to find out that it – and Rachel – weren't quite what he'd expected.

Frank's silhouette disappeared from the window as he probably trotted to the door to wait for me to come in. I took the opportunity of his absence to hop out of the car and come around to get the little stinker out of the passenger seat. My overnight bag in the trunk could wait for now.

Mocha's head went up again as I swung open the door, his tail now doing tentative figure eights.

'Don't worry,' I said. 'There's a utility sink in the garage and warm water.'

Dog in arms, I felt for the switch just inside the door and turned on the fluorescent ceiling fixture, for all the good it did. Boxes and furniture were stacked nearly to the rafters, blocking the light and creating shadows. As I slipped between a blue floral sofa and dark sideboard with etched mirrors, Mocha whined.

'I know,' I said. 'What was I thinking, keeping all this stuff? I won't live long enough for it to come back into fashion.' If late nineties department store chic ever made a return.

'But,' I said, shoving a box with my foot so I could switch on a bedroom lamp sitting on top of an old microwave cart, 'the furniture served its purpose. A couch to sit on while I nursed Eric. A cabinet to hide away Ted's mother's crystal.' Which he now had custody of. Thank God.

These days I not only didn't want the stuff from my pre-divorce house, but I made it a practice only to put things I loved in the current one. And if I couldn't find just the right nightstand at a resale shop or antique store? Well, I'd just use a borrowed folding TV table for now.

'For now' had been two years.

But then blending households with Pavlik would change all that.

I set Mocha in a white plastic laundry basket and plugged the sink before I turned on the water and adjusted the temperature.

On the clothes dryer next to the sink was the shampoo I used for Frank. For the sheepdog, though, I connected a hose and ran the warm water out the side door of the garage where he could stand on the concrete stoop while I lathered him up. 'Lucky you. You'll fit in the sink.'

I picked up the chihuahua and separated him from the blanketing. 'You're sticking a little.'

Unstuck, he sprung out like a cartoon cat trying to get a paw on each side of the sink. 'It's warm water,' I told him. 'You'll like it.'

Like hell he would. He bared his teeth and snarled at me.

Startled, I dropped the little dog in the water and backed away from the sink, hands palm-out.

Astonished to find himself in two inches of water, Mocha got to his feet and shook.

I backed up further.

The chihuahua whimpered and waggled a hesitant tail.

'Don't give me that,' I said. 'I'm not the one who just threatened to bite the hand that fed me hot pretzels.'

Another little whine and now he had his front paws on the edge of the sink.

'OK, fine,' I said, daring to get close again. 'I know you're scared, but you need to stay put so I can get you clean.'

Slipping one hand under the dog's belly, I settled him back into the water. 'Hey, you're a girl.'

In the dark, I'd just assumed male, probably because Frank was a boy. Not that the sheepdog and the chihuahua even appeared to be the same species.

A deep-throated *Ruff?* from the house signaled that Frank was at the door and getting impatient.

'He's not going to know what you are,' I said, squirting shampoo on Mocha's back. 'You're maybe five pounds, soaking wet, and Frank is a hundred, plus whatever he's eaten that day and hasn't pooped out.

'This sure isn't going to take long, compared with him.' I worked the shampoo into a lather and toward the little dog's back end. 'Argh. What's this?'

Having a sheepdog, I'd dealt with my share of snarls. But this one was monumental in comparison with the size of the dog. And, undoubtedly, it was the source of the stench. 'You're matted with dried poo back here, baby.'

I worked the warm water into the tangle, but the shampoo had met its match. 'Hang on a second. I have a comb here.'

Taking a fine-tooth comb from the back sink lip, I picked at the snarl with it, trying to be gentle.

But apparently not gentle enough. Mocha gave a yip and turned to snap at me.

I put down the comb.

'I think I'd better cut this out for both our sakes. I'll be right back.' I held up a hand, palm out. 'Stay.'

Mocha sat her matted butt down in the water with a cock of her head. 'Arrh?'

Taking her at her word, I made a beeline for the house. Then I realized my purse was in the car and doubled back to get my keys out of it.

Unlocking the door, I braced myself for Frank's happy dance. 'Don't jump. I'm happy to see you, too, but—'

Whoosh. The sheepdog was past me and out the door before I could form the next word. Dropping my keys, I ducked my head into the kitchen to grab the scissors from the junk drawer and dashed out after him. 'Frank! Leave the puppy alone.'

But the sheepdog had already disappeared into the garage. A crash, followed by a pained whine.

'Stay, Mocha!' I called, running for the garage. I didn't think Frank could get at the little dog if she stayed in the sink. Not that the sheepdog would intentionally hurt Mocha, but, given what Sarah had said about the dog park, I couldn't be sure he wouldn't sit on her.

Another crash, this one followed by a yelp as I stuck my head in the door. By the patchy light of the fluorescent tube, I could see past the couch to the sink. No Mocha.

A throaty growl. 'No, Frank!'

Circumventing the couch, I tried to locate the source of the sounds. 'Frank? Mocha?'

A high-pitched whimpering now, from behind a brown corduroy recliner in the corner. It had been facing out in the upright position, but now it was reclined. Mocha's poundage couldn't have done that, but Frank's tonnage certainly could, trapping the smaller dog in the corner behind it. 'Off, Frank! Do you hear me? Let the puppy up.'

Reaching across a box, I pulled the chair back into the upright position.

Frank was huddled whimpering in the corner. A few feet away Mocha lounged on a cocktail table, tidying herself with a self-satisfied air.

THREE

'Shame on you,' I said to Frank. 'A big dog like you, afraid of a little dog like Mocha.'

He gave me a 'puh-leeze' look and he was right. When it came to unreasoning chihuahua fear, I was the human pot calling the canine kettle chicken.

As I picked up Mocha, she threw my poor sheepdog a disdainful look.

That look disappeared as I plunked the chihuahua back into the bath water. 'Now that you two have met,' I said, pulling the scissors out of my pocket, 'let's get you poo-free.'

Snipping off a section of matted fur, I held it up to the light.

Something moved.

'Argh!' Kicking open the door into the yard, I tossed the hunk out into the night. I turned back to the little dog. 'You have fleas?'

She cocked her head and then, as if she'd just remembered, sat down abruptly and scratched, sending water everywhere.

I stepped out of the line of fire. 'I saved that butt of yours and you bring fleas into my house? Or at least my garage?'

Mocha had the grace to look embarrassed.

I picked up the shampoo bottle. A small miracle – it was flea shampoo.

'You are lucky, missy,' I said to the dog. 'If we didn't have flea shampoo, you'd be sleeping in Pavlik's car tonight.'

Which, come to think of it, was probably already flea-infested. As was the blanket I'd carried Mocha in.

I scratched at my arm. And me.

Poo was bad enough, but—

'Frank!' The sheepdog had finally moved from his corner, sliding sideways to try to make his escape by way of the door through which I'd just thrown the matted, flea-filled tangle. I slammed the door shut. 'Use the other door, mister. With a bit of luck, you didn't get close enough to her to pick up anything. We'll get rid of the flea-wad tomorrow.'

Mocha whined.

'I'm not talking about you,' I said to the chihuahua.

Frank looked crestfallen.

'Don't worry, we'll get Mocha back where she belongs, too.'

Or so I hoped.

Frank was waiting on the concrete porch steps when I approached with Mocha under one arm and dragging a metal dog crate with the other. I was wearing one of Pavlik's T-shirts and nothing else.

Frank took two steps back.

Since he'd seen me naked and had outgrown the crate when he was less than three months old, I knew he wasn't scared of either.

'It's OK,' I told the sheepdog. 'Mocha is going to spend the night in the crate.'

This would set both our minds at ease. The sheepdog could be sure he wouldn't be mauled by the tiny dog, and I wouldn't wake up with visions of flea circuses dancing in my head.

I'd bathed Mocha twice more, leaving the flea shampoo on for the five minutes the label suggested. I'd also washed the blanket in hot water, along with her nylon collar. Both were in the dryer now and I'd stripped and put my clothes in the washer and pulled on Pavlik's shirt from the 'clean and dry, but not folded' basket.

I was still feeling itchy, so a hot shower and shampoo were in order in the very near future for me, as well.

Opening the door of the house, I pulled the crate just into the living room. In a perfect world, with a dry dog and a nicer night, I could have left Mocha in the crate on the porch. Unfortunately, there really was no porch, just concrete steps up to a stoop, and the roof overhang wouldn't provide much protection from the rain that was threatening again. The garage was another option, but I felt bad leaving the frightened little thing out there alone.

Meanwhile, the frightened big thing sidestepped me, the

sheepdog giving me wide berth as I swung open the wire door.

I set Mocha in the crate and closed the door. 'You stay here, and I'll get the blanket, so you'll have something soft to lie on.'

The dog eyed me forlornly from behind the bars.

Feeling a twinge of guilt, I went to the garage to fetch Pavlik's now-clean blanket and Mocha's collar. When I got back, Frank, apparently emboldened by Mocha's incarceration, was sniffing the crate. Mocha's lip just curled in the start of a snarl as she caught sight of me.

The lip dropped and tail wagged. Frank backed off anyway.

'You're a wily little thing, aren't you?' Opening the door of the crate, I gave the long-haired chihuahua a good scratch behind the ear. Now that she'd begun to dry, her light brown and black coat was fluffing out around her neck and her tail was thick and luxuriant, curling up and over her back. 'I can see why they call you Mocha. You're pretty cute now that you're clean and dry – you know that?'

Frank groaned and collapsed by the couch.

'Not to worry,' I told him, spreading out the blanket so Mocha could lie down. 'We're not going to keep her.'

Frank didn't look reassured.

I closed and latched the crate door.

Frank sniffled.

'Aww, Frankie,' I said, sliding over to the sheepdog. 'First your space is invaded by Pavlik and now this.' I lifted the hair so I could see his eyes. 'You know you're still my main man, right?'

He licked my face.

'Good.' I let the hair drop. 'Oh, I forgot to put Mocha's collar back on.' Picking it up, I squinted at the tag again. The back was worn nearly smooth, but I thought I could just make out seven digits. 'Yes! A phone number.'

I glanced at the clock. Nearly two-thirty in the morning. Way too late to call the owners. Maybe a text? There was no guarantee that the number on the tag was a cell phone, but if it was, the good news that Mocha had been found would be waiting for her owners when they woke up.

If the cell didn't wake them when the text came through. 'That's a chance I'm willing to take. I'd want to know you were safe, no matter what time it was,' I told Frank, texting.

'Found Mocha and she's fine. Call or text after six a.m.,' I read back. 'Sound OK?'

Frank didn't opine.

I hit send and my cell phone rang. 'Well, that's odd.'

A photo flashed onto the screen. Pavlik. I'd forgotten to call or text when I got home.

'I'm so sorry,' I said into the phone. 'I completely forgot to call you.'

'That's all right.'

'No, it's not. But I picked up a poor little stray dog in the industrial park and—'

'You—'

'I know. It was probably silly of me, but she was so afraid.' I was debating whether I should tell him about the fleas, given it was his car and all. 'I was careful. Even took your big flashlight in case something jumped out at me.'

'That's good, but—'

'I know I should have called anyway. I'm just not used to having somebody worry about me, I guess.'

Silence on the other end.

'Not that I don't love it.' Still nothing. 'And you,' I added, fearing I'd broken some kind of cardinal couple rule and should make amends.

But then maybe it was the connection that was broken. 'Pavlik? Are you there?'

'Yes,' the voice on the other end said. 'Sorry, but . . .'

The sheriff let the sentence fade off, and I got a sick feeling in the pit of my stomach. 'Jake? Are you all right? Is it your mother?'

'Mom died about an hour ago.'

FOUR

Margaret 'Peggy' Pavlik had died at one twenty a.m. as the result of an apparent second heart attack, this one massive. 'Even being right there in the hospital, there was nothing they could do,' I told Sarah on the phone at seven the next morning.

'Are you going down there?' she asked. 'I should be fine here on my own.'

'Pavlik said I should wait to hear from him. I guess there are arrangements and all, and maybe it's easier without me there.'

Sarah had heard something that I didn't think I'd said. 'Don't tell me your feelings are hurt.'

I thought about that. 'No, not really. I mean, it's important for him to focus on his dad right now and what he needs. I guess I just don't know what's the right thing.'

'The right thing?'

I was feeling foolish. 'As a couple. I mean, should I ignore what Pavlik said and go down anyway to be by his side? Is that what a fiancée does?'

'Got me,' Sarah said, against the backdrop sound of steaming milk. She must be making herself a latte. 'But I wouldn't take my cues from those old movies you watch.'

Given that the last one I'd watched was *Gaslight*, I'd try not to.

'The sheriff doesn't strike me as the mixed-signals type,' Sarah continued. 'If he says he wants you to come later, he probably means just that. Not that he secretly expects you to don a white dress and track him down to fling yourself into his arms.'

Apparently, Sarah's last movie had been *Under the Tuscan Sun*. And while it was true that Diane Lane's decision to throw romantic caution to the wind and surprise Marcello hadn't gone as she'd expected, the movie did have a happy ending.

Although I've always thought the handsome stranger showing up in the last frame was a little . . .

But I digress. 'Amy is on vacation and you can't handle things alone. Friday's a busy day.'

'They'll wait,' Sarah said. 'Do what you have to.'

'I may drive down this afternoon, but what I have to do right now is return this dog to its owners.'

I'd told Sarah about finding Mocha, to which she'd said, 'Better you than me.'

And she didn't even know about the fleas.

Which reminded me. I needed to stop at the pet store for flea spray for Pavlik's car. I'd showered last night and again this morning, and washed everything that had been in hopping distance of the little flea bag, but the Corolla was a bigger problem. I figured I'd fumigate it and use my Escape in the meantime.

I picked up my keys. 'I texted the number on the tag last night and the owner had the dog-sitter just call me. Guess who it is?'

'Somebody who isn't doing a very good job, obviously,' Sarah said, suddenly irritable. 'Damn, you made me spill my shot.'

I hadn't made her do anything. Ever.

But I let it go. 'Your niece, Ariel. Which explains why she couldn't stay with Frank.'

'And I had to,' Sarah said dryly. 'Thank you very much, the two of you.'

'You're welcome. Anyway, she offered to come here, but I told her I'd drop Mocha off on my way to Uncommon Grounds.'

'Go home and shower in between. I don't want fleas.'

'Mocha doesn't have fleas.' It was the truth, as of two a.m. As far as I knew.

'Stray dogs have fleas. They roll in shit.'

I didn't know if she meant the latter literally or figuratively, like 'stuff.' Either way, though, I couldn't dispute it. 'I gave Mocha a flea bath, just in case. She's flea-free.'

'Sure, tell yourself that. It takes months to get rid of fleas. Hope you didn't let her sleep in the house.'

forest and no one is around to hear, it can still give you a headache.

'I'm very sorry if I caused your headache, Mr Lyle,' Ariel said, edging toward the house. 'I'll be sure to keep it down from now on.'

Ariel seemed anxious to get away from the neighbor, and I needed to get to the shop or suffer my own sonic attack from Sarah. And Bruce Willis had nothing on her.

But Lyle was still going. 'I'll prove my theory to Satterwite – or the police, if he won't listen to me – one way or another. There are microphones for detecting infrasound. An app, even.'

Now there was a surprise.

'I must run,' I said, catching Ariel checking her watch again.

'Got to get on with my day, too,' Lyle said, turning to head back down the path to his house. 'Good talking to you.'

'Same here.' Ariel didn't sound all that convincing.

'If you figure out where those firecrackers came from,' he said over his shoulder, 'let me know. I'm about to call the police.'

'I'm sure it's just kids,' Ariel called after him.

He waved his hand over his head and kept going.

'I'd hate for anybody to get into trouble,' Ariel said, a line etching her forehead.

'Don't worry. Nobody is going to jail for shooting off firecrackers.'

'Mr Lyle likes to complain about everything, but especially noise. George spent thousands of dollars soundproofing their movie room just so the Lyles wouldn't be bothered.' She was looking around frantically. 'Oh, dear. Where's Mocha gone now?'

'Into the garage,' I said.

'Oh, that's right.' Ariel was hurrying toward the front door. 'Thanks again for bringing her back, Maggy,' she said, turning. 'She's just a bundle of nerves, poor thing.'

The chihuahua wasn't the only one, I thought as the door closed behind Ariel.

'So what?' Sarah handed me a five-pound bag of coffee beans. 'Weren't you young once? A very long time ago.'

I let the comment go without pointing out that it was an even longer time ago for her. 'What does that have to do with the neighbor accusing her of sound-blasting him?'

'Nothing. I think Ariel was upset because you caught her boyfriend sneaking out,' Sarah said.

'The guy in the garage?' I tipped the beans into the bin marked *Sumatran* and handed her back the empty plastic bag. 'But Ariel's not a sixteen-year-old babysitter – she's an adult. What do I care if she has a sleepover?'

'I don't know.' Sarah was trying to stuff the stiff plastic bag in the already full recycling container under the service counter. 'Maybe she thought you'd tell the owners.'

'Yet when I assumed the guy *was* George Satterwite, Ariel glommed on to it.'

'Glommed on to it?' The bag popped back out and on to the floor.

I picked up the plastic and handed it back to her. 'Glommed on to my suggestion that he'd just gotten home.'

'Maybe he had.'

'I thought you just said it was her boyfriend that I saw.'

'That was my suggestion, and you' – she stabbed the bag down one side of the container – 'glommed on to it.' The plastic slipped out again.

'You could just take it out, you know.'

'It *is* out.' My partner stooped to pick up the bag and then leveled a stare at me. 'I thought you wanted me to put it in.'

'I meant you could take out the recycling. You know, instead of trying to stuff more into this container, you could empty it into the dumpster outside.'

'But then I'd have to *go* outside.'

Yes. Yes, she would. But yesterday's rain was past, the skies were sunny and the temperature was July warm. Still, as when dealing with a kid, there were times when it was just easier to do it yourself. I took the bag from her. 'I guess it could have been George.'

Sarah's eyes went exaggeratedly wide. 'You mean somebody was actually telling you the truth? What a novel idea.'

It was. 'But why wouldn't he come out and thank me for rescuing Mocha?'

'Maybe he doesn't like the little hairless ball.'

'Good attempt at a joke, but this is a long-haired chihuahua. Kind of cute. And, besides, a Mexican Hairless is an entirely different breed to a chihuahua.'

'What do I know?' Sarah said, shrugging. 'You're the one who wastes two full nights on that Westminster show.'

Westminster Kennel Club Dog Show LIVE from Madison Square Garden! It was Frank's and my favorite time of the year.

'It's interesting,' I said defensively. 'If you watched, you'd know, for example, that chihuahuas are only one of the breeds with Mexican ties. In fact, there's some thinking that the Chinese Crested has DNA—'

'Now you're just messing with me.'

I shrugged and picked up the recycling basket. 'Fine. Don't be educated,' I said, going to the back door. 'But if you're so smart, tell me one thing.'

'What?'

Opening the door, I stepped out. 'Tell me why Ariel said what we heard were firecrackers, when I'm pretty sure they were gunshots.'

The door closed behind me.

'I hate it when you do that.'

'Do what?' I asked my partner.

'You know what. The dramatic exit.'

'Keeps your attention.' I slid the now-empty basket under the counter. 'Besides, it wasn't much of an exit. I'm back already.'

'Sure, for Act Two.' Sarah waved me over to a table.' Tell me what you're talking about.'

'OK, but—' I stopped and cocked my head. 'Where is everybody? I know I missed the morning commuters heading downtown, but shouldn't the senior crowd be here by now?'

'Brookhills Manor is having some sort of festival today. Food and drink is free, which means we're likely to see nary a codger.' Sarah shrugged. 'Besides, their numbers are down anyway. Deaths, arrests . . .'

It was always my fault. 'I—'

'I'm just saying it's bad for business,' Sarah continued, undeterred. 'Now tell me about your newest crime.'

'I didn't say there was a crime.' I poured two cups of coffee.

'Only that there was a gunshot.'

'Gunshots, plural.' Setting one cup in front of my partner, I sat down across from her with the other. 'Or at least I think they were gunshots. They have a flatter, less echoey sound to me than firecrackers.'

'And the corpse-stumbler would have heard enough to know.'

Corpse-stumbler was one of many of Sarah's less affectionate nicknames for me. 'I haven't heard anybody actually get shot, you know.'

'I guess "corpse," by definition, is already dead when you find it.'

'Come on,' I said, taking a sip of hot coffee before setting the cup down. 'You'd know the difference between a firecracker and a gunshot, too. I've only been to the firing range with Pavlik, but you own a gun. In fact, the first one I actually saw close up was yours.'

And thank the Lord she'd had it.

'You're welcome,' Sarah said, as if she'd read my thoughts. 'What's your point? You say you heard a gunshot that Ariel – innocent that she is – mistook for a firecracker. That's not unusual.'

She was right. The sheriff's department regularly got reports of gunshots that turned out to be firecrackers or fireworks. And vice versa. 'My point is who's shooting guns in broad daylight in Brookhills?'

'Your sheriff was just shot at a Brookhills senior center and you're asking me that?'

I leaned forward across the table. 'I guess I'm just worried, Sarah. About Ariel.'

Sarah sat back, reclaiming her personal space. 'Why?'

'This.' I pulled the crumpled napkin out of my jeans pocket and flattened it out. 'I think this is blood.'

Sarah pulled the napkin toward her and studied the smudge of reddish brown. 'Maybe. But what does it have to do with Ariel?'

I closed my eyes. And opened them. 'I'll see you by seven thirty.'

All the way to Mocha's house, I was scratching at imagined flea bites. George and Marian Satterwite were Mocha's parents, according to Ariel, and they lived in a nice, if homogenous, neighborhood called Pinehurst. Their house was a big white colonial with pillars, surrounded by a whole lot of other big white colonials with pillars. 'You must have gotten the fleas while you were lost, 'cause I doubt they allow them here.'

In reply, the chihuahua flipped sideways and started licking herself.

'I think you're pretty clean after those three baths, but have at it.'

As I turned into the driveway, though, I caught a whiff of something. 'Geez, Mocha. That better be a fart.'

The little dog got up and circled on the passenger seat, sniffing her butt.

'Did you poop?' I asked, rolling down the window.

'Oh dear.' Ariel was hurrying up to the car and must have heard me. 'I'm so sorry, Maggy. She has IBS.'

'Irritable bowel syndrome?' I asked, as Ariel swung open Mocha's car door. 'I didn't know dogs could get that.'

'Oh yes,' she said, bundling the little dog out. 'When she gets nervous.'

'Well, she's home now, so all is well.' I climbed out of the car and came around to give Ariel a hug.

'Thanks to you. I wish you would have let me come pick her up.'

'Dropping her off wasn't a problem. And it's always good to see you.' I wiped a smudge off her cheek with my thumb.

'Thanks, Mom,' she said with a grin, swiping at her face. Like the mermaid Ariel, this one was petite, but her hair was brown, not red. And no fins or tail.

'Sorry, once a mom always a mom.' I pulled a crumpled napkin out of my jeans pocket and offered it to her. Without spitting on it, I might add.

Ariel shook her head. 'Mocha is always a nervous wreck when George is out of town. Marian travels internationally, so Mocha is used to her being gone for extended periods. But when Dad is gone too, puppy gets worried. Right, Mocha?' She gave the pooch a smooch. 'We make lots of poops.'

Lovely. I wiped my own hand on the napkin and stuck it back into my pocket. 'One other thing – she must have picked up fleas on her jaunt. I washed her with flea shampoo last night, so hopefully she's not going to infect the household.'

'Oh, thank you, Maggy.' She glanced back at the house and set the dog down. 'I was so worried when she went missing last night.'

'Just last night?' Given Mocha's bedraggled condition, I'd assumed it had been longer.

'Yes, around eleven or so.' She saw my face and blushed. 'You're thinking about the fleas. I'm so sorry about that. I thought we'd gotten rid of them.'

I glanced again at the immaculate white house. 'You mean, Mocha already had fleas when she ran away?'

'About a month ago, but you know how it is. You have to keep de-fleaing everything – not just the dog, but the house and grounds – over and over, to get rid of the eggs and larvae and all.'

I tried to control my shiver. Meanwhile, Typhoid Mocha was joyfully sniffing a viburnum bush next to the open door of the house.

'George didn't want Marian to know,' Ariel was saying, 'which made it more difficult to treat.'

'Mrs Satterwite didn't know her dog had fleas?' What was I being so superior about? I hadn't mentioned the fleas to Pavlik.

'This was while she was gone on a trip, and George thought it best. Poor Mocha would have been relegated to the crate on the porch. And Marian would undoubtedly have blamed the Lyles' dog, Harry.' Ariel gestured toward the path that led around the house and to the property beyond. She put her hand up to shield her mouth, as if the neighbors would be able to hear from there. 'Ryan Lyle can be a little difficult, so—'

The sound of the Satterwites' garage door opening interrupted her. Mocha scooted in underneath it and I caught a glimpse of the bumper of a brownish vehicle and a man's khaki-clad legs before the door reversed course and went right back down again. 'Oh, is Mr Satterwite home?'

'No. I mean yes.' The girl seemed nervous all of a sudden. 'Yes, just got home.'

I cocked my head. 'The reason I ask is that I may have to go back down to Chicago today for a few days, and if one of the Satterwites is back, I thought you might be available.'

'To sit?' Ariel looked relieved. 'Yes. I mean no. I mean not immediately. I have somebody else that . . .'

I took pity and waved her off. 'Not to worry, I'll work it out. Just glad I found Mocha's home.'

'Oh yes, and me, too. I'm so grateful, Maggy. I've just been so upset—'

POP! Pop!

We both jumped. Inside, Mocha yipped, then another nearby dog started up howling, then another and another, until we had a veritable canine cacophony of assorted yapping and yelping.

'The neighborhood kids and their firecrackers,' Ariel said. 'They think it's funny that it drives the dogs crazy, but it's just plain cruel.'

A man of about fifty came hurrying up the path from the house behind the Satterwites'. 'Did you hear that? Harry's hiding and whimpering like a little puppy, which is no small feat for a hundred-and-ten-pound German shepherd.'

'Firecrackers,' Ariel said. 'It's so inconsiderate.'

'Any idea which way they came from?' he asked, a little out of breath.

'It seemed to echo all around,' Ariel said. 'Didn't you think, Maggy?'

'I—'

'Ryan Lyle.' The man stuck out his hand.

I shook it. 'Maggy Thorsen.'

'Maggy found Mocha.' Ariel was glancing at her watch. 'She ran off last night.'

'I saw your post on the message board. Glad she's back safe.' He rubbed his forehead. 'I had a pounding headache again last night. Was it movie night?'

I was confused by the non sequitur, but Ariel seemed to

know where he was going with the question, if not necessarily how to answer it.

'Yes.' Her eyes shot sideways and then back. 'But the back door of the theater was closed, and I'm sure I had the acoustical drapes pulled.'

'You did, but that doesn't necessarily stop the infrasonic noise. Just the masking mid and upper range.' Ryan Lyle turned to me. 'Infrasound is low frequency sound that's below the range of human hearing. It's been known to cause illness.'

The term seemed familiar. 'Isn't that one of the theories for the symptoms the diplomats at our Cuban embassy experienced? Some sort of a sonic attack?'

'Exactly.' He turned back to Ariel. 'What movie was it, may I ask? And when?'

'*Death Wish.*' Ariel seemed uncomfortable. 'Between ten and midnight, maybe?'

'I'll see if I can find its decibel level,' Lyle said, pulling out his phone.

'But Mr Satterwite—'

'Thinks I'm a hypochondriac,' Ryan Lyle said. 'I know. And likely Becky and Harry, too. But the fact is we're sick with headaches and nausea nearly every night. And George Satterwite doesn't want to admit he's responsible.'

'For noise you can't hear?' It was none of my business, but I couldn't help running a little interference for Ariel, who had simply watched a movie. Something I dearly loved to do myself.

Lyle didn't take offense at my question. 'I know it sounds counterintuitive, but apparently this low frequency sound can travel long distances – they call it propagating – and your body reacts to it, even if your ears don't consciously pick it up. There's plenty of research on the subject all over the internet.'

There were a lot of things all over the internet. 'But how would you ever know if you can't hear it?'

'That's just the problem,' Lyle said. 'You feel unwell and don't know why. You might suspect the air quality in your house or an allergy or a virus, but never—'

'A sound you can't hear.' Apparently if a tree falls in a

forest and no one is around to hear, it can still give you a headache.

'I'm very sorry if I caused your headache, Mr Lyle,' Ariel said, edging toward the house. 'I'll be sure to keep it down from now on.'

Ariel seemed anxious to get away from the neighbor, and I needed to get to the shop or suffer my own sonic attack from Sarah. And Bruce Willis had nothing on her.

But Lyle was still going. 'I'll prove my theory to Satterwite – or the police, if he won't listen to me – one way or another. There are microphones for detecting infrasound. An app, even.'

Now there was a surprise.

'I must run,' I said, catching Ariel checking her watch again.

'Got to get on with my day, too,' Lyle said, turning to head back down the path to his house. 'Good talking to you.'

'Same here.' Ariel didn't sound all that convincing.

'If you figure out where those firecrackers came from,' he said over his shoulder, 'let me know. I'm about to call the police.'

'I'm sure it's just kids,' Ariel called after him.

He waved his hand over his head and kept going.

'I'd hate for anybody to get into trouble,' Ariel said, a line etching her forehead.

'Don't worry. Nobody is going to jail for shooting off firecrackers.'

'Mr Lyle likes to complain about everything, but especially noise. George spent thousands of dollars soundproofing their movie room just so the Lyles wouldn't be bothered.' She was looking around frantically. 'Oh, dear. Where's Mocha gone now?'

'Into the garage,' I said.

'Oh, that's right.' Ariel was hurrying toward the front door. 'Thanks again for bringing her back, Maggy,' she said, turning. 'She's just a bundle of nerves, poor thing.'

The chihuahua wasn't the only one, I thought as the door closed behind Ariel.

'So what?' Sarah handed me a five-pound bag of coffee beans. 'Weren't you young once? A very long time ago.'

I let the comment go without pointing out that it was an even longer time ago for her. 'What does that have to do with the neighbor accusing her of sound-blasting him?'

'Nothing. I think Ariel was upset because you caught her boyfriend sneaking out,' Sarah said.

'The guy in the garage?' I tipped the beans into the bin marked *Sumatran* and handed her back the empty plastic bag. 'But Ariel's not a sixteen-year-old babysitter – she's an adult. What do I care if she has a sleepover?'

'I don't know.' Sarah was trying to stuff the stiff plastic bag in the already full recycling container under the service counter. 'Maybe she thought you'd tell the owners.'

'Yet when I assumed the guy *was* George Satterwite, Ariel glommed on to it.'

'Glommed on to it?' The bag popped back out and on to the floor.

I picked up the plastic and handed it back to her. 'Glommed on to my suggestion that he'd just gotten home.'

'Maybe he had.'

'I thought you just said it was her boyfriend that I saw.'

'That was my suggestion, and you' – she stabbed the bag down one side of the container – 'glommed on to it.' The plastic slipped out again.

'You could just take it out, you know.'

'It *is* out.' My partner stooped to pick up the bag and then leveled a stare at me. 'I thought you wanted me to put it in.'

'I meant you could take out the recycling. You know, instead of trying to stuff more into this container, you could empty it into the dumpster outside.'

'But then I'd have to *go* outside.'

Yes. Yes, she would. But yesterday's rain was past, the skies were sunny and the temperature was July warm. Still, as when dealing with a kid, there were times when it was just easier to do it yourself. I took the bag from her. 'I guess it could have been George.'

Sarah's eyes went exaggeratedly wide. 'You mean somebody was actually telling you the truth? What a novel idea.'

It was. 'But why wouldn't he come out and thank me for rescuing Mocha?'

'Maybe he doesn't like the little hairless ball.'

'Good attempt at a joke, but this is a long-haired chihuahua. Kind of cute. And, besides, a Mexican Hairless is an entirely different breed to a chihuahua.'

'What do I know?' Sarah said, shrugging. 'You're the one who wastes two full nights on that Westminster show.'

Westminster Kennel Club Dog Show LIVE from Madison Square Garden! It was Frank's and my favorite time of the year.

'It's interesting,' I said defensively. 'If you watched, you'd know, for example, that chihuahuas are only one of the breeds with Mexican ties. In fact, there's some thinking that the Chinese Crested has DNA—'

'Now you're just messing with me.'

I shrugged and picked up the recycling basket. 'Fine. Don't be educated,' I said, going to the back door. 'But if you're so smart, tell me one thing.'

'What?'

Opening the door, I stepped out. 'Tell me why Ariel said what we heard were firecrackers, when I'm pretty sure they were gunshots.'

The door closed behind me.

'I hate it when you do that.'

'Do what?' I asked my partner.

'You know what. The dramatic exit.'

'Keeps your attention.' I slid the now-empty basket under the counter. 'Besides, it wasn't much of an exit. I'm back already.'

'Sure, for Act Two.' Sarah waved me over to a table.' Tell me what you're talking about.'

'OK, but—' I stopped and cocked my head. 'Where is everybody? I know I missed the morning commuters heading downtown, but shouldn't the senior crowd be here by now?'

'Brookhills Manor is having some sort of festival today. Food and drink is free, which means we're likely to see nary a codger.' Sarah shrugged. 'Besides, their numbers are down anyway. Deaths, arrests . . .'

It was always my fault. 'I—'

'I'm just saying it's bad for business,' Sarah continued, undeterred. 'Now tell me about your newest crime.'

'I didn't say there was a crime.' I poured two cups of coffee.

'Only that there was a gunshot.'

'Gunshots, plural.' Setting one cup in front of my partner, I sat down across from her with the other. 'Or at least I think they were gunshots. They have a flatter, less echoey sound to me than firecrackers.'

'And the corpse-stumbler would have heard enough to know.'

Corpse-stumbler was one of many of Sarah's less affectionate nicknames for me. 'I haven't heard anybody actually get shot, you know.'

'I guess "corpse," by definition, is already dead when you find it.'

'Come on,' I said, taking a sip of hot coffee before setting the cup down. 'You'd know the difference between a firecracker and a gunshot, too. I've only been to the firing range with Pavlik, but you own a gun. In fact, the first one I actually saw close up was yours.'

And thank the Lord she'd had it.

'You're welcome,' Sarah said, as if she'd read my thoughts. 'What's your point? You say you heard a gunshot that Ariel – innocent that she is – mistook for a firecracker. That's not unusual.'

She was right. The sheriff's department regularly got reports of gunshots that turned out to be firecrackers or fireworks. And vice versa. 'My point is who's shooting guns in broad daylight in Brookhills?'

'Your sheriff was just shot at a Brookhills senior center and you're asking me that?'

I leaned forward across the table. 'I guess I'm just worried, Sarah. About Ariel.'

Sarah sat back, reclaiming her personal space. 'Why?'

'This.' I pulled the crumpled napkin out of my jeans pocket and flattened it out. 'I think this is blood.'

Sarah pulled the napkin toward her and studied the smudge of reddish brown. 'Maybe. But what does it have to do with Ariel?'

'It was on her face. I wiped it off with my hand, thinking it was make-up or something, and then wiped my fingers on this napkin. She also seemed nervous. And there was the man in the garage.'

Sarah stood up abruptly. 'Are you saying you think he hit her?'

'Honestly?' I stood up, too. 'I don't know. But I can't get it out of my head that she seemed anxious to get back inside. So I left.'

'And now you wonder.' She fished in her apron pocket and came up with her phone, putting it on the table. 'Let's give her a call.'

She punched up the contact.

'A-r-i-*a*-l?' I read upside down as the call rang through. 'Isn't it *e*-l?'

'Now you're telling me how my niece's name is spelled?'

It was a bit of a sore spot because I was constantly correcting my partner's spelling on our menu boards, where Guatemalan was just as often 'Guatamalan', cinnamon was 'cinamon,' and Reuben (the sandwich), 'Ruben.'

'No. But I know the Little Mermaid character is spelled with an "e," and I assumed Arial was named after her.'

'Shows all you know.' Bumped to voicemail, Sarah picked up the phone and snapped, 'Call me! Now!'

'Maybe she's busy and can't answer,' I said.

'Too busy being beaten up?'

'Try a text.'

'Fine.' Sarah tapped in a message and then turned her phone so I could see. 'It's this font.'

'"Call me NOW," I read. 'Looks all right to me, though I hate all caps.'

Sarah gave me an exasperated look. 'She was named after the font.'

'Arial. Got it.' I wasn't about to ask why. Or how.

Sarah told me anyway, still punching away. 'Her father supposedly worked at IBM.'

As if that explained it all. Although maybe it did, since I had some vague recollection that, unlike print typefaces like Times Roman and Helvetica that have been around for years,

Arial was developed for the computer.

Finished with the text, Sarah stood up. 'Let's go check on her.'

I felt as if I'd put a freight train in motion. 'You haven't given her a chance to reply. Maybe she's just fine.'

'Even if she does come back to me and says she's OK, we can't be sure she's not doing it under duress.' Sarah already had her apron untied.

I followed her to the office. 'Are we closing?'

Sarah slipped on the long, baggy jacket that she always wore with her trousers and started rummaging through a desk drawer.

I tried again. 'Should I put up a sign saying we'll be back in twenty minutes?'

My partner found what she was looking for and turned. 'Maybe a little longer.'

She had a pistol in her hand.

FIVE

'And *I'm* dramatic?'

Sarah was driving her yellow 1975 Firebird and I was riding shotgun. Or just 'gun' in this case. Sarah's purse – with the little semi-automatic – was on my lap.

'What?' she said. 'Aren't you the one who says that women need to trust their instincts more? That when something feels wrong, it might be because it *is* wrong. We're trusting your instincts.'

With a gun in our collective purse. 'Maybe my instincts suck.'

Sarah downshifted as we approached the corner. 'So? There's nothing to be lost. We'll say "hi" to Arial. Tell her we were talking about her and decided to stop by on our way home from work.'

'At noon.'

'OK, on our lunchbreak.'

Sarah tossed me a look as we made the turn on to the Satterwites' street. 'What a ninny you are.'

Not usually. But I did have trouble trusting my instincts, as Sarah put it. Which was why Pavlik had given me the 'trust yourself' lecture that I'd shared with Sarah. Oh, it was fine to get a feeling or suspect something. Toss it around in my head. Ruminate. Conjecture. Theorize.

But to actually act on it? With a gun?

'That's the house,' I said, pointing. 'We're not taking this gun in there, are we?'

The Firebird slid to a stop on the street behind a Volkswagen Beetle. 'Of course not. I brought it along to leave it in the car.'

'Oh, good,' I said, setting the purse on the floor.

'You don't understand facetiousness?' Sarah said, reaching over the console for the purse. 'Since when?'

'So sue me for wanting to believe you were sincere.'

I handed her the purse and swung open the door. We still had a gun, but at least I wouldn't be carrying it.

Sarah unzipped the side of her bag and stuck her hand in it as we hurried up the driveway.

I grabbed her arm. 'You are not going to pull that gun out.'

'No, I'm going to leave it inside the purse.'

'Enough with facetious.'

'That wasn't facetious.' She turned, hand still in the bag. 'This is a concealed carry bag. There's a little opening I can shoot through, see?' She poked the barrel out and wiggled it.

I put my hand to my forehead and looked around to see if anybody was watching us. No human beings on the street, but a taxi was just turning the corner. 'For God's sake, put that thing away. A car is coming.'

Sarah grinned. 'Is that a pistol in your handbag or are you just pleased to see me?'

Deep breath. 'Why in the world did you buy a purse you can shoot people through?'

'Not *through*. That's the whole point.' She beckoned for me to start walking again. 'No reason to ruin a perfectly good purse by shooting it. Besides, your gun could get hung up. Or start a fire.'

'In your purse?' I was staying put where I was. 'There is no reason for you to have a gun. We're not in the Wild West.'

'I didn't hear you objecting when I arrived at your front door that day, gun in hand.'

'I didn't object because I was terrified. I thought you were going to shoot me. Didn't you notice my hands in the air?'

Sarah shrugged and kept walking. 'I thought it was gratitude. You know, a "praise God" kind of thing.'

She rang the doorbell.

I stood behind her feeling a little silly now that we were here in this ordinary neighborhood – actually, much nicer than ordinary – standing in front of this also much nicer than ordinary house. Why had I gotten Sarah worked up enough to bring a gun of all things? 'For all we know, the Satterwites have a cat, too, and he scratched Arial. And the guy I saw in the garage was George Satterwite coming home and he just didn't want to talk to anybody. Don't you ever feel like that?'

'If I say yes, will you shut up?' Sarah snapped.

Which reminded me that I didn't hear Mocha inside. Either she was the first dog I've ever met who didn't bark at a door-bell or it hadn't rung. Reaching past Sarah, I pushed it again. This time I heard the chime, but still no sounds of life from inside. 'Nobody home. Maybe George drove Arial home and Mocha is with them.'

'Arial has a car.' Sarah took her hand out of the bag and hiked a finger. 'It's that Beetle we parked behind. She must be here.'

'You know, I don't think this door is . . .' I touched the door and it swung open.

'Can I help you?' a voice behind us asked.

A dark-haired woman in a white linen business suit was standing on the walkway, trailing a small roller-bag.

'Yes, we were just looking for Arial Kingston.'

'We understand she's dog-sitting here,' Sarah said, hand back in her purse. 'And you are?'

'Marian Satterwite.' She was frowning. 'Was that door open?'

'Yes,' I said. 'Nobody was answering the bell, so I went to knock on the door and it swung open.' It was mostly true, except for the knocking part.

'Well, that's odd.' She stepped past us into the white marble foyer, beckoning for us to follow.

Trusting woman. We might be axe murderers. Or have a gun in our purse.

'I'm just back from Sydney,' she said, rolling the carry-on to one side and setting her purse on the foyer table. Also white marble. 'But George should be here, which means Arial may already have left.'

'But her car—'

Marian interrupted Sarah and said to me, 'Aren't you that coffeehouse owner, Maggy something or other?'

'Thorsen,' I said, putting out a hand. 'And Sarah Kingston here is my partner. Have we met?'

'Not really,' Marian said. 'But I went to your shop – your old shop before the shopping center collapsed in that freak May snowstorm. Who could have imagined?'

'Not us,' Sarah said.

What really had happened that day was a long story. Much longer than we had time to get into here. 'We've reopened in Brookhills Depot. You'll have to stop by again.'

'Thank you, I will. And thank you, too, for taking such good care of Mocha.'

'Oh,' I said, surprised. 'You know about that.'

'Of course,' she said, picking up her purse. 'That's why I recognized you. I had a text from Arial saying that Mocha had run off and you'd brought her back. So good of you. Let me give you something for your trouble.'

The woman thought she was being nice, but I was a little offended. 'Not necessary. I have a dog, too, and I know you'd do the same for Frank if he was in trouble.'

She'd already set down the bag and was going through a stack of mail. 'And what kind of dog is darling Frank?'

'An Old English.'

She cocked her head, puzzled.

'Old English Sheepdog.' Lest she think I was talking about the furniture polish.

'Oh, yes.' Her nose wrinkled. 'Such a big dog. Whatever do you do with him?'

'Do with him?' I asked. 'I'm not sure what you mean.'

'Well, a dog like Mocha can go anywhere and no one seems to object. I imagine with a real dog like yours – the size, all that hair – that's not so true.'

A real dog? What did she think Mocha was? 'It's true that Frank would make a terrible purse dog.' As I said it, I chin-gestured to Sarah's own purse. The gun muzzle had poked back out.

She tucked it back in and zipped up.

'Anyway,' Marian said, setting down the mail and turning. 'I can call Arial, if you like, and see where she is.'

'No need,' Sarah said. 'I've got her number.' And yours, Sarah's tone said.

But Marian just smiled graciously. Of course it would be graciously. The woman was wearing a white linen suit that wasn't even wrinkled. Living in an immaculate house. Dissing my giant hairball.

But her dog was the one that had fleas, I reminded myself 'Let's just check the theater before you go,' Marian was saying. 'Arial wouldn't have heard the bell from in there.'

'She did mention the theater when your neighbor stopped by,' I said.

'Not Ryan Lyle, I hope.' She had started down the hall, clearly expecting us to follow. 'George built the room at the back of the house and insulated it so it wouldn't disturb the neighbors, but he didn't take Ryan's overactive imagination into account. Oh dear,' she said, pausing to scuff at a spot on the floor with the toe of her pump. 'Mocha must have tracked something in.'

I had to squint to see the tiny paw prints tracking down the hall toward the front door. Frank's were more platter-size.

'Anyway,' she said, continuing on to a wide double-door entrance that only needed a marquee to complete the picture. 'It doesn't look like Arial is here, but you must see this room. It's George's pride and joy. We met at a movie studio, you know, in Los Angeles. He was in production on a film I was doing.'

'You're an actress?' I was studying her face, trying to figure out if I should know her.

'Heaven's no. Wardrobe and costume design. I loved it, but then we moved here.' She shrugged. 'I stayed in fashion, but as a buyer now.'

'Which is why you travel so much, I suppose?'

'Yes. I—' She stepped into the room and screamed.

SIX

The theater room was maybe twenty feet wide by thirty feet long with an enormous screen at the far end of it. Thick curtains partially covered the windows and a door on the back wall of the room. The dozen or so white leather recliners that were scattered around the perimeter made the recliner in my garage look like a poor, tattered relation. These had push buttons and mahogany cup holders. A cashmere coat was draped casually over the arm of one, making it look especially natty.

But it was what was lying on the white marble floor in the center of the room that had our attention.

A man was sprawled face down there in a pool of coagulating blood. As Sarah and I hesitated near the door, Marian stumbled to him and knelt. 'George,' she wailed, pulling him into her arms with difficulty. 'Dear God, please . . . Oh!'

She jumped up and back, letting her husband's bloody head slide down and hit the floor unceremoniously.

'Nice,' Sarah whispered to me. 'Talk about adding traumatic insult to fatal injury.'

'Give the woman a break,' I whispered back. 'She just found her husband's body.'

'A stiff,' Sarah agreed. 'Literally.'

'But he's not!' Marian Satterwite exclaimed, turning.

'Sure he is,' Sarah said. 'The shoulders are rigid and the arms—'

'I see it and it's disgusting. But it's not George.'

Sarah and I cocked our heads in tandem. 'No?'

Marian Satterwite was backing away from the body. Her formerly immaculate suit had a wide slash of red down the front from the man's bloody head. 'I have no idea who this man is.'

I was studying the body. 'He's wearing cargo pants.'

Sarah looked sideways at me. 'You're getting way too used

to this sort of thing when that's all you have to say in this situation. Did you also notice a chunk of this guy's forehead is blown off?'

'I'm not critiquing his fashion choice. Just wondering if it's the man I glimpsed in the garage.'

'He was wearing cargo pants?' Sarah asked.

'I assumed they were khakis because I only saw him from the knees down. But they could just as easily have been cargo pants, I guess.'

'Yeah,' Sarah said. 'These pockets are above his knees, so—'

'Will you two stop!' Marian exploded. 'There's a dead man bleeding on my floor.'

'From the looks of it, he's pretty much done bleeding,' Sarah said. 'And what do you want us to do about it? It's your house.'

'You should call nine-one-one,' I added helpfully. 'From your landline, if possible.'

But Marian was looking around. 'Where is my husband?'

'Again,' Sarah said, 'it's your house, your husband. How should we—'

'I'm not sure,' I said, interrupting. Marian had had quite a shock, no matter who the dead man was. She didn't need to deal with my partner's prickliness. 'When Arial and I were speaking, I noticed a man in the garage and asked if your husband was home. She said yes, hesitantly.'

'Hesitantly?' Marian seemed bewildered. 'Why?'

'I don't know, and maybe I even imagined the hesitation. But at the time I thought she might have had an overnight guest and didn't want to admit it.'

Marian's eyes opened wide. 'The "overnight guest" being this man?'

I lifted my shoulders and dropped them. 'Maybe. I just had a quick look at somebody in the garage with a car.'

'A car? We have an SUV. A Lincoln Navigator.'

Of course they did. I held up my hands. 'Car, SUV, motor home, whatever. All I saw was a flash of bumper. Kind of raisin-colored.'

She frowned. 'Perhaps burgundy velvet metallic?'

Sure, why not. 'I guess.'

'That's our Navigator.' She started out of the room. 'Then George *is* home.'

'Weren't you going to call nine-one-one?' I was following her back up the hall toward the door, Sarah on my heels.

'The man is clearly dead,' she said over her shoulder. 'We can't help him. I'm concerned about my husband.'

'Who may have killed the man who is clearly dead,' Sarah muttered from behind me. 'And where the hell is Arial?'

Who may know the whereabouts of the husband who may have killed the man who is clearly dead.

Taking a right at the foyer, Marian pushed through a door and we followed her into the garage. 'It's gone.'

She was right. There was no giant raisin SUV or khaki-legged man: just a little white Mercedes and no man. I assumed the Mercedes was Marian's. She seemed to favor white.

Speaking of the absence of color, Marian looked down at her skirt and saw the red streak, now darkening a bit at the edges. 'Oh, yuck.'

That was putting it mildly.

'Your husband must have taken the Navigator,' I said. 'Did he know the man in the theater, do you think?'

'I think that I don't know,' Marian snapped. 'I told you. That man is a stranger to me.'

Yet he was dead in her house and her husband, assuming he had come home, had taken off again in the car either voluntarily or involuntarily.

Marian seemed to read my mind. 'Just what are you insinuating?'

'That your husband might have killed the guy in the theater and then scrammed in the Navigator. It's what she does.' Sarah shrugged. 'Is somebody going to call the police?'

'It really should be her.' I gestured toward the homeowner.

'I don't have my phone,' she said. 'And we don't have a landline.'

Likely story. And the cell was probably with her purse and the wheelie bag in the front hall not twenty feet away. 'Fine, I'll call.'

'It *is* kind of your department,' Sarah said.

'But Pavlik is in Chicago . . . Oh, no,' I said. 'I forgot to call and see how he's doing.'

'Who is Pavlik?' Marian asked Sarah as I pulled out my cell.

'Boyfriend.'

'Seriously?' Marian said. 'There's a dead man in the house and you're going to call your boyfriend?'

OK, enough. 'First of all, as we've been saying—'

'Ad nauseum,' Sarah supplied.

'The dead man is in *your* house.'

'And her boyfriend is the sheriff.' Again, from Sarah.

'*And* his mother just died. But fine.' I held up my hands in mock surrender. 'Let me forget him and everybody else and their needs and dial nine-one-one for you.'

I placed the call and, after talking to Dispatch, slipped the phone back in my pocket. 'I think I'll wait to call Pavlik when I have some privacy.'

'You don't want to tell him you're standing over another body?' Sarah asked.

'Not until I'm no longer doing so.'

'Well, thank you anyway,' Marian said, sounding subdued. 'And I'm sorry about your boyfriend's mother.'

'Thank you,' I said politely. 'The authorities will be here soon. We'll want to tell them about your husband's car.'

'You mean the fact that you say it was here and now it's gone?'

'And apparently so is he,' I said.

'I don't understand,' Sarah said. 'Marian, you didn't know the Navigator had been here when we walked into the house with you, right?'

'Yes.'

'So you couldn't have known your husband was home. Why did you jump to the conclusion that he was the dead guy?'

It was a good question, I thought.

Marian didn't agree. 'It wasn't exactly a leap. George was due home this morning and there was a man lying on the floor of my husband's home theater.'

OK, maybe Marian wins. 'Your husband took the Navigator on his trip, then?'

'Yes, drove to Minneapolis, if you can believe it.'

I could, since Eric went to school at the University of Minnesota in Minneapolis. I regularly made the five- to six-hour trip myself, as did Eric. He was usually on the five-hour end, me on the six.

'I told George he should fly,' Marian continued. 'It's not like we don't have the money. And besides, I have the miles and tons of upgrades.'

'Maybe he just likes to drive.'

'That, and he likes the flexibility of driving, he says. It does come in handy, I suppose.'

Sarah was beckoning us back into the main house, her phone in her hand. 'Arial's still not answering her cell. Maybe we should go through the house. If she walked in on the killer, she could be lying hurt somewhere.'

'Or maybe she caught a stranger in the house and shot him herself,' Marian said, stepping into the foyer. 'I should see if any of my jewelry or art is missing.'

'I suppose it's possible the man was a thief,' I said. 'But if so, it's more likely Mr Satterwite caught him in the act. Arial was outside with me when we heard the shots.'

Mrs Satterwite's head snapped back. 'You were here when this happened and didn't report it?'

Says the woman who made *me* call nine-one-one. 'Arial thought it was the neighborhood kids with firecrackers. But now – after the fact – I do wonder if what we actually heard were shots.'

Truth was I didn't wonder. I was certain. I had even been certain at the time. Why *hadn't* I done something?

'What time was this?' Marian asked.

'Maybe seven-fifteen this morning.'

'What was this man doing in our house at that time of the morning? Arial must have invited him, the slut.' The last word seemed to have slipped out.

'Hey,' Sarah said. 'That's my niece you're talking about.'

Marian cocked her head and peered at Sarah. 'Who are you and why are you here?'

'She's my business partner,' I explained. 'And your dog-sitter's aunt.'

A raised eyebrow. 'Quite the coincidence.'

Not really. It was the reason we were there. 'If I were you, I'd hope somebody else was in the house besides your husband and the victim when Arial and I heard the shots.'

'What do you mean?' she asked. 'Who else would there be?'

'I have no clue. That's what I was asking—'

'For Pete's sake, do the math,' Sarah said to her, leapfrogging me. 'Two people would be your husband and the dead guy. Meaning Maggy is right and hubby killed anonymous here and took off.'

Marian put her hands up to her ears. 'I won't listen to any more of this. For all you know, George is out there somewhere in danger.'

'At the hands of a third person. Which is exactly what I was trying to get to,' I said. 'Have you checked your phone?'

Now she did go to her purse and retrieve her phone. 'There's nothing from George.' Her eyes got big as she turned to me. 'Or did you mean I should check it for a call from the kidnapper?'

'I'm just thinking of all the possibilities,' I said. 'Do you and George own a gun?'

'Way to slip in the loaded question,' Sarah whispered.

'Of course we don't have a gun,' Marian said. 'Who asks a question like that?'

Sarah held up her hands. 'Hey, there's a dead guy in the room at the end of the hall with his head blown off. Somebody has a gun.' She tucked her bag a little more securely under her arm.

Marian opened her mouth to answer, but then turned on her stacked heels and stalked off down the hall toward the theater.

Sarah and I followed, but when Marian took an abrupt left before we got there and then disappeared into the first door on the right, we hesitated.

A door slammed hard. Sarah shrugged. 'Must need a bathroom break.'

Or more likely a Sarah break. 'You should lock that gun in the car before the sheriff's department gets here.'

'You think they're going to search me? It's registered. And I do have a concealed carry permit.'

I gestured to the theater. 'Man with head wound.' Then to her. 'Woman with gun.'

'Ballistics won't match, but I take your point. Thing is, I wanted to look around for some sign of Arial before they get here, and we don't have much time. I just keep thinking she might be here somewhere needing our help.'

I nodded, understanding. I hoped the gun wouldn't be an issue, but if it was, we'd deal with it.

Trying to move quickly, we took a right where Marian had taken a left and found two guest bedrooms. In one, the bed had been stripped of its sheets and pillowcases.

'Arial's room?' I guessed.

'Probably,' Sarah said. 'Besides being a pain in the butt, my sister is spooky clean. Probably the prototype for the original Stepford Wife. She pounded it into Arial.'

In addition to naming her after a typeface. But Sarah's problems with her sister aside, it seemed only considerate of Arial to have stripped the bed and maybe thrown the sheets in the wash, knowing that the Satterwites were coming back today. 'I don't see a suitcase or overnight bag, do you?'

'No, but maybe she'd already tossed it in her car. She uses the VW like a rolling closet.' Sarah's own car was immaculate.

I stuck my head in the adjoining bathroom. 'A few things still in here. Toothbrush, toothpaste – the stuff you throw in your bag last minute.'

'Unless a killer grabs you first.'

Or you're in a hurry to leave the scene of a crime, I thought. But whose crime? Not Arial. She'd been with me.

The other guest room shared the same bathroom and had been turned into an office. The computer was on, and I couldn't help but take a peek. 'This is one of those message boards where people talk about what's going on in their neighborhood. You know, what roadwork is being done, whose dog ran away . . . Oh, yes – here's Mocha. Arial must have posted it last night when she went missing.'

I scrolled down. 'And here's one posted today headed

"Firecrackers" and another about a peeping Tom.' I clicked again. 'Damn, it's not letting me any further. I need a password.'

'Can you use this?' Sarah tapped her finger on a sticky-note next to the computer with two possibilities: Satterwites2 and Mochalicious.

'Cute.' I tried them both. 'No, that's not it, but—'

We heard a toilet flush on the other side of the house. 'You're wasting time.'

Pumping neighbors for information was seldom a waste of time, but Sarah was right in this case. 'Maybe I can join with a made-up address from my own computer later.'

'Wonderful. How about we check the closet for my niece's body in the meantime?'

I swung open the door and found nothing but winter clothes. 'All clear. Just a spare closet. Let's see what's down that other hallway.'

'Besides Marian?'

'Yup.' We tapped on the half-open door that Marian had disappeared through and it swung open on the master suite. Creeping in, we saw a bed that had either been made or hadn't been slept in at all. The duvet, the pillowcases, the throw cushions – everything looked crisp and fresh. A hallway off the bedroom yielded his and her closets on each side.

'This is bigger than your living room,' Sarah said, sticking her head into one.

'No, it's . . . well, OK, maybe it is.' I mentally measured rooms by how many Franks would fit. Lying Franks, of course, took up one and half times a sitting Frank. My living room was an eleven-lying-Franker. I'd put Marian's closet at a thirteener, give or take a foot.

At the end of the closet corridor was a door. 'The master bath, I presume?' I whispered to Sarah. As if in confirmation, the sound of running water started up.

'Let's get out of here.'

I hesitated. 'She shouldn't shower before the detectives see her.'

'Wanna rap on the door and tell her?'

'I think not. Come on.' We tiptoed out of the bedroom, careful to leave the door half-closed as we'd found it.

We had time to retrace our steps to the other side of the house, where we checked the kitchen and pantry. We were in the laundry room – sheets on top of a load of darks in the hamper waiting to be washed – when the doorbell rang. 'Brookhills Sheriff's Department,' a voice called.

'Let her get it,' Sarah whispered.

'She may be in the shower.'

'Washing off the evidence.' Sarah peeked out the door toward the foyer. 'You want to tell your sheriff's deputies that?'

'Not really, but—'

The click-clack of Marian's heels down the opposite corridor interrupted, and we waited until she'd sailed into the main hallway before following.

Relieved to see that Marian was still wearing her soiled suit, I exchanged looks with Sarah as the homeowner opened the door.

'Thank goodness you're here, officers.'

They were Brookhills County sheriff's deputies, as opposed to City of Brookhills police officers, but the deputies at the door didn't correct her. Two crime-scene technicians followed them in and we stood aside as Marian led them to the theater room.

In the pool of sunlight from the open door, I noticed more of the tiny paw prints Marian had pointed out in the corridor. 'Huh.'

'Huh, what?'

I bent down. 'I think this is blood.'

'You sure?' Sarah went to scratch at one of the prints with her fingernail, and I slapped her hand. 'Oww.'

'No touching. We've already broken enough rules. And no, I'm not sure, but it sure looks like dried blood to me.'

'They're leading to the door. Doesn't the faithful dog stay and stand guard over the body?'

'Depends on the dog. Frank would be stepping over my body to get to the pantry.'

'Better than eating you.'

That was true. I might not care at that point, but his reputation would take a hit. Eat your master and you could pretty much kiss finding a good home goodbye.

'Maggy?' Detective Mike Hallonquist had followed the deputies in.

'Hi, Mike,' I said, straightening. 'You remember Sarah Kingston?'

'Sarah,' Hallonquist said, touching his hat. 'I understand you called this in, Maggy.'

Mike's a nice guy. He didn't even add 'again.'

'I did. But as a favor to the woman who owns the house, Marian Satterwite.'

'She found the body,' Sarah said.

Hallonquist seemed pleasantly surprised. 'You weren't here?'

I can't lie to law enforcement. 'We may have been standing behind her.'

Sarah gave me a disgusted look. 'At least ten feet. She screamed before we even got into the room.'

'And what room would that be, ma'am?' The question came from a female detective, who'd just come in and closed the door behind her.

The woman was tall, maybe six feet, with gray-blonde curls and, like pretty much any other investigator I'd come across, a notebook in her hand. I didn't think I'd ever seen her before.

'The home theater at the end of this hall,' I said.

'Detective Cindy Angles,' Hallonquist said, 'this is Maggy Thorsen and Sarah Kingston. They own the local coffeehouse.'

'Nice to meet you, Detective Angles.'

'Same,' she said with a nod.

No 'Call me Cindy,' but I didn't expect it. This was business.

'Detective Angles is my new partner,' Hallonquist said.

Hallonquist's last partner had taken his own life. It had been tough on everybody in the department, but Mike, of course, more than anyone.

'You have a good one here,' I told Angles, nodding to Hallonquist.

Her stance softened just a bit. 'No question about that, ma'am.' She was studying me. 'Maggy Thorsen. The name is familiar. Have we met?'

'Are you new to the department?'

'Yes.'

'Then probably not,' I said.

'Give yourself time.' I'd forgotten Sarah was there.

'Maggy is . . .' Hallonquist looked at me for help.

'I'm . . . Jake Pavlik's fiancée.'

Sarah's mouth dropped. 'Is that the first time you've said it out loud?'

'Pretty much,' I said. 'Which reminds me that I need to call him.'

'I heard about the sheriff's mother,' Hallonquist said. 'Give him my regards and we'll talk after you get off the phone.'

The door swung open again and we moved aside to let two more technicians with plastic bins pass by. 'Of course. Though I think I'll wait to call when I get home.'

'She doesn't want to tell him she's stumbled over another body,' Sarah said.

'I'll tell him,' I retorted. 'Just not from the crime scene.'

'Smart.' Angles cracked a grin as she flipped the page on her notebook.

Evidently, my reputation had preceded me.

SEVEN

We filled in the detectives as we moved in pairs – Sarah and Angles ahead of Hallonquist and me – to the theater room.

Since I considered Joe Friday's 'Just the facts, ma'am' pretty good advice when speaking to investigators, I kept it short. Finding Mocha last night, my visit this morning to return her, the man and car in the garage, the firecrackers or shots and, then, our return to make sure Arial was all right and the subsequent discovery of the body.

'You've never seen the victim before?'

I shook my head. 'Any ID on him?'

'Of course not. That would make it too easy.'

Meanwhile, Sarah was talking to Angles. 'I have no idea where Arial is, but damn right I'm worried. She could have walked right into a murder after Maggy left.'

Angles made a note. 'I assume she has her cell phone with her. Do you have the number?'

Sarah fumbled in her purse for her phone, probably not wanting to accidentally pull out the semi-automatic instead.

I came to her rescue. 'I talked to Arial this morning, so I have her number in my recent calls.' I punched it up and showed it to Angles.

She wrote it down.

'I did try to call her maybe half an hour ago,' Sarah said, taking advantage of my diversion to pull out the cell and shove the gun to the bottom of the purse. 'No answer.'

'But it did ring?' Angles asked.

Sarah nodded.

I had a thought. 'Maybe Arial left her phone in her car out front.'

'We've already been through it,' Hallonquist said. 'Lots of stuff, but no phone.'

'We can track down the phone even if she doesn't answer,' Angles said. 'We'll keep you posted.'

'She means they'll use her phone to find the body,' Sarah said when the two detectives crossed the room to talk to Marian.

'It's one possibility.'

Sarah's eyebrows shot up. 'Way to be reassuring, Maggy.'

I put my hand on her arm. 'If I said anything vaguely reassuring, you'd have accused me of being a Pollyanna or lying to you.'

'Well, yeah. Maybe.' She shrugged my hand off. 'But you could have tried.'

'Fact is, Arial could have been taken against her will. Or she could have had something to do with the murder and run away – with or without the murderer, who might or might not be George. Or, third possibility, Arial is totally oblivious to what has happened and is out with the dog.'

'Which is getting less and less likely as time goes on.'

She was right. How far could Mocha's little legs have taken her, especially after last night's adventure? 'Maybe they walked to the dog park?'

'From what you said, the rat doesn't even like other dogs.'

'She doesn't like Frank, which is different.'

'Because he's not a dog's dog? I'll grant you that.' Sarah leaned against a polished cherry column about four feet tall and the thing slid sideways.

'Careful. That's a very expensive speaker, I think.' Given the amount of sound equipment in the room, Ryan Lyle's complaints didn't seem quite as ridiculous. 'I wouldn't be leaning on it, if I were you.'

As Sarah stepped away from the thing, the front grill fell off, clattering to the floor.

Marian Satterwite flinched, but didn't turn from the conversation with Hallonquist and Angles. 'And I texted him from the international arrivals lounge in San Francisco yesterday morning. Such a relief to be able to shower and change after a long flight, but then I had the flight to Chicago and then yet another to Milwaukee. That last flight was canceled, of course. Those puddle-jumpers are canceled more than they fly.'

'Fix this,' Sarah hissed, picking the grill up.

Angles glanced at us over her shoulder and then turned her attention back to Marian. 'You were supposed to get back last night, then?'

'Yes. But, as I said, I ended up having to stay over in Chicago.'

'I hope the airline put you up in a hotel,' Angles said.

Marian shivered. 'I wouldn't call it a hotel. At least I'd carried on my luggage, so I had clothes and toiletries with me.'

Angles smiled and shook her head. 'However do you do that? I barely fit enough clothes in my carry-on for a weekend in Madison.'

Marian shrugged. 'You almost have to, when you travel as much as I do. It's so much safer than checking if you have to change flights.'

'I suppose that's true,' Angles said. 'But I'm still impressed. And what about your husband?'

'He checks, mostly. Or drives.'

'I meant when was the last time you heard from him?'

'Oh,' Marian said, embarrassed. 'I had a message when I landed in Chicago saying he had to stay in Minneapolis an extra day but would be driving back this morning. Of course, when I saw the man on the floor, I just assumed . . .'

Sarah nudged me with the grill. 'Take this.'

I took the thing, knowing that shushing her so I could eavesdrop would just earn me a thundering 'Why are you shushing me?' As I went to put it back on, it sucked right out of my hand and on to the speaker front. 'Magnetic.'

'What will modern science think of next?' Sarah said. 'Now shush.'

'. . . From Minneapolis,' Angles was saying. 'Do you know when he sent the text?'

'It could have been anytime while we were in the air between San Francisco and Chicago, because I got the message around six when we landed. It was a group message to both the dog-sitter and me, though, so her phone might have an exact time.'

'If we could find her.' Sarah was poking at what looked like a shiny black futuristic microphone lying on the top of the speaker. 'What's this?'

'It's a diamond tweeter,' Marian said loudly. 'And don't you dare touch it again or George will kill you.' Realizing what she'd just said, she put her hand to her mouth and looked at the detectives. 'I didn't mean that.'

'Of course, you didn't,' Cindy Angles assured her. 'And honestly, I wouldn't blame him if he did. Those are Bowers and Wilkins speakers, aren't they?'

'They are,' Marian Satterwite said, seeming surprised. 'But I'm afraid that's pretty much all I know, other than not to touch them. George is the audiophile.'

'And if you like dogs, cats and goldfish, does that make you a pet-o-phile?' Sarah whispered to me.

This time I did shush her. 'Put Manic Mary back in the box, will you, please?'

'That's hurtful,' Sarah said, not looking at all hurt. 'I didn't ask to be bipolar.'

'No, but you sure take advantage of it at times. You can't just say anything you want.'

'I kind of can.'

'Well, you shouldn't. Now shush!'

That earned me an over-the-shoulder glance of my own from Angles.

'. . . Nowhere near that level,' the detective was saying. 'But I can tell that this is a sweet system. You have B and W subwoofers, too?'

'Four. One in each corner,' Marian confirmed. 'It's overkill, given the size of the room and the proximity of the neighbors. The acoustic curtains help some, but then he couldn't resist adding those.' She pointed up.

'Height channels,' Angles breathed, as if she'd just discovered a pot of gold floating overhead instead of four round ceiling speakers.

'Geez,' Sarah said. 'The detective is a little over the top on the subject of speakers, don't you think?'

'She's bonding with Marian,' I whispered. 'She's no rookie.'

'The gray hair didn't tell you that?'

'Her age doesn't necessarily mean she's not new at being a detective.' I was examining what Marian had called the acoustic curtains.

'Looking for a place to hide?' Sarah said.

'Wondering how much noise these would block. The sound of the bullets was pretty clear, but then Arial and I were standing right outside the house and the front door was open.'

At Arial's name, Sarah's brow furrowed. 'Think they'll put out an APB?'

'Probably. For both George Satterwite and Arial. Did you give Angles her address, so they can go over to her place and check?'

Sarah shook her head. 'Kid doesn't have a place – at least not a permanent one. She's usually dog-sitting, house-sitting or both, so paying rent is a waste, she says.'

'But what does she do in between jobs?'

'Crashes on a friend's couch. Or comes by our place.'

'Kind of a cool way to live,' I said. 'I mean, if you're young enough.'

Sarah shrugged. 'Her clients go away for a week or a month at a time and don't have to worry about anything, because she's there. I guess it works for everybody.'

Mike Hallonquist rejoined us, notebook in hand. 'Maggy, you said you were here a little after seven?'

'Yes, on my way to work.'

'And you didn't see George Satterwite.'

'Not to my knowledge.' I knew I sounded like a congressional witness. But Pavlik had taught me to be precise when I gave evidence. 'I mean, I saw the legs of a man in tan or khaki pants in the garage. It could have been him' – I gestured to the body, now under a blue tarp – 'or I suppose it could have been George if he was wearing something similar.'

'Mr Satterwite's Navigator was in the garage?'

'Again, I just got a glimpse, but it was a large vehicle and the right color. And now it's gone.'

Hallonquist flipped to the next page in his notebook. 'And when you heard what Arial Kingston called firecrackers and you thought were gunshots – what time was that?'

'A few minutes after I got here. Maybe seven-fifteen. Is that consistent with the time of death?'

Hallonquist frowned. 'We'll see.'

I didn't think I'd get more than that. And it was likely Mike didn't know any more at this point himself. 'I like Detective Angles.'

'She's a good investigator,' Hallonquist said. 'And as much as I loved Taylor, and you know I did' – I nodded – 'it's kind of nice to be paired with somebody who has people skills.'

I laughed. Let's just say Al Taylor was brusque until he warmed up to you. And then he was merely prickly. 'And I bet you get your chance to play bad cop, too, sometimes. Angles seems experienced.'

'She is – twenty years on the job in Madison.'

I watched as Hallonquist rejoined Angles near the body. 'That's odd.'

'That Detective Audiophone moved here from Madison?'

'No, and it's Audiophile.'

'Then, what?'

'Wait a second. Let me just check.' I walked to the body and then back to the door, Sarah scurrying after me.

'Will you tell me what your problem is?'

I crouched down to see better. 'My problem is there are no Mocha prints at the body. Nothing until the doorway.'

'So?'

I stood. 'So how did she get to the hall?'

EIGHT

S arah and I reopened Uncommon Grounds just in time to
catch the evening commuter crowd and close again.

Sarah had invited me over for dinner, so after leaving
UG, I stopped at the pet store for flea spray and then ran home
to feed Frank and lightly spray the living room and porch
before I went out to fumigate Pavlik's Corolla. I didn't know
how effective the stuff could be, since it smelled of cloves.
Then again, baked hams seldom had fleas.

Standing outside the car after I'd emptied the spray can into
it, I debated leaving the windows open or closed. Open would
allow the smell to dissipate and the dying fleas to evacuate
and expire elsewhere. Rolling them up would seal in the fleas
with their killer overnight.

I chose door number two and checked my phone. Still no
message from Pavlik and it was nearly seven-thirty.

Changing out of my clothes, I set the washer on flea cycle
and showered before driving to Sarah's house in Brookhills
Estates. The Estates was an upscale neighborhood – sort of
the Victorian version of the Satterwites' Colonial haven.

Sarah's was a rose Painted Lady on the left side of the street.
Approaching the door, I was hit for the umpteenth time by the
contrast between the gracious – even fussy – home filled with
florals and the plain-spoken woman who opened the door in
her uniform of Hepburnesque (Katharine, not Audrey) trousers
and floppy jackets.

'How's this theory?' she said, before I could say anything.
'Mocha was so scared she levitated.'

'Hi, Maggy.' A tall young man with sandy blonde hair had
appeared behind Sarah. 'Hey, Sarah. Can I take the Firebird?'

'Over your dead body,' Sarah said.

'Nice, huh?' Sam was grinning at me.

'You broke it once, Sam,' I said to him. 'She's not going
to give you another chance.'

'Can't blame a guy for trying.' He slipped past Sarah to get outside. 'See you all later.'

'Good kid,' I said, watching him trot down the walk. 'Has he decided on colleges yet?'

'He wants Northwestern, but we'll see.'

Northwestern was pricey, but I had a feeling that what Sam wanted, Sam was going to get. Except for driving Sarah's vintage Firebird.

'Anyway,' I said, stepping into the house, 'good guess on the levitating dog. It's much more fun to contemplate than the obvious answer.'

'Which is what?' Sarah asked, leading me into the parlor.

'That somebody picked her up and carried her to the hallway. Which begs the obvious question: who?'

'That's easy.' Sarah waved me toward the coffee table where a cluster of Chinese takeout boxes were center stage, flanked by plates, silverware and two glasses of red wine. 'The murderer, of course.'

'Or Arial?' I asked, sitting down on the couch.

'But she was outside with you, you said.' Sarah was frowning as she sat down across from me. A door opened and closed somewhere in the house.

'Yes, but she went into the house as I left,' I said, helping myself to rice. 'Mocha had already gone in through the garage. If she found the dog in the theater near the body, Arial would have picked her up.'

'Arial picked up who?' Sarah's other charge, Courtney, flopped down on the couch next to me and picked up a fork.

I exchanged looks with Sarah as the pretty blonde girl leaned forward to stab a piece of sesame chicken.

'Another dog-sitting client. Maggy's looking to hire her away,' Sarah said, with a warning glance at me. 'Have you talked to her lately?'

'Uh-uh,' she said, shaking her head as she chewed. And swallowed. 'But I can dog-sit for you, Maggy, if she can't.'

'I'm afraid it's overnight, Courtney.' I was following Sarah's lead, and the fact was I did need a dog-sitter for Peggy Pavlik's funeral, which I assumed would be Sunday or Monday. 'Sarah doesn't think that your staying over is such a good idea.'

Courtney scowled, a deep vertical line etching her forehead above her nose. 'Sarah is overprotective. Did you know there are kids my age who live on their own? They sleep in the park or on heating grates. Your house would be safer than that.'

Sarah looked incredulous. 'You're comparing yourself to the homeless?'

And comparing my house – albeit favorably – to a heating grate. But the fact was Courtney and her brother, Sam, could well have been homeless if Sarah hadn't stepped into their lives.

The girl had the grace to blush. 'No, of course not. I'm just saying that I'm old enough to dog-sit overnight. It's not like I'm even babysitting. It's Frank. He's practically a person, right, Maggy?'

Sarah was giving me the eye. I spooned sesame chicken on my rice to give myself time to think.

In truth, I agreed with Courtney that Sarah was being over-protective. But three years ago, a single and forty-something Sarah had taken on the responsibility of raising Courtney and her brother, Sam, who were twelve and fifteen, respectively, at the time.

When you raise a child from infant, you have time to grow alongside it. No sweat carrying the seven-pound newborn and, as he gets bigger, you get stronger. Hoisting that two-year-old on to your hip or, two years after that, scooping up the cranky four-year-old is no problem.

Well, in Sarah's scenario, she'd been tossed a couple of hundred-pounders out of the clear blue sky and had caught them. I admired her and would give her all the support I could.

'Frank can sometimes be a handful,' I said.

Courtney waved her hand in the manner that, had she been of a different era, would have been 'pshaw.' In her generation it was more 'whatever.'

'Anyway,' I said, 'I'm waiting for Pavlik to call me back, so I don't know exactly when I'll leave.'

'Oh!' Courtney said, bouncing. 'Are you two going on vacation?'

'Unfortunately not,' I said. 'The sheriff's mother died last night, so I'll be joining him in Chicago for the funeral.'

Courtney's eyes teared up. The girl was not only at an emotional age, but she'd also lost her own mom and the wound remained tender. 'That's so sad. Why aren't you already there with him?'

The question hit a little too close to home. I'd called Pavlik and gotten a text back saying they were with the Rabbi and he'd call as soon as he could. Three hours later, I still hadn't heard from him. 'Right now, he has to focus on his dad and what needs to be done, so I don't want to . . .'

The word I was searching for was 'insinuate,' but I didn't think Courtney would understand it.

'Insinuate yourself?' she suggested.

'Well, yes,' I said, surprised. '"Insinuate" is just the word. I'm impressed.'

'I read,' she said, getting up. 'Well, anyway, if you do need a sitter, just let me know. If Sarah won't let me stay over, maybe Frank can come here.'

The thought of Frank thundering through Sarah's house made me grin. 'That could be just the solution.'

'Sure it could,' Sarah said dryly, 'right about the time hell freezes over. Courtney, why don't you text Arial and see where she is? If we can't find her, we'll talk.'

'Okey-dokey.' The girl snagged another piece of chicken and got up to leave.

'Don't you want to fix a plate?' I asked.

'No, I'm good.' We heard her bedroom door close.

'You realize that even if she does find Arial, she's not going to tell you,' I said. 'She wants the dog-sitting job for herself.'

'So I'll check her phone,' Sarah said, in a way that made me think it wouldn't be the first time.

'She doesn't mind if you read her messages?' I added a little Mongolian beef to my plate to balance the savory with the sweet sesame chicken already there. Nobody can say I'm not a gourmand.

'Mind?' Sarah took a sip of wine. 'There's no mind or don't mind. She's a fifteen-year-old. *Mi casa*, me cell phone.'

I took it all back. Sarah might be new to parenting, but she was a better mother than I was. Or at least a tougher one.

Luckily, Eric had survived nonetheless. 'Have you called Arial's mom and dad? Have they heard from her?'

'Her dad is not in the picture, never has been. And Arial likes her mother just about as much as I do.'

'This is the sister who lives in Milwaukee with your mom?'

'More that she lives *on* my mom. But yes, Saint Ruth is my only sibling.'

Sarah had told me she hadn't seen either Ruth or her mother in years, despite the fact that they were less than fifteen miles away. She hadn't expanded on the situation other than to say Ruth had a martyr complex. Hence, I assumed, the canonization.

'Still, don't you think you should call her? Or your mother.'

'No, I don't.' She raised her eyebrows. 'Now, you were saying about Mocha, the magic levitating fleabag?'

I wasn't going to get anything else out of Sarah on the family front. 'Only that Arial might have run in and picked up the dog to keep her away from the body.'

'And then set her down again in the hall, not realizing she had blood on her feet?'

'Exactly. And even if Arial did realize, I'm sure getting the dog away from the body was higher on her list of concerns than keeping the hall clean.'

'A few paw prints would be nothing compared with that pool of blood,' Sarah agreed. 'Then what?'

'Arial took Mocha and ran?'

'But why? Why not just call the police?'

I set down my plate and picked up my wine glass. 'I don't know. Maybe because of who the victim was or what he was doing there? Maybe she didn't want to be associated with him.'

'That sounds sketchy.' Sarah shifted uncomfortably in her chair. 'Of course, it's also possible the murderer grabbed her.'

'That would explain why Arial's car is still there. But here's another "why" for you. Why would the killer do that?'

Sarah shrugged. 'She was a witness.'

'But—'

Sarah waved me down. 'I know what you're going to say. He killed one person, so why not just kill her?'

'Actually, I was going to say she wasn't a witness. We were outside.'

'Maybe the guy was still standing over the body when she got in.'

Maybe he was. Comfortable right there in his own house. 'I'm thinking George is our most likely suspect. You?'

'Seems so. And he's missing, too.' She picked up a white cardboard carton and put it down again. 'We should have checked Arial's car for her suitcase and purse.'

'The deputies did. They weren't there.'

'I assume they think she took them with her, then. Meaning she left voluntarily.'

'Probably.' I ducked my head. 'I mean, that's probably what they think.'

'At least that would mean she's alive.' Sarah forced a smile. 'Good to have a line into the sheriff's department, even when your SO isn't here.'

'Significant Other?' I guessed. 'I haven't heard it used as an acronym.'

'I don't think it's caught on,' Sarah said.

'An SO does sound a little like something you wouldn't want to call your significant other.'

'Well, you won't have to worry about what you call him after you're married,' Sarah said, shifting the subject. 'Don't suppose you've set a date?'

'No.' I thought I felt a vibration and pulled the phone out of my pocket. No text. No missed call. My stomach gave a twist. 'Well, listen. I hate to eat and run, but I think I'm going to go home and try Pavlik again.'

'You love to eat and run,' Sarah said, following me to the foyer. 'And as for Pavlik, he's probably just busy.'

'I know. And I'm not hurt or anything.' I opened the door. 'I just feel like I should be doing something for him, and I'm not sure what.'

'You can solve a murder.'

I paused to consider. 'I don't think he'd consider that helping him.'

'Maybe not.' Sarah handed me my purse. 'Go home and call HE.'

'He?'

'Husband equivalent. That one hasn't caught on either.' She went to close the door behind me.

I put my hand out to stop it. 'They'll find Arial,' I told her. 'If not, you'd better.'

The door closed.

I was lying in bed spooning Frank when Pavlik called.

'Is everything all right?' I asked him. Then, 'Sorry, that was a silly question. Of course, nothing is right. How is your dad holding up?'

'He's . . . I guess he's dealing with it in his own way.' Pavlik's voice was tired. 'You know my mom was Jewish. We didn't really practice, but suddenly my dad wants to do everything according to tradition. So . . . we buried my mom this afternoon. Just made it before sundown.'

'Today?' I didn't think I'd heard right. 'But your mom died just last night. Or this morning, really.'

'Dad insisted. According to Jewish law, the body should be buried within twenty-four hours.'

I sat up. Frank didn't stir. 'I thought there was some leeway these days, so family could get home and such.'

'I know, but he was dead set on having the burial before Shabbat.'

That's right. It was Friday and the Jewish observance had started at sundown. 'Besides,' Pavlik was saying, 'there really is no family, except me and my dad.'

And me? Though I didn't say it.

'And Tracey, of course.'

'Susan brought Tracey down?' This I did say. Susan was Pavlik's ex-wife.

'They were already here in Chicago, luckily, visiting Susan's folks.'

'Well, that's . . . good.' I'd almost said 'convenient,' which would have come out bitchy, when I really didn't mean it to.

Or maybe I did. A little. Pavlik had buried his mother, and I hadn't been there. He didn't even seem to think I should have been there. Yet his ex-wife was.

'Susan and my mom were close,' Pavlik was saying.

I took a deep breath. This wasn't about me, I reminded myself. 'I'm sorry. I wish I could have been there.'

I said it simply and honestly and, I hoped, without any undercurrents.

'Me, too,' Pavlik said. 'And I'm sorry, too.'

'You don't have to be sorry.' Though I was glad he was.

'I should have called you right away when I realized what he had in mind. Told you to come down. But I honestly thought I could talk him into waiting until after Shabbat. Believe me, there's no way I saw my Gentile father turning into Tevye from *Fiddler on the Roof.*'

I smiled and lay back, dislodging Frank, who jumped to the floor to scratch. 'I guess he was doing what he thought your mom would want?'

'I guess. Or repaying all those years she played Mrs Claus to his Santa.'

'No,' I said. 'Really?'

'From the tasseled red hat to the tip-tilted shoes. It was for their company Christmas party.' A pause. 'She was always such a good sport about it.'

'I wish I'd had time to get to know her better.'

'Me, too.' Another pause, this one longer. 'Now, tell me about this murder you're involved in.'

NINE

'Mike Hallonquist has a big mouth.'

'For what it's worth,' Pavlik said, 'Mike called me about a crop of identity theft cases we're turning over to Cybercrimes, not to tattle on you.'

Yet he had, no doubt, told Pavlik all about the body at the Satterwite house and my involvement.

Which I tried to downplay, of course. 'I don't know the Satterwites and certainly not the dead man. I was just there to return their dog.'

'To Sarah's niece, Arial, the dog-sitter. Who happens to be missing. Any idea where she's gone?'

Right to the point. It was one of the things I loved about him. And not.

'I wish I knew,' I admitted. 'Sarah is frantic.' Or what passed as frantic for Sarah, who normally preferred not to show anybody she cared about anything.

'How do you think Arial is involved?' Pavlik asked.

'In the murder? Got me. We both were outside when the shots were fired.' It wasn't an answer that summed up or expanded on all my conjecture, but it was just the facts. Ma'am.

'So Hallonquist tells me. That doesn't mean she didn't know what was going on inside.'

Frank hopped back on the bed and laid down, his sheer mass stripping the covers half off me. I tugged them back best I could as I thought. 'She did seem distracted. Even afraid. And she had blood . . . oh, shit!'

'What?'

'I wiped the blood from her cheek on to a napkin.'

'Why is that a problem?' Pavlik said. 'We can test it. Maybe it was hers and the victim assaulted her. Or if it was his—'

'I washed it.'

'What?'

'The napkin was in my jeans pocket, and I took them off when I got home today' – after I'd de-fleaed his car – 'and threw them in the washing machine before I went to Sarah's.'

'And started it?'

'The washing machine? Yes, on hot.'

'Not your normal MO,' he said. 'You usually leave them in the machine for a couple of days before you start it. And after washing they're lucky to get to the dryer before they mildew. Of course, even once in the dryer, it doesn't mean—'

'Yes, yes,' I said. 'And it all drives you crazy.'

'A little,' admitted the man who irons his jeans. 'But apparently you're turning over a new leaf. Unfortunate timing, but . . .' I heard him shrug.

I groaned. 'No new leaf. Just fleas.'

'What?'

'Fleas. Mocha, the stray dog I returned? She had fleas, and even though I shampooed her—'

'Wait. Didn't you pick her up in my car?'

'Yes.'

'No.'

'I'm sorry,' I said. 'But I did wrap her in a blanket before I put her in the car.'

'My blanket?'

'Afraid so. But I washed it in hot water.'

'And what about the car? I know you're not fond of the Toyota, but—'

'Don't worry. I got flea spray and fogged the whole thing. Closed up the car so it would be more effective.'

'So now I have a car full of dead fleas.'

You can never win. 'Beats the alternative, right?'

'I suppose,' Pavlik said, sounding a little sheepish. 'It's just that I hate fleas. Muffin was infested when I rescued her, and I had bites and welts all over me. It took months to get rid of them.'

'The welts?'

'The fleas.'

Muffin was Pavlik's pit bull, who'd died recently. Toothless, the poor pittie had been kept for breeding until Pavlik rescued her from a fight ring.

So Pavlik had lost both his dog and his mom in the last month.

'When are you coming home?' I asked.

'Not soon. We're sitting Shiva.'

Seven days of mourning. His dad really was embracing the traditions. 'Well, the fleas should be gone by then. But in the meantime, I'll come down.'

'Uh-uh,' Pavlik said. 'Even I don't want to be in the condo with my dad for seven days.'

'But you'll do it.'

'Because it's what he wants. Or thinks he needs, for my mom.'

My fiancé was a very good man.

The next morning was Saturday and I started work at six a.m., meaning I was up at five. First things first, though. I needed to check something I should have done the night before. Padding out to the garage in my sweat socks and robe, I opened the washer. Empty.

Damn. Not only had I turned on the washer, as I'd told Pavlik, but I'd transferred the clothes to the dryer when I got home from Sarah's. And turned it on. It was a once-in-a-blue-moon occurrence, as Pavlik had said.

Although the sheriff apparently had more experience with fleas, we were on the same page, abhorrence-wise. The nasty little bugs gave me the creepy-crawlies. I'd figured if they'd abandoned the Toyota and hopped on to me during the flea Armageddon I'd staged, the soap and hot water of the washer and the heat of the dryer would kill them. All of the above certainly would have done in the napkin.

Sure enough. Turning the jeans pocket inside out, white matted bits wafted out on to my bare feet.

'Think I should try to save what's left?' I asked Frank, who had followed me out and was drinking out of his auxiliary water dish nearby.

He lifted his head, water dripping from his beard, but didn't answer. I dumped the jeans on the dryer and pulled out the lint filter. Shreds of the destroyed napkin, of course, tangled with Frank fur. Hesitating with my hand over the waste basket,

I instead put the whole wad in the red Solo cup I kept next to the sink. Who knew? Maybe there were some new developments in forensics I didn't know about that made the blood on a washed, dried and shredded napkin DNA-able.

Remains stashed, I picked up the jeans from the top of the dryer and tried to shake out the wrinkles. 'Pavlik would iron these.'

Frank turned and stalked back to the house.

'You're right,' I said. 'He's him and I'm me. Besides, this pair is tight enough that the wrinkles don't stand a chance against my thighs.'

Saturdays at Uncommon Grounds were kind of a crapshoot. Our shop was in the historical Brookhills Junction train station and the core of our customer base was business people commuting in and out of Milwaukee on the train. For weekend business, we depended on locals and visitors, which was an ever-changing prospect depending on what was going on in town.

The farmers' market held on Saturday mornings from Memorial Day through Labor Day in the Town Hall parking lot affected business, too. It opened at seven and sometimes folks would stop by Uncommon Grounds on their way there. Or they might just as easily get their coffee fix from one of the vendors there.

Like I said, crapshoot. For a while, we'd bought a booth at the market, but it was a big time and manpower commitment – and, frankly, a pain in the butt. No electricity, for one, so we couldn't make espresso drinks and the coffee had to be brewed ahead and transported in five-gallon insulated containers.

And then there was the outdoorness.

Depending on which Saturday, May through September, we could spend seven hours huddling under the lift gate of the van when it rained, using socks from the vendor across the way for mittens when it was cold, staving off sunburn and heat prostration when it was hot and humid, and swatting wasps away from our cinnamon rolls pretty much the whole season.

We finally called it quits.

Well, to be specific, Sarah had called it quits after she was stung the third time. I didn't argue.

Anyway, the farmers' market must be going great guns, because this Saturday morning at the shop was unusually quiet. Boring, even. About nine thirty, Clare Twohig, who owned the antique store next to us, stuck her head in. 'Morning, Maggy. Could I get a latte?'

'Sure, Clare,' I said. 'To go, I assume?'

'No, actually, I'll sit out here on the porch with a real cup, if you don't mind. I have the puppies with me.'

'Puppies?' I perked up.

'Yes,' she said. 'They're a year old now, but still puppies.'

When I took the latte out to her, I saw that each of Clare's 'puppies' had to weigh sixty pounds. But they hadn't lost any of that wiggly puppy exuberance.

'Oh my God,' I said, setting down her drink and leaning over to scratch the smaller of the two behind the ear. 'They're beautiful.'

'Thank you,' she said, and then laughed. 'I say that like I gave birth to them. Though I do admit I treat them like my kids.'

'So introduce me,' I said, settling down on the top step of the porch. 'Who's this?'

'The boy licking your face is Spike,' she said. 'And the girl you're petting is Terra.'

'Hi, Spike – such a good boy,' I said, dodging his tongue so I could talk without getting it in the mouth.

Spike was lanky with long legs and a narrow waist. His fur was brindle-colored, like a boxer but long and luxurious, his bushy tail curling up and over his back. Terra was mostly fawn-colored with a pink-tipped nose and big brown eyes that seemed outlined with chestnut eyeliner. The silky white hair on her haunches nearly brushed the ground like a petticoat peeking out.

'Such a pretty girl,' I said as she offered me a toy. 'What in the world are they?'

Clare sipped gingerly on her steaming latte. 'Honestly, I don't know. They're both rescue pups.'

'Have you had them long?' I asked as I took Terra's offering.

'Since they were eight weeks old.'

I held up what Terra had given me. 'Is this a dismembered arm?'

'Dismembered monkey arm,' Clare said. 'But yes. Spike pulls the stuffed animals apart and then Terra carries the body parts around.'

Terra tugged on the hand end of the arm, and I let her have it back. She gave me a you-obviously-don't-understand-the-concept look and offered it again. 'They can't be brother and sister.'

'No, each was the last pup adopted from two different litters. Their foster mom had them in the pen together so they could keep each other company, and I just couldn't separate them. I took both.'

'I'm not surprised. How could you choose between these two?' Spike was back, flopping over like a rag doll so I could rub his belly. 'Is the shop closed today?'

Clare checked her watch. 'No, but we don't open until noon. I'm meeting with an IT guy now to work on my computer system. I'm considering keeping these two with me today to see how they do with the customers. Think anyone will mind?'

'I *think* if you keep the door open, these two will attract customers in droves,' I said. 'I'm not sure how your antiques will fare with the table-height tail swishing around, though.'

Spike wagged said tail, and Claire slid her cup away. 'I took them to the dog park to run off energy this morning, so I'm hoping they'll just sleep once they get inside.'

Fat chance, from what I was seeing. But puppies – even at a year old – are kind of like kids. They go and go until they finally collapse to rest up for another round. 'Sarah was telling me about the new dog park. I haven't been there yet.'

'It really is nice. Your Frank would love it. Lots of trees to anoint and open spaces to run. Be careful, though, or they'll suck you in to help.'

'Spoken from experience, I take it?' I stood up, wiping hands covered in sweet puppy spit on my jeans.

'Oh, yes. And how could I refuse? I come practically every day, with not just one but two dogs. And Becky and Doug work so hard.'

'Sarah mentioned Doug, but who's Becky?'

'She's the one who raised the money and got the support to build the park in the first place. Quite the go-getter.'

I smiled. 'So what did she go-get you to do?'

Clare sighed. 'The annual – or what will become the annual – barbecue and fundraiser.'

As a person who'd planned events in a former life, I could only think, in Sarah's words, 'better you than me.' 'That's really good of you.'

'It's next month, in August. You have to come with Frank.' She got up and unlooped the dogs' leashes from the deck railing. 'We're roasting a pig.'

A roasted pig with Frank around. What could go wrong? 'It sounds like fun, but I'm not sure we'd be welcome. I understand that Frank wasn't on his best behavior there when Sarah and Courtney took him.'

Clare looked surprised. 'Really? What happened?'

'Sat on a Pekingese.'

'Ohhh, yes. Princess,' she said. 'I heard about that.'

Yup. One visit and Frank was canine-non-grata at the dog park.

Clare saw my face and put her hand on my arm. 'Don't worry, Maggy. Frank's not blacklisted or anything. You just need to take him to the park more often, so he's socialized. People understand.'

'Even the owner of the Peke?'

'Lydia?' She wobbled her head. 'Not so much, but Frank isn't the first one to try to put Princess in her place.'

Which apparently was under his butt.

I gave both puppies a last scratch. 'You guys be good, you hear?'

Terra accepted my scratches graciously as if her due, then politely picked up her monkey arm in preparation for leaving.

Spike reared up on his back legs, planted his two front paws on my shoulders and gave me a sloppy ol' French kiss.

'They say dog mouths are cleaner than human toilets,' Sarah said as I recounted my meeting with the Twohig kids.

I took a sip of coffee and swished it around. 'I think it's "cleaner than human mouths."'

'Same thing.'

Not really. 'Anyway, they're adorable.'

'And the only customers we've had today,' she said, looking at the cash register tape.

'Sad, but true. If this continues, we may have to think about closing on Saturday.'

'And then reopen for the Goddard Gang on Sunday mornings?'

The Goddard Gang was a group that frequented Uncommon Grounds every Sunday and could range anywhere from half a dozen people upward to twenty, so they were nothing to sneeze at. Especially since many made return visits during the week. 'Kind of weird to be closed on Saturday and open on Sunday, I suppose.'

'Kind of.'

'I guess we'll just have to weather the occasional slow Saturday, then.' I shrugged. 'Or consider going back to the farmers' market and renting a booth.'

'Over my wasp-stung body.' Sarah opened the lid of the stainless-steel cream pitcher on the condiment cart and let it drop again. 'Now there's a filthy animal for you. Yellow jackets are like flying garbage cans. I—'

'Hello?' Marian Satterwite came around the corner from the side door that led to the train platform and, beyond that, our parking lot. She stopped short and glanced around at the empty shop. 'Are you open?'

'Sadly, yes,' Sarah said.

'The "sadly" has nothing to do with you,' I explained to Marian, lest she take Sarah's remark personally. 'It's just that business today has been abysmal.'

'That's because it's such a lovely day and everybody is outside,' Marian said, coming to the counter. 'The farmers' market is packed with people.'

I shot Sarah a look.

'No.'

'Yes, it was,' Marian said, misunderstanding. 'Very busy.'

'Busy like bees.' Sarah leaned over the service counter to

fetch a quart of half-and-half from the fridge on the other side. 'Or wasps.'

'Anyway,' Marian said, turning to me, 'that's not why I'm here. I was wondering if Mocha might have wandered back to your place.'

'No,' I said. 'She hasn't come back, then?'

'No,' the woman said, setting her handbag on the counter. 'It's worrisome.'

'What about your husband?' I asked.

'You think he knows where Mocha is?'

It wasn't what I'd meant, but her question had sparked a question of its own. 'Whose cell number is on Mocha's tag?'

Marian frowned, thinking. 'George's, I think, since he's easier to get hold of given my travel schedule. But we got that tag when Mocha was a puppy, so I can't be sure.'

'It was worn,' I said. 'But I texted that number late Thursday night when I found Mocha.'

'And got a reply?' Now I had Marian's attention.

'Yes. Almost immediately, saying he was out of town but would have Arial call first thing in the morning.'

'And did she?'

'Six a.m.' When Marian seemed horrified by the early hour, I elaborated. 'I'd said to call any time after six. We start early here.'

'Some of us do, at least,' Sarah said.

That seemed unfair, since I'd opened today. But then my partner *had* covered for me Thursday. And Frank-sat.

Marian just cocked her head. 'George must have relayed the message to her then.'

'You still haven't heard from him? Or Arial?' I asked.

'Not a word.'

'And yet you're here looking for your dog,' Sarah muttered as she crossed back to the condiment cart with the cream.

'Who are you again?' Marian asked to Sarah's back.

'Sarah Kingston is my partner here and Arial's aunt, as you'll recall,' I said before Sarah could turn and illuminate the woman in her own inimitable way. 'We haven't heard from Arial, either.'

'Interesting, if not surprising, that she hasn't surfaced.

I can't believe it's a coincidence that a man was killed in my house while she was dog-sitting and now she's missing.'

'Of course not,' I said. 'She could have been abducted by the killer or even be dead herself.'

'Geez, Maggy.' Sarah had started to fill the cream pitcher and now stopped, shoulders slumped.

'I'm not saying that's what happened,' I assured my partner. 'I just meant that the situation is as serious for Arial as it could be for Marian's husband.'

'Exactly so,' Marian said. 'Have you considered the possibility that she ran off?'

'We have,' I said, nodding toward Sarah. 'If Arial came back in the house and found the man's body in the living room, she may have been frightened for her own life and fled.'

'But she'd have contacted us by now,' Sarah said. 'Or called the police for help.'

'I meant,' Marian said, not looking at either of us, 'that she might have run off with the person responsible.'

Sarah was approaching a slow boil, but I held up my hand. There was something in the way Marian had said it. And the look on her face. 'That person being your husband? You think Arial ran off with George?'

'May I remind you once again,' Sarah said, 'that we're talking about my niece?'

'And my husband,' Marian reminded us both.

'So that means you really think your husband shot this guy?' Sarah asked. 'Why? You said he was a complete stranger.'

'To me.' Marian walked to the front window and put her hand on the sill for support as she gazed out. 'But maybe he wasn't a complete stranger to Arial.'

She turned, her face ashen. 'What if your instinct was right, Maggy, and Arial did have an overnight guest?'

'That's a killing offense in the dog-sitting world?' Sarah snapped.

Marian pivoted to face her. 'It might be, if you were already having an affair with her.'

TEN

'She has you beat in the drama department,' Sarah said to me.

Maybe. But it's not a dramatic exit if you don't leave. And Marian was still standing in our coffeehouse.

'Arial and your husband were having an affair?' I asked her.

She shrugged.

'C'mon, that's ridiculous,' Sarah said. 'Arial's barely twenty years old. You have to be in your forties.'

Marian leveled a stare at her. 'So you see my point.'

Sarah blushed. I had forgotten it was even possible, but there it was, all over her face.

'I meant "you" plural,' Sarah said, 'as in you and your husband. But, yeah, I do get your point. I just don't think that Arial would . . .' She let the sentence peter out and turned her attention back to refilling the creamer.

Under normal circumstances, Sarah being at a loss for words was something to be savored. Today it was just plain sad.

I turned to Marian. 'According to your theory, your husband came upon Arial cheating on him with the guy in the theater, killed him and then he and Arial ran off together?'

She shrugged again. 'Unless he killed her, too, like you said.'

'I never said that,' I protested, though I had, in a way. 'Do you have any proof of this affair?'

'The girl washed the sheets, for one,' Marian said. 'Every time I get home, the sheets are in the wash. What's she so afraid that I'm—'

'Oh, for God's sake.' Sarah had picked up the carton of half-and-half to return it to the kitchen and now slammed it down hard enough on the cart for cream to erupt.

'Arial has good manners,' I said to Marian as I tossed a dish rag to Sarah. 'Don't you offer to strip the sheets when you stay at someone's house?'

She blinked. 'No. I assume they have people for that.'

Now I thought Sarah was going to bean her with the rag.

I put up my hand. 'Let's just assume that you're right and washing the sheets was a way of getting rid of the evidence she was sleeping with somebody while you were gone. Why do you think it was your husband? It just as easily could have been the dead guy.'

'Sure, Maggy, put a positive spin on it,' Sarah said sarcastically.

'I'm just asking why Marian thinks her husband is cheating.'

'The sheets, like I said. And charges on the credit card George won't explain. He didn't even tell me you'd found Mocha.'

'It was the middle of the night,' I told her. 'Maybe he didn't want to wake you.'

'Yet he woke her.' She folded her arms. 'A woman knows.'

This woman hadn't. 'Let's stick with facts. A man is dead. Your husband is missing. Arial is missing, and so is Mocha. If they were running off together, why would they take your dog?'

Marian seemed surprised I had to ask. 'The two of them are crazy about the little mutt.'

The mutt she'd come looking for. 'Mocha wasn't your dog, then?'

'She was at one point.'

I remembered Arial saying Mocha's IBS kicked up when George was gone, but she was used to Marian being away. 'I suppose with your traveling so much, it was difficult.'

'I took her along when I could, but that meant I had to carry the dog on and check my luggage.'

God forbid the woman should have to go to the baggage carousel.

'Then,' Marian continued, 'that crazy handbag rescue woman started harassing me and she got nippy—'

I held up a hand. 'Wait. Handbag rescue?'

'Yes,' she said. 'Somehow they think it's abuse to carry a cute little dog in your purse. What else would it be doing? Sitting at home licking its butt? Scratching its balls?'

Even if Mocha were a boy, I didn't think the latter was

anatomically possible. Though it did sound like something Frank would enjoy. Certainly more than being dragged around in a handbag. 'And this handbag woman got snippy with you?'

Marian looked at me as if I'd lost it. 'Well, yes. But I was talking about Mocha. She bit me.'

Ahh. Nippy, not snippy.

'Well, anyway,' Marian said, gathering up her own bag, 'I need to get to the sheriff's department. Detective Angles has some photos she wants me to look through.'

This time I blinked. 'You mean like a photo lineup?'

'Yes, of known associates of the dead man.'

'Then they've identified him?'

'They must have, if they know who his associates are.' Her expression said, *Try to keep up.*

'But you don't know?' I asked. 'I mean, you still don't know who he is.'

'His name? Not a clue,' she said, opening the front door. 'And I can't imagine I'll recognize any of his friends, either.'

I stood by the window as she walked down the steps to the street.

'"Known associates."' Sarah had come to stand next to me. 'By definition, does that mean *criminal* associates?'

I thought about it. 'When law enforcement uses the term, it sure seems to. And the fact they were able to identify him so quickly without an ID on his person may mean his fingerprints are in the system.'

'Maybe he is a thief, then,' Sarah said, 'come to rob the house, and George Satterwite caught him in the act.'

'And shot him?'

'Sure,' Sarah said. 'Castle doctrine says you have the right to shoot somebody who breaks into your castle, which these days translates to your home or business.'

Says the woman with the gun-purse. 'You took the semi-automatic out of your purse, right?'

'Right,' Sarah said, nodding.

I wasn't sure I believed that, but short of frisking her, there wasn't much I could do about it at the moment. 'Wouldn't George have to know that the victim entered unlawfully?'

'He'd have to *reasonably believe*. Finding a stranger in his home theater would probably qualify.'

'But what was he afraid the victim was going to do? Boost a woofer? Haul off a leather chair?'

'You heard what Marian said. There's a bunch of expensive equipment in there.'

'Which is still in there.'

'Because George defended his property.'

Sarah and I were never going to agree on this gun thing. 'If George had been away, how would he know that Arial hadn't let this guy in lawfully?'

'Think about the scenario,' Sarah said. 'Arial is outside with you and hasn't had a chance to tell George a stranger is in the house.'

'But they'd already been in contact,' I objected. 'George gave her my message about Mocha.'

'Doesn't mean she told him she was having a sleepover. She probably figured the guy would be gone before George got home. But instead he walks in early, sees the guy and *blam*. King George protects his castle.'

'By shooting an unarmed man.'

'You have to remember it doesn't matter what the actual circumstances are. It's what George *believes* they are.'

'*Reasonably* believes. Any reasonable person would ask the stranger what he was doing there. Not shoot him. Besides, Marian said they didn't have a gun.'

'Even better,' Sarah said. 'The bad guy has the gun. Satterwite disarms and shoots him.'

If so, the man belonged in movies, not watching them.

'And what about Arial?' Sarah continued. 'You said she had blood on her face before you heard the shot. Maybe the perp hit her.'

Thanks to me, the fleas and the washing machine, we'd never know if it was her blood. 'If Arial was in trouble, why didn't she say something to me on the driveway? Ask for help.'

'You said the door was open.'

'True. You're saying she was afraid he'd hear?'

'Or she knew the guy was holding George hostage and

couldn't take a chance. Maybe the shots you two heard were a struggle for the gun.'

Hmm. 'But if George did overpower him, why not call the police after the shooting?'

'Fear? Or ignorance? Not everybody knows about the Castle law.'

'They couldn't take a second and get out their phones to Google "self-defense in Wisconsin"? Beats going on the lam.'

'Fine. Then what's your theory? That Marian is right and Arial and George decided to run off together, stepping arm-in-arm over the corpse on their way out?'

'Maybe they had been planning it all along and saw this as their opening?' I mulled that over. 'But now there's a manhunt on for the two of them. There are easier ways to play musical partners. Divorces aren't pleasant, but at least George stood to come away from a divorce with half the marital property. Better than nothing.'

'Maybe Marian has the money and an iron-clad prenup.'

It was possible, of course. Marian Satterwite pretty much stank of money. 'And for all we know, George could have cleaned out the bank accounts when he left.'

'Call Pavlik,' Sarah urged, taking a real shine to the theory.

I didn't know what the rules of Shabbat were. Could you talk business? Especially this kind of business? 'I'm not sure how much he'll be able to tell me.'

'What good is being engaged to the sheriff, then?'

'One of the reasons we're together is that I do, very occasionally, recognize lines that I shouldn't cross.' I was talking about official investigations, but Shabbat and sitting Shiva were very new rules. I didn't want to mess with them, either.

Sarah was unusually quiet.

'I do have a thought, though,' I said, breaking the silence. 'I can ask Marian.'

Sarah seemed skeptical. 'She's kind of a bitch.'

'She is. Which is why it's odd that she's trying to find Mocha, don't you think? She obviously doesn't even like her.'

'Last year's fashion accessory and a nippy one at that.'

'I'd bite Marian, too, if she stuffed me in a bag.' I wiped

up a coffee ring with a napkin from the condiment cart. 'There has to be another reason why she wants Mocha back.'

'Vindictiveness? She knows her husband loves the wee-bag and doesn't want him to have her.'

'If she thinks Mocha is with George and Arial, why come here looking for her? No, I think there's another reason.'

Sarah took the soggy napkin from me. 'You're going for one of those dramatic flourishes again. Just tell me.'

'Actually, I'm not.' The woman ruined all my fun. 'I honestly don't know why she wants Mocha. But I'm sure going to ask her.'

Because I had opened, I was done at noon. I left Sarah playing solitaire on her phone and drove to the Satterwite house, figuring Marian would have had plenty of time to talk to Cindy Angles and get home.

I was right. She answered when I rang the doorbell, a mop in her hand.

'Don't you have people for that?' I asked.

'Yes, but not until Monday, and I can't stand having a mess. All those people tramping in and out.'

'Please tell me you're not cleaning up the crime scene?'

'The theater? Of course not,' she said. 'I'm sure they have special . . . people for that.'

'There are firms that handle crime-scene clean-up, but it's your responsibility to hire one once the county clears the scene. The sheriff's department doesn't do it.'

'Really?' She looked astonished, as if she expected the Brookhills Sheriff's Department's Merry Maids Division to show up. 'But it's not my fault a man was murdered in our home.'

'It's not the sheriff's department's fault either.'

'Well.' She leaned the mop against the wall. 'That's inconvenient.'

The woman was all heart. And whether as a result of her mopping or the people tramping in and out, as she put it, I was having trouble locating the tiny Mocha paw prints.

'Look on the bright side,' I said. 'Once they find the murderer, you can send the bill to him.' Assuming it wasn't her husband.

'And what about the victim?' she said, her face brightening.
'He had no right to be here. I'll ask Detective Angles to put
me in touch with his family once they're notified.'

Appalling thought. *Imagine the nerve of your father/brother/
husband/son leaving blood and brain matter all over my nice
clean theater floor.*

I glanced sharply at Marian.

'What?'

'I'm sorry,' I said. 'I'm sure it's a lot to take in. Were you
able to help Detective Angles?'

'Of course not. As I told you – and her – I didn't know the
man.'

'I assume the detective gave you his name, though.'

'Yes.' She leaned down to flick at an imaginary crumb.

I waited for a beat before prompting, 'What is it?'

'His name? Michael, maybe?' She shrugged. 'It was so
mundane it barely registered.'

Nothing except her own self-interest seemed to register with
Marian, so I decided to go for the financial jugular. 'I was
thinking about what you said about your husband. Have you
checked your bank accounts?'

She straightened. 'My bank accounts? Why are my bank
accounts any of your . . .' Her eyes went big. 'You think
George might have absconded with my money?'

I shrugged. 'And his.'

'No,' she said tightly, 'mostly mine.' Going to the door, she
swung it open. 'I appreciate your stopping by, but I have things
to do.'

As I retraced my steps down the front walk, she was already
on the phone.

Frank was waiting at the door when I got home and blasted
past me as I opened it.

Instead of watering the nearest bush, though, he stopped in
the middle of the yard and looked around.

'What?' I said.

Cocking his head, he trotted to Pavlik's Toyota and
sniffed it.

'Are you looking for Pavlik?' I asked him. 'Or Mocha?'

At the name Mocha, I could have sworn I saw his lip curl. Pavlik, then.

'You got all huffy about sharing our bed with the sheriff,' I told Frank. 'And now you're missing him?'

Frank sighed and collapsed to the ground.

'Yeah, me, too. Who knew?'

Frank hoisted himself back to his feet and followed me toward the house, with a quick detour en route to the nearest tree. Once inside, I tossed my purse on the couch and sat down to call Pavlik. Frank hopped up next to me, something he rarely does.

I gave him a scratch as the call rang five times and went to voicemail.

'Hi, it's me,' I said. 'Just calling to see how it's going. I . . .' I hesitated. 'Frank and I miss you.'

I hung up and Frank plopped his head on my lap. 'Yeah, I know. Why couldn't I just say that *I* miss him? Somehow adding you to the equation makes it seem less risky.'

Frank sighed.

I settled back against the couch pillow and rubbed his head. 'What am I afraid of? That Pavlik doesn't miss me? He's already told me he does.' I sat up. 'But he's there, I'm here, and it seems easier for him that way. Which is why I'm going along with it. But is that the way it should be?'

Frank pushed himself up, hopped off the couch and padded into the kitchen.

'OK, maybe you're right,' I called after him. 'I most certainly am being a weenie. Good having this talk, though.' I followed him into the room and picked up his leash. 'Let's go to the dog park.'

Apparently, just the thought of sitting on a Pekingese was enough to cheer Frank up. He smiled all the way to the dog park, and by the time I stopped the car on the street adjacent to the gate, there was slobber sliding down the passenger seat window and pooling on the armrest.

This was one happy sheepdog.

Not having anybody to sit on, I couldn't raise the same level of enthusiasm until we got to the park. Rolling hills, lots of trees, lots of dirt – it was, admittedly, a doggy paradise.

'Wait, Frank,' I said as I swung open his door. Frank usually didn't take off, but he also was not a dog that walked well on a leash, probably because I seldom used one. It seemed prudent today to get him to the gate. 'Let me put this—'

Wham, and he'd blown past me and was already at the gate. The park's airlock system reminded me of a prison intake (don't ask me how I know), with a door into a holding area and then another into the secured area.

'Dogs are required by the city to be on leash until they get inside,' a woman said from inside the gate. 'And I hope he's licensed. The police have been doing surprise inspections.'

A little breathless as I caught up with Frank, I snapped the leash on his collar. 'Sorry. And yes, he's licensed.'

Though the tag had expired a year ago.

'Is that Frank?' The woman was squinting at the sheepdog.

'It is.' I opened the first gate so Frank could step in. 'You've met?' I was hoping this wasn't the squished Peke's owner.

'He was with Courtney the other day,' the woman said. 'And a rather unpleasant woman from what I remember?'

'That would be Sarah,' I said, taking Frank's leash off again. 'I'm Maggy Thorsen.'

'Frank's mom,' she said, nodding. 'Good to have him back. You know, three times and we expect you to volunteer.'

That clicked. 'You must be Becky.'

'Courtney told you about me?' she said. 'What a nice girl and so good with the dogs. She told me she didn't have one herself, so you can't be her mother.'

'No, the unpleasant woman is,' I said. 'And it was Clare Twohig from the antique store who told me about you. She helps out here?'

'One of our best,' Becky said, hand on the gate latch to go in. 'And Spike and Terra are adorable. Ready?'

'Ready?' I repeated. 'Ready for—'

At my word, she swung open the gate and dogs came bounding toward us from every direction. Frank froze.

'In you go, boy,' Becky said, nudging the sheepdog through

the opening with her toe. 'Can't have anybody getting out on us.'

She looked expectantly at me, and I stepped through, too.

I love dogs, but this felt a bit like being run down by the Hound of the Baskervilles times ten or fifteen. Big, medium, small. Long hair, short hair and hairless. None of them were interested in me, of course, but if Frank had a tail, it would have been curled underneath him. As it was, the poor sheepdog had no defense against the butt sniffing. Not that he wasn't doing his share.

'Let 'em get it out of the way,' Becky said. 'It's the way they say hello. Dogs are much more honest and straightforward than human beings.'

Somebody comes up to me and honestly and straightforwardly sniffs my butt, I'm going to deck them.

Or sit on them.

I looked at Frank with new understanding. Respect, even.

'He's doing pretty well, don't you think?' I said, as the sheepdog touched noses with a German shepherd.

The big shepherd backed off and looked as if it might growl, then did that little bow dogs do when they want to play and dashed away the length of the park, inviting Frank to follow. It took a second, but Frank got the drift and trotted after, choosing the center of the sidewalk rather than deal with the brush the shepherd was leaping over.

'We put that walk in for people,' Becky said, 'but the dogs use it like a race track.'

A very slow race, in Frank's case. My poor sheepdog was losing steam.

The shepherd turned and barked a 'come on!', causing Frank to kick it up to high gear. Which meant he was in second. Frank was more furry bulldozer than sleek Maserati.

'That's my Harry,' Becky said, nodding toward the shepherd.

Harry. 'Do you live in the Pinehurst area? I think I may have met your husband yesterday.'

'With the firecrackers that apparently weren't firecrackers at the Satterwites' house?' Becky Lyle asked. 'I talked Ryan out of calling the police. Now I wish he had.'

'I'm not sure it would have made any difference,' I said.

'I suppose not.' She was looking over my shoulder. 'Damn, there's Princess.'

A Pekingese watching from the wings waddled purposefully on to the sidewalk and stopped, blocking Frank's path and barking. Sarah had said 'dust mop,' but right now this dog looked more like a wooly caterpillar about to be squished. 'Does the dog have a death wish?'

'Any Peke can be stubborn, but Princess is in a class of her own, and Lydia, her owner, does nothing to discourage it. Honestly?' She put her hand up to shield her next words. 'I loved seeing Frank take her down a few pegs.'

'That's all good, but she looks like she's out to take revenge.' Harry had circled back and was now alongside Frank, the two of them slow-loping toward Princess who still stood on the path alone.

High Noon, doggy-style. I just wasn't sure which one was Gary Cooper.

'Princess?' A woman with shoulder-length white hair limped on to the sidewalk and picked up her powder puff. 'You stay away from that mean doggy.'

Frank stopped, glancing around uneasily.

'You, Frank,' I called. 'She's talking about you.'

'Shoo!' The woman flapped her hand in my dog's face.

I started toward them but Becky put a restraining hand on my arm. 'You really don't want to get into it with her.'

Didn't I? I shook off Becky's hand. 'Don't worry. I'll kill her with kindness.'

Patting Frank reassuringly as I passed, I stopped in front of Lydia. 'Oh, what a sweet puppy. Is she friendly?'

Princess bared her teeth and growled at me.

Lydia shushed. 'I'm sorry. Usually, Princess is so friendly.'

I heard Becky mutter, 'Sure she is.'

'I think she's defensive because she's so frightened of him.' She pointed a gnarled finger at Frank, who was absorbed in licking his penis. He looked up.

'Yes, you again,' I said to him. 'And it would help if you put that away.' He lowered his leg to cover his privates.

Then to her, 'I'm very sorry Frank sat on your Princess. I'm afraid he doesn't see very well.'

'Oh dear.' Lydia stashed Princess under one arm as she leaned down to peer at Frank. 'Blind?'

'Oblivious,' I said, nodding.

She opened her mouth and closed it again, not seeming to know what to make of me. Or Frank.

'Anyway,' I continued, 'that's no excuse for sitting on your little Princess here.' I held my hand out, palm up, so I didn't frighten the little dog, and it still snapped at me. 'Who seems delightful.'

'She . . . umm, well, thank you.'

Having defused the situation – yet scored a couple of self-satisfying passive aggressive points – I watched Harry pick up a stick and offer one end of it to Frank.

'Oh dear,' Lydia said again. 'He can't see that, can he?'

Truth was if it wasn't a hot dog, Frank didn't consider it worth his time of day. Yet, as we watched, he tentatively grabbed at it.

Harry, having got his attention, pulled the stick away and backed off, tail wagging.

'Go get 'em, Frank,' I said. 'Go get the stick.'

Frank looked at me.

'Go on!'

He took off.

'Oh, that was so heartwarming,' Lydia said. 'He overcame his disability. We can all take a lesson from that.'

I felt guilty for misleading the woman, although she'd pretty much misled herself. Still, I tried to show interest in her fur-wrapped set of teeth.

'How much does Princess weigh?' I asked.

'Eight pounds three ounces.' She gave the Peke a kiss on the nose. 'Right, Princie?'

'Princie' was squirming and Lydia leaned down to set her on the ground, almost tipping over herself. 'She just hates to be carried around.'

I glanced over to see Frank running – actually running – after Harry. I wasn't necessarily one for making small talk, but since I had the time . . . 'Funny you should mention that. I was just talking to a woman with a chihuahua—'

The woman shuddered. 'Such yippy little dogs.'

'I didn't find that.' I was defending a chihuahua? But Lydia's comment, especially given the manners of her own dog, smacked of canine elitism. 'Mocha seemed—'

'Mocha? You mean Marian Satterwite's poor dog?'

'Yes,' I said, feeling a stab of fear for the little fleabag. 'Why? Did something happen to her?'

'Happen?' Lydia raised her eyebrows. 'Other than spending her life in that horrible woman's purse?'

I think I'd found Marian's 'crazy handbag rescue woman.'

'How would Marian Satterwite like to have *her* hair fall out? Or little legs atrophy?'

'Mocha's legs atrophied?' I asked, horrified.

'Well, no,' Lydia said primly. 'But they would have if we hadn't staged an intervention with the husband.'

'Are you with a rescue organization?'

She was nodding as she reached into a pocket and pulled out a business card. 'Oh, sorry,' she said, using her thumbnail to dislodge a liver treat before handing the card to me.

'It's hell in a handbag,' I read. I thought the expression actually was 'hell in a hand*basket*,' but it didn't seem the time to debate it. Besides, it was a damn good slogan.

'That is a damn good slogan,' I said, handing back the card.

'No, keep it,' she said. 'You see somebody with a dog in a purse, give it to them.'

I slipped the liver-spotted card into my pocket. 'Can you just assume the dog is being abused? Some dogs might like an occasional ride in a purse, right?'

'Occasional, maybe,' Lydia said. 'But dogs aren't meant to be fashion accessories. Even the smallest dog needs exercise and takes work. Do you think Paris Hilton is cleaning poop out of her Gucci purse? I think not.'

I thought probably likewise.

'These dogs are discarded when they do what comes naturally,' Lydia continued. 'Be dogs. Then, after having spent every day in close contact with a human, they suddenly find themselves alone in shelters or abandoned on the side of the road. Can you imagine? Poor puppies have all sorts of psychological and physical problems. Chihuahuas, pugs, bichons, Pomeranians—'

'Is Princess one of your rescues?' The Pekingese was following Frank and Harry at a safe distance.

Lydia rolled her eyes. 'You tried to pet her. Would you want to stuff her in a bag?'

'No way.'

'Pekes have a reputation for being willful,' Lydia said. 'I respect that. And it usually keeps them out of handbags.'

'I had no idea this was such a problem.'

'You don't hear so much about it here in the US,' Lydia said. 'In the UK, though, they saw a huge boom in illegal breeding and smuggling. No surprise – there was an eighty percent rise in demand for these little dogs. Then, as the purse-dog fad dwindled there, rescues saw a corresponding rise in the number of handbag breeds abandoned.'

'People have always bought dogs of all types for the wrong reason,' Becky said, coming up behind us. 'We see them here every day.'

'It's just these dogs are so small and defenseless—' A snarl made Lydia break off and we turned to see that Princess had Frank and Harry cornered.

Lydia blushed. 'Well, not all of them. Let me take Princess home before she does damage.'

We watched as she gathered up the Pekingese. Frank and Harry followed them to the gate.

'They want to make sure she's gone,' Becky said as Lydia and the peke disappeared.

'Maybe it's a crush,' I said as the two dogs bounded back.

'These two?' Becky said. 'They do have fun together.'

'I agree, but I meant Princess. I think she has a crush on Frank or Harry or both. Did you see her following them around? She's like a girl on the playground teasing a boy she likes.'

'Maybe you're right,' Becky said with a smile.

'Well, I suppose it's time to get Frank home. But thank you for this place.'

'Hey,' Becky said. 'Believe me, you'll pay for it in volunteer hours.'

I had a feeling I would. Calling Frank, I started toward the gate and then turned as he stopped to water one last bush.

Which reminded me. 'Is there a restroom here?'

'I wish.' Becky picked up a broom and was sweeping the walk. 'We had one, but the homeless were using it overnight. Not that *not* having one is any better.' She made a face. 'They just make do.'

I hoped it wasn't a pun. 'People sleep right here at the park?' I glanced around.

'Don't worry. They're harmless; it's just very sad for them and not very . . . hygienic for us. They come in mostly after hours, when the park is empty. Doug has been stopping by late and handing out information and offering transportation to St Anne's, our local homeless shelter.'

'You'd think that would be so much more preferable to sleeping outside. This time of year, it's not so bad. But in winter?' I shivered.

'I know, but there are all sorts of reasons people are on the streets.' She pointed toward a figure lingering on the edge of a wooded area. 'There's one, I bet. Hood up, even on a warm day.'

'And no dog?'

Becky sighed. 'That's not a clue, I'm afraid. A lot of the homeless have dogs, the poor things.'

'The homeless or the dogs?'

'Both. Though maybe the dogs have it better. I've seen people on the street go without eating to feed their dogs.'

'Probably the only friends they have.'

The figure had faded away into the trees. 'I want to help, but I also have to keep this place safe.' She gave Frank a scratch. 'Have a good night, you two.'

'Thanks.' Leaving the park, I slipped Frank's leash on and we headed home.

My sheepdog was sound asleep in the backseat and snoring before we did a mile. The park really was good for him. Frank didn't get nearly the amount of exercise he probably needed and the socialization would be an added benefit. For both of us.

'Wakey-wakey,' I said to Frank as we pulled into the driveway. 'We're home.' Turning off the engine, I saw movement on the porch. The scenario had a familiar feel.

'Mocha?' I called, as I got out of the car. 'Is that you?'

ELEVEN

While I was glad to see the chihuahua, Frank seemed less so. I sat down on the porch steps and Mocha hopped on to my lap. Frank hovered near the Escape.

'Geez, Mocha,' I said to the little dog. 'How did you get here?'

She licked my face.

The distance from the Satterwite house to mine was maybe two miles. Not all that far, unless you had a three-inch stride.

'Pretty impressive,' I told her. 'Especially since you'd have to cross Brookhill Road.' I sniffed. 'Didn't poop yourself this time, I smell. What about fleas?' She wrapped herself around counter-clockwise, so she could gnaw on her back leg. 'You're kidding, right?' She stopped.

'Quite the joker,' I said, standing up with her. 'I guess we should call your mom before it gets dark. She'll be worried.'

Or not.

As I unlocked the door, Frank pushed in behind.

Mocha growled at him.

I held her up – nose to nose. 'Listen, Missy. This is Frank's home and you're a visitor. You be polite while you're here – you understand me?'

She didn't say yes, but she didn't say no, either. I put her down to get my phone, so I could call Marian.

Frank was already in the kitchen, slurping down water from his bowl. As I pulled out my phone, Mocha padded over.

'Grrrr,' from the little dog.

'Mocha,' I warned, 'I told—'

Frank lifted his head from the dish and shook, sending water and spittle in every direction.

Mocha backed away, eying Frank warily.

Pleased with himself, the sheepdog went back to drinking, one eye on the suddenly sodden little dog.

Maybe they'd work it out themselves. Though Mocha likely wouldn't be here long enough for it to matter. As far as I was concerned, Frank and I were in for the night. If Marian wanted the chihuahua, she could come get her.

As I was about to dial, my phone rang.

'Pavlik,' I said into it. 'I didn't know if you could talk on the phone while you were sitting Shiva.'

'Actually,' he said, keeping his voice low, 'we're on the cusp between Shabbat, when you can't sit Shiva, and Shiva, which I guess we're starting now.'

'So Shabbat ends at sunset and that's when Shiva starts?'

'Honestly, I'm not sure,' Pavlik said. 'My dad is Googling this as we go.' A hesitation. 'I miss you.'

'I miss you, too,' I said, warmth spreading through me. 'Are you sure I shouldn't drive to Chicago?'

'Positive,' Pavlik said. 'I love my dad, but he's gone temporarily off the deep end.'

'The woman he loved died suddenly,' I said.

'He says I should marry a nice Jewish girl.'

At least I was nice. Mostly. 'It probably won't help to assure him that I'm as Jewish as he is?'

'Not at the moment,' Pavlik said regretfully. 'I'm hoping this will pass.'

'Or you'll marry a nice Jewish girl?'

Pavlik laughed. 'I'm marrying the girl I want to marry. And,' he sighed, 'I know my father will come around. It's just with Mom dying so suddenly and Dad acting this way . . .'

'You feel like you've lost him, too.'

'Exactly.'

One word, but I heard the catch in his voice. 'I'm coming down.'

'No.' One word again, but this one emphatic enough to hurt a little.

'You truly don't want' – now my voice caught – 'me there? I want to help.'

'Please, please don't take this the wrong way, but it'll just be easier for me to deal with him without you here.'

'I understand.' I tried to keep my voice even, best I could.

'You really do? Or are you just saying that?'

'I'm just saying that,' I said, pulling out a kitchen chair and sitting down. 'But I'm sure I will understand once I give it some thought. It just hurt my feelings for a second.'

'I know. And that's the last thing I want to do.'

'I know.'

Awkward silence.

I broke it with the only thing I could think of. 'Arial is still missing, and Sarah and I were talking. Was any money taken from the Satterwites' accounts?'

'How could you know that?' Pavlik asked. 'Hallonquist just told me that not ten minutes ago.'

'Just a hunch.' I was feeling pretty pleased with myself. 'Marian came by looking for Mocha and she seems to think Arial and George took off together.'

'That's one of our theories, too. But with or without the girl, George Satterwite is out there somewhere, probably of his own accord.'

'But maybe he was forced to withdraw the money. How much was it, anyway?'

I'd apparently crossed the invisible line because Pavlik hesitated before saying, 'Not enough to make us think he did it under instructions from a kidnapper.'

Presumably, that would be a larger withdrawal – or quick series of withdrawals – with the kidnapper in the wind and George either released or dead before the transactions could be traced.

'You're thinking George kept the withdrawal small hoping nobody would notice?'

'Possibly. Debit and credit cards were used, too.'

'None of this necessarily means Arial is with him.'

'Then where is she?'

'I don't know. But wherever it is, I hope she's safe.' I stood up and pulled two dishes out of the cupboard, scooping dog food – a mountain in one, a molehill in the other. 'Speaking of being safe, guess who showed up at my door tonight?'

'Since I have faith that you wouldn't be harboring a human fugitive, I assume the dog?'

'Yup, Mocha.' Dinner about to be served, both dogs had stopped eyeing each other suspiciously and were sitting side by side at my feet. 'Wait.'

'All right.'

I set down the dishes. 'No, I meant the dogs should wait until I said it was OK for them to eat.'

Of course, at the word 'OK' Frank buried his face in the dish. Glancing over at him, the chihuahua followed suit. 'I've got to get another release word. I use "OK" too often in conversation.'

'Why do you think the dog came back?'

'Probably didn't want to go home to Marian. Did you know there are purse-dog rescues?'

'I. . . well, no. I didn't. This chihuahua is Marian Satterwite's purse dog?'

'Was. Until Mocha bit her or the rescue people got hold of her. I'm not clear on which was the tipping point. I did meet the rescue woman at the dog park today, though.'

'That new one on Wilson? I took Muffin there once. Nice place.'

'It is.' Frank had finished his food and swiveled his head toward Mocha's. The little dog just raised its top lip and Frank hesitated. 'I suppose I should call Marian.'

'You haven't already? He has fleas.'

'Mocha's a she. And it seems she's cured.'

'Until the eggs hatch.'

My shoulders dropped. 'Now, why did you have to say that? I'm going to itch all night.'

'You're planning to keep her all night? Not in our bed, I hope.'

'No, of course not. I may even call Marian to get her. I just thought it was odd that she came looking for her this morning when she doesn't even like the dog.'

'Where did she come looking?'

'Uncommon Grounds, but only to ask if I'd seen her. Oh! Do you know if Hallonquist noticed the doggy footprints in the hallway? I think Mocha might have tracked the victim's blood down the hall to the door.'

'Not sure, but from what Hallonquist said, there was plenty of blood to be tracked. What difference would a few paw prints make?'

'I don't know, but when I stopped by the house around noon today, Marian was cleaning the floor and the prints were gone.'

'Headline: "Rash of cleanliness sweeps the nation, destroying evidence."' He was teasing me. 'I wouldn't worry about it. If it was of note, crime scene already took a sample.'

'I suppose.' I remembered something else. 'Marian said she was going to see Detective Angles to look at "known associates" of the victim. That means you have an ID?'

'Mitchell Walker. Age twenty-nine.'

Mitchell, not Michael. 'Does he have a record?'

'Not really. Got into trouble for selling papers he pulled off the internet in college. Changed a few grades. There was a shoplifting charge from a convenience store that was dropped. The usual.'

'The usual? These are the things any kid does when they're away at school?' Not my kid.

'Believe me, in my world, this is small potatoes.'

I supposed it was. And Pavlik had spent most of his life and career in Chicago, where the violent crime rate was higher than Milwaukee's and certainly higher than Brookhills'. 'Then what "known associates" would Angles have been showing Marian?'

'Classmates maybe. Or it might have been a pretense.'

That was an interesting thought. 'Detective Angles called Marian in to look at pictures in order to have a chance to pump her for information?'

'Cindy's a good detective. We're lucky to have her on our force.'

'I liked her,' I said. 'Oh, on the subject of blood. I found the napkin with the blood from Arial's cheek on it.'

'And?'

'And, as I feared, it was washed, dried and pretty much shredded. I kept the pieces. Think anything could be raised from it?'

'That, I very much doubt.' There was a voice in the background. 'I have to go. But do me a favor?'

'Anything,' I said.

'If you find any more evidence, just pile it in a basket, and I'll take care of washing it when I get home.'

'Deal.'

TWELVE

'First time Pavlik ever said *that* to me.'

'You mean called your place home?' Sarah asked.

It was late morning on Sunday, and we were cleaning up after the Goddard Gang.

'No,' I said, straightening up from a table I was wiping. 'But that, too. I was talking about not washing anything. This is the guy who starches his jeans.'

Sarah picked up the bussing tray of dirty cups. 'Well, whatever he's doing, it's working for him.'

Was this my partner lusting after my boyfriend? 'Hey!'

'What?' Setting the tray on the counter, she turned to give me a dirty grin. 'I'm just saying he always looks well put together.'

'Yeah, yeah, yeah. He's good-looking.'

'*And* rides a Harley. I think that's the perfecta of men. Or should I say *perfectamundo*?'

'Been watching the Fonz on re-runs of *Happy Days*?' I didn't know Sarah was into seventies sitcoms.

'Actually, no. I've been betting the ponies down at Arlington racetrack. A perfecta is—'

'Getting the first two finishers in order. I know,' I said, moving on to the next table. 'And the "*mundo*"?'

'"World" in Spanish. A tribute to your tiny Mexican house guest.' Sarah was very pleased with herself. 'Have you called Marian?'

'To come get Mocha, you mean? No.'

Sarah raised her eyebrows. 'And why is that? Don't tell me you don't like the woman.'

'You know that I don't. I told you I stopped by her house yesterday afternoon and asked whether anything was missing from their accounts. She told me it was none of my business.'

'You expected otherwise?'

'Not really. But it's one reason I don't want to call her about Mocha. That and I just can't get past the feeling that the dog may hold the key to something,' I admitted. 'Or Marian thinks she does.'

'Because she came looking for a dog she doesn't necessarily even like?' Sarah disappeared and then reappeared in the service window to heft the tray of dirty dishes.

'That and the fact she wiped up the paw prints in the hall.'

'Wiped up everything in the hall, from what you said.'

I thought about that. 'You're right. I suppose there could have been something else that we didn't notice. It's just odd that she felt compelled to clean. She has people for that.'

'You don't have people and it still isn't your thing.'

It was true. 'I know. Yet it seems to be the recurring theme over the last couple of days. Marian mopping the hallway, Arial stripping the sheets so Marian thinks she's having an affair, me washing and drying the bloody napkin to oblivion. If we all kept our hands out of the sudsy water, we might actually have some clues.'

'And fleas.' Sarah was loading the cups into the dishwasher.

'Yes. Definitely fleas. I—' I stopped.

Finishing with the cups, Sarah closed the dishwasher door. 'Are you going to wipe that table or just stand there?'

'Just stand here,' I said. 'Thinking.'

'Would you care to tell me about what?'

'About how Mocha got to my house. I found her at the freeway exit and drove her to my house in the middle of the night. Then Friday morning I drove her back to the Satterwites. She'd have to be one smart dog to find her way back to my house on foot.'

'You didn't see *Lassie Come Home*?'

'No, and neither has anybody else in the last seventy-five years. Probably time for a remake. But the point is, it's not my home this lassie should be coming home to.'

'You think somebody drove the little mutt there and dropped her off? Why?'

'Maybe to protect her? Or because they couldn't take her along wherever they were going.'

'"They" being Arial and George Satterwite?'

'Arial is the only one who knows where I live.'

Sarah met my eyes. 'Then she's alive.'

I put my hand on her shoulder. 'I've always believed that.'

'I wish I had been as sure.' She collapsed into a chair. 'My sister is a real piece of work, but I didn't want to have to talk to her for the first time in years and tell her that Arial was dead. Not that she would have cared.'

'Is it truly that bad?' I sat down across from her. 'Arial is her daughter.'

'Arial, in Ruth's words, is a mistake from a one-night stand with a guy she met online, who turned out to be married.'

'The guy from IBM?'

'Or Microsoft, or Cisco, or Apple, or Intel. It changes every time Ruth tells the story. Truth is not her strong suit.'

'Was this hook-up in college? We all do stupid things when we're young.' Like trusting that the person on the other end of the computer or smartphone was who they said they were.

'Ruth was still in school. But then there's my mother. You asked about naming the baby after a computer font? Ruth liked the name Ariel, with an "e," like the Little Mermaid. My mother suggested this spelling. Thought it was clever and meant it as a dig, of course, at Ruth's computer hook-up.'

'No.' I had a sick feeling in my stomach. 'But your sister didn't have to agree to it. Does Arial know?'

'Of course. They never made any secret of it – thought it was funny, in fact. Like I said, the story would adapt to the audience, but it would always end with how they'd "done right by her," as if somehow it was Arial's fault and Ruth was noble for rising above.'

Saint Ruth.

'I'm so sorry,' I said.

Sarah pushed the chair back and stood up. 'Me, too. Happily, by some miracle Arial survived and even turned out more well-adjusted than I am. She says families are families, no matter how shitty they treat each other.'

I had started to stand up, too, and stopped.

'What now?'

'I just realized I didn't wash all the evidence. Or, at least, some of it may have survived.'

'Again, I ask, what?'

'The poo.'

'The poo,' Sarah repeated.

'Yes.' I tossed her the rag I'd been using to clean tables. 'Mocha had pooped herself, she was so scared.'

She let the dirty cloth fall, and then picked it up gingerly by one corner before dropping it in the sink. 'So you told me. In graphic detail, thank you.'

'You're welcome.' I approached the counter. 'But what if it wasn't poop? What if it was blood or something else significant that she dragged her butt in?'

'How does one significantly drag one's butt?'

'You know what I mean. And something else has been bothering me.'

'I can't wait to find out what.'

'Do you remember how stiff Walker was?'

'I do. As well as how underappreciated my stiff joke was.'

'Rigor mortis starts in the small muscles in the head and face. I think it takes a while to get to bigger ones like the shoulders. If he was killed at seven-fifteen, we found him five hours later. I'm not sure that's enough time.'

This got Sarah's attention. 'But you heard the shots.'

'Maybe Arial was right, and they were just firecrackers,' I said. 'I don't know.'

'There's a lot you don't know,' Sarah said. 'But the coroner must have a time of death, right? They'll have taken into account the rigor mortis and all.'

'True,' I said, considering. 'I'll ask Hallonquist.'

'Why not Pavlik?'

'He's still in Chicago, and I don't know if he'll pick up my call.'

'You two kids have a fight?'

'No, it's Shabbat. Or by now, I guess, Shiva.'

Sarah looked confused.

'It's a long story.' I was untying my apron.

'Then I prefer not to hear it,' she said. 'And where do you think you're going? We don't close for another three hours.'

'So we'll close early. There's nobody here. You want to come with me?'

'Beats sitting around an empty store.' She was already untying her own apron. 'But where are we going?'

'My own backyard.'

'Let me get this straight,' Sarah said. 'We're looking for fleas?'

We were on our hands and knees, wearing blue plastic gloves and searching through the crab grass outside my garage door.

'A needle in a haystack would be easier to find, you know,' Sarah continued grousing.

'The fleas are probably long gone,' I said. 'Hitched a ride on the next warm-blooded mammal that passed by.'

Frank, who was sniffing a nearby maple tree, lifted his head.

'Present company excepted, I hope,' I told him.

Mocha had spent the day in the crate. She and Frank were making progress, but I couldn't imagine what both the house and the dogs would have looked like after a day left to their own devices. Now the smaller dog was safely exploring the garage while we huddled out here in the backyard.

'We're looking for dog hair. That should be a whole lot easier.' Sarah had probably perfected sarcasm at the age of five and facetiousness hot on sarcasm's heels.

'Not just dog hair. A whole wad of dog hair, matted with poop. Or blood.'

'Gets better and better.' She didn't lift her head. 'You might cut the grass back here occasionally.'

'I do. Occasionally.' Just not recently.

'What's this?' Sarah said, holding out a clod of something.

'I think it's just dried mud.' I looked more closely and sniffed. 'Nope. Poop.'

'Isn't that what we're after?'

'There's no fur there. That's likely just a Frank poop I missed.'

'The last time you didn't cut the grass.'

'Exactly.'

Sarah tried to drop it and her glove came off with it. 'Damn it. These latex gloves suck.'

'I'm allergic to latex. They're nitrile.'

'And must be just fine for dying your hair. But they don't stand up to poop-hunting.'

'I'll tell the manufacturer.' I handed her another glove from the box. 'And I don't dye my hair.'

'Sure you don't,' she said, slipping it on.

'I don't.' I had people – or a person – for that. And it was more a touch-up.

Frank had wandered over and was nuzzling something on the ground.

'Leave it,' I said, and picked it up, fumbling a bit with my gloves.

'See?' Sarah said. 'I told you these gloves su—'

'This is it!' I said, holding it up.

'If it is, Frank just contaminated the thing,' Sarah said skeptically. 'You turn it over to the cops, it'll place him at the scene. Your sheepdog will fry.'

'Funny,' I said, examining the evidence.

'What's the verdict?' Sarah was sitting back on her heels, looking relieved. 'Hidden treasure map, congealed blood or just your basic poop?'

'Probably not the former. But as for the rest, I don't know.' I stood up and opened the garage door. 'Wait, Mocha,' I said, and the little dog, who'd trotted to the door when I opened it, went back to sniffing Eric's old tennis racket in the corner.

'What do you mean?' Sarah asked, coming into the garage. 'You knew Frank's poop was poop when you saw it.'

'I'm very familiar with Frank's poop.'

'That's kind of creepy, you know that?' She glanced out at the sheepdog, who was laying down another one.

'I said familiar, not intimate. I pick up a lot of it.' Tons, it seemed.

'Well, does the blob there smell like poop?'

'Dried poop doesn't smell all that much unless it gets squished, but yeah, I'm getting a whiff. But that doesn't mean it's not mixed with blood or something else.'

'I don't know why you wanted to find this so bad,' Sarah said. 'We know the little fart stepped into the guy's blood.'

I puffed out my chest. 'Maybe it will help pin down the time of death. Or . . . or . . . I don't know.' My chest deflated.

My partner shook her head in disgust. 'You don't know. And you've had me crawling around all afternoon looking for shit.'

'Sarah!'

'Why is poop an OK word and sh—'

'Enough!' I set the clod of fur and whatever on the ledge next to the sink and slipped off my gloves. Retrieving the box from outside, I pulled out a clean glove. Slipping it on to my hand, I picked up the clod with it and then neatly snapped the glove off inside out, clod contained, and knotted the glove at the wrist.

'That was pretty cool,' Sarah said grudgingly. 'Did Pavlik show you that?'

'No. It's poop-bag inspired, but they're in the house and I didn't want to go in with dirty hands.' I dangled the glove and its contents. 'You're right that I don't know what this could possibly prove. But it's the only piece of evidence I've come into contact with that I haven't destroyed. I'm turning it over to Hallonquist. Can you get Mocha?' I gestured toward the dog who had come to sit at my feet, apparently thinking the glove contained something good.

'You want me to pick it up?'

'The dog? Yes. We need to go in the house. What's the matter with you? You like dogs.' Sort of.

'It's got fleas.'

'It's a she, and I killed the fleas.'

'Fleas are like zombies. You only think they're dead until they bite you.'

'Pick up the dog.'

For once, Sarah did as she was told and followed me into the house, Frank at her heels.

Instructing Sarah to put Mocha safely in the crate in the corner of the living room for now, I punched up Hallonquist's number and put it on speaker.

'Detective Angles.'

Damn. 'Detective Angles, this is Maggy Thorsen. I thought I'd dialed Mike Hallonquist's number.'

'You did, but Mike is pulling together some information for a case, so I offered to get his phone. Can I help you?'

'Is the case Mike is working on the murder at the Satterwite house? Because that's what I'm calling about.'

'No, it's not. Can I help you?' she repeated.

I guess she'd have to. Or, at least, I'd ask her to help.

'Has Forensics determined a time of death for the man who was killed?'

'Walker?' Angles seemed surprised. And not forthcoming. 'Why do you ask?'

I wondered if she went to the Jake Pavlik school of policing. He always answered a question he didn't want to answer with another question. That I didn't want to answer.

I decided not to lead with the poop. 'The Satterwite's dog, Mocha, showed up at my house last night.'

'I'm sure Mrs Satterwite will be happy to hear he's all right.'

'*She's* all right. Mocha is a girl. And, yes, Marian has been looking for her. I just think it's odd that the dog was on my doorstep instead of the Satterwites'. She doesn't know where I live.'

'"She" being the dog, I assume?'

'Yes, Mocha. Though Marian doesn't know where I live either.'

'But wasn't Mocha just at your house?'

'Only overnight. And I picked her up just off the freeway and drove her home. And then drove her to the Satterwites.'

'I don't own a dog, but I hear they're pretty good at finding their way home. Landmarks and such.'

'But this isn't home,' I said, as I had with Sarah. 'Or at least, her home. And you haven't seen her, but Mocha is a chihuahua. The little thing isn't big enough to see out of the car window. Even if she was some kind of doggy genius, how could she navigate by landmarks she didn't see?'

There was silence after I finished.

'Detective Angles?'

'Sorry. I was just . . . You believe that somebody dropped

her off?'

'Yes.'

'Like Arial Kingston or George Satterwite.'

I glanced over at Sarah, who just shrugged. I took it as permission to answer freely. 'Arial would know where I live.'

'Interesting.' I thought I heard the sound of pen to paper. 'You say this was last night?'

'The dog was on the porch waiting when I came home from the dog park about five.'

'Still light, so maybe one of your neighbors saw something.'

'It's possible. You might want to talk to them today. Most will be off to work tomorrow.' I flashed Sarah a smile.

'I'll swing by.'

'Good idea,' I said. 'And be sure to stop by here for Mocha. Who knows, there might be evidence on her.'

Sarah was shaking her head as I hung up the phone. 'You're going to give her your glove of poop, aren't you?'

'You bet I am.'

THIRTEEN

The first time the doorbell rang, it was pizza delivery.
'I don't know why you couldn't wait to eat until after Detective Angles was here and gone,' I said, carrying the flat box into the kitchen.

'Hey, evidence hunting is hard work. I'm starved.' Sarah was getting out the paper plates.

'Pepperoni, right?' I lifted the lid of the box.

'Pepperoni and artichokes. Gotta get our veggies.'

Interesting combination. But I was game.

'What kind of red wine do you have?' Sarah was now in my wine cabinet. Which was really just the shelf above the Ritz Crackers boxes and spray cheese.

I grabbed the latter two. 'Hors d'oeuvres?'

Sarah cocked her head. 'Sort of miniature cheese pizzas without the sauce, don't you think? We might as well go right to the main event.'

'You're right.' Putting the cheese and crackers back, I took a bottle of wine from the next shelf. 'A red blend OK?'

She wrinkled her nose. 'I think my elevating the mundane pepperoni pizza with the addition of artichoke hearts calls for a single varietal.'

Snob. 'Cabernet?'

That got her nod of approval and she pulled out three wine glasses.

'Why three?'

'The detective.' She was working on opening the bottle.

'She can't drink,' I said. 'And I think I'll wait to have a glass until after she's been here.'

'Worried about being impaired?' Sarah pulled out the cork and splashed wine into two of the glasses. 'You're handing over a dog, not being questioned.'

Right again. I picked up both glasses. 'Let's take the pizza into the living room.'

Sarah hesitated. 'Frank will slobber on the coffee table and, therefore, the pizza.'

'He doesn't do that,' I said, leading the way. 'At least not when we're eating.'

'He did when I was here.' Sarah had the pizza box with the paper plates and napkins balanced on top.

'Well, that's your fault, then,' I said, setting the glasses on the table to help her unload. 'You have to tell him no.'

'Just say no? You're telling me he drools on command?' Sarah piled two triangles of the pie on to a plate, trailing melted cheese across the glass coffee table. And here she was, complaining about Frank. Drool was a cinch to clean up compared with coagulated mozzarella.

I handed her a napkin. 'Sit, Frank.'

The sheepdog obediently sat about a foot away from the table. A string of drool hit the floor, just missing the table.

'See? No drool on the coffee table or the pizza.' Taking a paper plate, I loaded it with a slice of pizza and took it back into the kitchen.

'Was it something I said?' Sarah called.

'Hang on,' I said. 'I should have done this the first time we were in here.'

'Done what?'

'Feed the dogs.' I cut a quarter of the slice into Mocha-sized bites and the rest into Frank-hunks and sprinkled some kibbles on top.

'I don't know why you bother,' Sarah said from the doorway.

'Bother what?' I slid Mocha's share on a fresh paper plate.

'Cutting it up and adding dog food. Frank won't even notice. The whole thing will be gone in one gulp.'

'It makes me feel like a better doggy parent than if I just hand him a slice right out of the box.' Returning to the living room, I set Frank's plate down in front of him and went to slip Mocha's into the crate. By the time I turned back, Frank's pizza had disappeared and he seemed to be contemplating eating the greasy plate.

'See?' Sarah said.

Frank let out a harrumph and slid down into a supplicant position, as I picked up the plate. 'Beg all you want,' I said, 'but that's it. You don't want to lose your svelte figure.'

Hefting himself back on his feet, Frank ambled nonchalantly toward the crate. If sheepdogs could whistle, that's just what he'd have been doing as he angled ever nearer.

Mocha, who was still working on her first tiny morsel, glanced up and lifted her top lip into a snarl. Frank veered off.

'She's got your number, buddy,' I told him. 'If you slowed down and chewed your food, you'd still have some left, like Mocha.'

The sheepdog turned and stalked out of the room.

'She'll be gone soon,' I called after him.

Choosing a piece with extra artichoke hearts for myself, I was just about to take a bite when the doorbell rang. 'That would be Detective Angles.'

'Perfect timing,' Sarah said, setting aside her empty plate. 'I'm done.'

'And I thought Frank eats fast,' I said as I set down my slice and went to answer the door.

'Detective Angles,' I said, opening it. 'Come in.'

'Thank you.' She stepped into the front hall.

'Did you talk to the neighbors?'

'For all the good it did.' She sniffed. 'Is that pepperoni pizza?'

'With artichokes. Would you like a slice?'

'I'd love one, to be honest,' she said, entering the room. 'I'm just coming off duty and haven't had a thing to eat all day.'

'Then you'll want a glass of wine to go with your pizza.' Sarah held up the bottle.

Angles glanced at her watch. 'Yes, thank you. I'm off the clock.'

'Hang on,' I said. 'There's just one thing you might want to see first.' I ducked into the kitchen and came back with the glove.

'A latex glove?'

'Nitrile,' Sarah said, passing me to get the third wine glass from the kitchen table.

'It's what's *in* the glove,' I said. 'I cut a tuft of hair off Mocha that's tangled with what I think might be blood—'

'And is undoubtedly poop,' Sarah added, setting the glass on the coffee table. 'The fleas are gone, though.'

Angles was holding the knotted glove at arm's length. 'You're kidding.'

'No, they really are gone. Though God knows where to.' Sarah poured the wine. 'Hope Cabernet is OK.'

'Perfect.' Angles bounced the glove up and down from the knot I'd tied in it. 'Did this come off the dog today?'

I felt my face redden. 'No, actually. It was Thursday night – or really early Friday morning – when I found her wandering in the industrial park. I know that's before Walker was killed, but—'

'What time?'

'Did I find Mocha, you mean?' I asked.

Angles nodded.

'I left Chicago about midnight and it's a ninety-minute drive here without traffic. So it would have been about one-thirty when I saw her on the Brookhills off-ramp.'

'So one-thirty a.m.?'

'By the time I lured her into the car and got her home and into the tub it was probably approaching two.'

Another nod. 'Let me log this and lock it up. Back in a second.'

I cocked my head as the door closed behind the detective. 'I wonder if she's supposed to take it back to the lab tonight.'

'Probably,' Sarah said. 'And she probably would do it pre-pizza if she actually thought it was evidence.'

I sat down and took a sip of my wine. 'Actually, she seemed more interested than I expected, asking about the timing and all. Maybe I'm right and the rigor means Walker was killed earlier.'

'Earlier like midnight, instead of seven a.m.?'

'Closer to eleven, when Arial said Mocha took off.'

'If you were right about the rigor, then you were wrong about the gunshots.'

Can't be right about everything.

A tap on the door.

'Come on in,' I called.

Angles re-entered and stopped by the crate. 'So, this is the Satterwite pup?'

'It is,' I said. 'Are you taking her with you?'

Frank peered around the corner hopefully.

'There's no reason to, unless there's something I don't know.' She took a piece of pizza from the box and sat down. 'So tell me.'

'Like I said, she showed up at the door late yesterday afternoon.'

'And just to be clear, this was the second time she's been here?'

'Right. The first time was when I found her on the exit ramp around one-thirty Friday morning and returned her to the Satterwites' house around seven. Then yesterday – Saturday – she was on the porch when Frank and I got home from the dog park.'

'So the dog resurfaces, but still no sign of Arial Kingston.' This was directed to Sarah.

'Are you asking if she dropped off the dog? I don't know. I wasn't here.'

Angles swiveled to get a more direct sightline to Sarah. 'But she's your niece. She hasn't been in touch?'

'No.' Finding herself abruptly in the hot seat, Sarah glanced at the wine glass in her hand and set it down.

'What about the rest of the family?'

'There's just her mother and grandmother, and they're estranged.'

'I know. I called your sister.' I noticed the detective wasn't touching her own wine. 'She seems to think if anybody knew where Arial was, it would be you.'

'She seems to think wrong.'

Sarah's innate crankiness was coming off as defensive – never a good thing with the police. 'Sarah and her sister don't get along either, as you can probably tell. But believe me, if Sarah knew where Arial was, she'd tell me.'

'Of course I would.' Yet Sarah wasn't looking at me.

Angles would have noticed the interplay – or lack thereof.

'Anyway,' I said, 'I think Mocha might have stepped in the blood at the scene because her paw prints led down the hall and away from the body.'

'The sheriff told me about that. I had to tell him that Forensics missed it.'

Score another one for the scrub bucket over the evidence bag. 'He probably wasn't happy about that.'

'He was not. What do you think the paw prints indicate?'

She was asking me? 'Well, I was thinking about that. There were no prints in the theater room near the body; they started just inside the door to the hall. We're thinking somebody picked Mocha up to get her away from the body and then put her down again in the hall.'

'And presumably that same somebody dropped her off at your door the next day.' Angles' eyes shifted to Sarah.

Well done, Maggy. I'd managed to divert the conversation right back to Arial.

I hoped to grill Sarah about her niece's whereabouts later. But for now, I wanted both Kingstons off the hook. 'I didn't want to call Marian Satterwite and tell her I had Mocha until you had a chance to see her.'

Angles stood up and wandered over to the crate, where Mocha had finished her dinner and was tidying herself up. 'Did you check for injuries?'

'Injuries on Mocha? I didn't see any. Why?'

Angles was on her knees next to the crate and swiveled her head toward me. 'You said you believe she had blood on her. An injury seems the obvious reason.'

Then why hadn't I thought of it?

'Come here, sweetie,' she crooned to the chihuahua as she opened the door.

The dog stayed where she was.

'She's a little shy,' I said. 'She's been through quite an ord—'

'Pizza, fleabag?' Sarah was holding up a piece of crust.

Mocha sprung out of the crate and landed on her lap.

'Food motivated,' Angles said, standing up. 'That makes a dog easy to train, they say.'

First theaters, now dog training. The woman knew a little something about everything.

'Frank certainly is food motivated,' I said. 'But he's also smart enough to know when I don't have a treat in my hand and it's safe to ignore me.'

At the word 'treat,' Frank stuck his nose in the room.

'Oh, you have an Old English,' Angles said, catching sight of him and going to give him a rub. 'He's beautiful.'

'Thank you,' I said. 'He's my son's, really, but Eric is away at college.'

'How old?'

I assumed she meant the sheepdog. 'Nearly four.'

'You're a lover, yes, you are.' Angles was kneeling on the floor getting a pizza-tinged facewash from Frank. 'How do the two of them get on?'

'Frank and Mocha? Not well – at least, not dependably well. Which is why Mocha was in the crate.'

'I can't believe this big sweetheart would hurt a fly. Oof.' In a bid for a belly-rub, Frank had flipped over and knocked Angles on to her rump.

'Actually, it's Mocha who snarls at Frank.'

Still on Sarah's lap, nibbling the crust, the little dog batted her eyes, all innocence.

'Oh, I'm sure she couldn't hurt him, either. You should let them sort it out themselves.'

Easy to say, when you haven't had to unwedge your terror-stricken sheepdog from under a chair. Though admittedly the two canines were chilling out a bit, if not necessarily warming up to each other. 'I'll give that a try. Though I doubt Mocha will be here long enough for it to matter. Are you certain you shouldn't take her with you?'

Frank gave Angles a big sloppy kiss at the thought, but the detective said, 'No reason to. You probably should give Mrs Satterwite a call and let her know the dog is all right. Or I can, if you like.'

'I will,' I said quickly. 'I understand there's still no sign of her husband?'

'Either with or without Arial Kingston.' Angles patted Frank before levering him off her so she could stand up. 'Marian Satterwite thinks they were having an affair, so we're investigating that possibility.'

'She mentioned that to us yesterday.' I turned to Sarah. 'Maybe that's why Marian came to the shop. Not to look for Mocha, but to see what you might know about it.'

'An affair that Arial was having with a married man?' Sarah said, gently rubbing Mocha's ear between her thumb and forefinger. 'Why would she tell me about that?'

'I thought you're close,' Angles said.

'Not close enough for that. I'm her aunt, not her girlfriend. She'd know I wouldn't approve.'

'Interesting,' Angles said, about nothing in particular. 'Well, thank you for the pizza and wine.'

'And poop.' Sarah didn't raise her eyes from Mocha, who had flipped over à la Frank and was getting her belly rubbed now.

'That, too.' She opened the door. 'I'll tell Mike what he missed.'

'You said he's on another case?' I asked, following her. Angles was obviously a good detective, but I got a lot more information out of Hallonquist. Angles seemed to expect some in return.

'Just until he turns it over tomorrow.' She flashed me a smile as she stepped out on to the front stoop. 'Believe me, he's more than ready. Computers are not his thing.'

'I'd take computers over homicidal maniacs any day,' I said to Sarah as the door closed. 'But I'll be glad to have Mike back on the case.'

I sat down across from Sarah and Mocha and picked up my wine. 'Now do you want to tell me where Arial is?'

'Arial?' Sarah acted puzzled.

'You didn't look at me when you said that you'd have told me if you knew where Arial was.'

'Actually, you're the one who said that.'

'And you agreed.'

'I did?' She was running her hand through the thick fur on Mocha's haunches.

'You did. Now will you put that dog down and tell me what you're not telling me?'

'I can tell you there's nothing I'm not telling you about Arial,' Sarah said, finally looking up. 'But wouldn't you rather I told you about the crease from a bullet on Mocha's back leg?'

FOURTEEN

Damned if Angles hadn't been right.

I set down my glass. 'You sure it's a bullet wound?'

I crossed to sit next to Sarah on the couch, Mocha between us, as Frank wandered back in. The sheepdog did a double-take at seeing his nemesis still out of the crate. Then, seeming to sense something was wrong, he padded over and lay down in front of the three of us, his head resting on my foot as a pillow.

'Not so much a wound as a graze,' she said. 'See?'

I did see. The angry inch-long scratch was on the dog's right haunch. 'I don't remember seeing that when I bathed her.'

'She's pretty furry there,' Sarah said. 'I felt it more than saw it.'

'You sure it's not just a bad scratch? Maybe a cat attacked her or something.'

At the word 'cat,' Frank raised his head and glanced around. I patted him reassuringly.

'You know when you said a gunshot sounds different than a firecracker?'

'I can't quite explain it, but I know it when I hear it.' Or so I'd thought.

'That's how this is.' She held the fur apart. 'Do you see it's darker on the edges?'

'Maybe.' I got closer. 'Like from gunpowder, you mean?'

'Or the heat of a bullet,' Sarah said. 'It just looks different.'

I sat back. 'Please don't tell me you know this because you shot somebody.'

She was silent for a moment and then shrugged out of her baggy jacket and pushed up her left sleeve. 'See this?'

I gingerly touched a caterpillar-thick three-inch-long scar that crossed her arm just above the elbow. 'That's from a bullet?'

Last year, when Sarah had taken up tennis and appeared in a skirt, I teased her that I'd never seen her bare legs. Now I realized this was also true of her arms.

'Shooting range accident,' she said, pushing her sleeve back down.

'Yours or somebody else's?'

Her eyes narrowed. 'I'm not totally inept with a gun.'

'So, yours.'

'Maybe.' Sarah pulled her jacket back on. 'I don't want to talk about it.'

'How—'

'I told you I don't want to talk about it.'

Then we wouldn't talk about it. Now.

'And that makes you sure that this' – I pointed at Mocha's graze – 'was made by a bullet?'

'Absolutely not.'

'It absolutely wasn't made by a bullet?'

'I'm absolutely not sure it was caused by a bullet. But I think it was.'

I wasn't going to ask her why again. We'd only go full circle back to that which we must not talk about.

'Why didn't you mention the wound when Detective Angles was here?' I asked instead. 'She's the one who brought up the possibility of Mocha being injured.'

'And didn't pursue it.'

No, the detective hadn't, which was odd. But then maybe she thought it didn't matter to the case. 'Should we call Angles to come back?'

'And have this poor baby taken away and poked and prodded?' She actually picked up the dog and kissed her on the lips. Mocha looked as astonished as I was.

Frank, who was dozing, didn't comment.

'Assuming you're right' – I held up my hands – 'and I have no reason to doubt you, Mocha would have been in pain.'

'Explaining why Arial picked her up and only put her down to get her things and run.'

It made sense, given what I knew of Arial. 'Do you think this kind of wound would have bled much?'

'Maybe not a lot, but some.'

'The graze isn't where the matted fur was.'

'Which probably means you just gave the detective a load of shit.'

I didn't scold her this time. She was right. 'We have to tell the investigators that Mocha was shot.'

'It's probably not going to matter. Besides, maybe I'm wrong and it was a cat who scratched her, like you said about Arial. Or even Frank.'

'Now who's not trusting her instincts?' And blaming my sheepdog. But I had the feeling Sarah was prevaricating again for a reason. 'So where is she?'

'Right here.' She pointed at Mocha.

'You know who I mean.'

'I do.' She moved Mocha to one side and stood up. 'I honestly don't know where Arial is.'

'What about Courtney?'

'She's at home.'

I waited.

She gave in. 'I think she may be in touch with Arial, but she's not saying. As for me, I'm just glad to know Arial's OK.'

'Then you agree she's the one who dropped Mocha off?' I asked, picking up the pizza box to take to the kitchen.

'Yes, that.' She gathered up the oft-lifted yet seldom-drunk-from wine glasses. 'But it was the blood I was talking about. It's been worrying me.'

'The blood on Mocha?'

'No, the blood on Arial,' Sarah said. 'When Mocha was wounded, Arial would have picked her up and done kissy face or some such thing.'

'And the blood transferred to Arial's face,' I said, following her out to the kitchen. 'That's plausible.'

'Or it's a combo of Mocha's blood and the blood of the guy who was killed, assuming Mocha got into that.' Dumping the wine down the sink drain, Sarah slipped the glasses into the dishwasher. 'Either way, it wasn't Arial's.'

'Right,' I said, taking the glasses back out to wash by hand. 'That might explain the blood, but it still doesn't tell us where she is.'

It was only when the door closed behind Sarah that I said

out loud what I was thinking. 'I said it might explain the blood on Arial. But does it really?'

Mocha, who was still on the couch, did her best curious-dog expression.

I sat down next to her and gently traced the graze, which was starting to scab over. 'The blood was on Arial's face when she greeted us. That was before you went into the garage and before we heard what I thought were shots.'

Mocha got up and braced her tiny front paws on my shoulders to lick the tip of my nose. When Frank tried that, it usually ended up with me toppling over, him on top of me.

'Thank you,' I said. 'That's a very nice kiss, but I wish you could talk.'

She barked.

'I know. You speak, but I can't understand.'

She had nothing to say to that.

'If that was Walker's blood on your rump, then he – and probably you – were shot before I found you very early Friday morning.'

Mocha turned to lick her wound.

Had she been nursing the injury the night I picked her up? Possibly. It was dark when I'd bathed her, and I'd have assumed any scratching or licking she did was because of fleas, not an injury.

A time of death closer to eleven or midnight would account for Walker's rigor. But what it didn't explain was the very thing Sarah thought it did. 'If Walker was killed earlier and Arial got the blood on her face when she picked you up before you ran away, what was Arial doing between then and when I arrived with you at seven?'

Mocha stood up and barked.

'Waiting for you?' I thought about that. I'd sent the text to George Satterwite's phone around two thirty a.m. and got an immediate reply. Arial had called right at six a.m. and offered to pick up the dog. Was that because she preferred that to my coming to the Satterwite house?

Or was that what both she and George preferred? Had he been there with her the entire time?

The two of them could have swung by my house for Mocha

shortly after we spoke at six and been on their way. Instead they had to wait until I arrived at seven. In the garage with the Navigator packed and ready to leave, George might have jumped the gun by opening the door when I was still there. But, 'Why wouldn't Arial have washed her face between eleven p.m. and seven a.m.?'

It also was possible the blood wasn't Mocha's, despite what Sarah thought. If Walker was already dead, Arial could have transferred his blood to her face while trying to move the body or even getting rid of the gun.

I hated thinking these things about Sarah's niece. Especially without having all the facts, the most important being Walker's time of death. Cindy Angles hadn't been about to give it to me. I wondered if Pavlik would.

Debating the wisdom of interrupting Shiva, I picked up my phone from the coffee table and saw I had two missed calls, both from Pavlik. Oh, God – the last time I had missed his calls, his mom had died. I hoped something hadn't happened to his dad now.

'I'm coming home on the first train tomorrow,' was the way he answered the phone. 'Can you pick me up at the Milwaukee station?'

'Of course I can,' I said. 'But what happened? Don't you have six more days of sitting Shiva?'

'One nearly broke us,' he said. 'My father stood up from his low chair tonight, stretched his back and said, "I don't know how observant Jews do this, but they're better men and women than me. Your mom will just have to take it on faith – any faith – that I loved her."'

'That's it?'

'That, along with offering to rent a car for me so I could drive home tonight.'

'That eager to get rid of you, huh?'

'Dad's former military and law enforcement, just like me. The two of us sitting in a room doing nothing but staring at each other – it was unnatural. And if anything, it made us realize even more how much we missed my mom. She, apparently, was the glue that held the two of us together. I'm not sure that without her . . .' He let it drop.

'Maybe that's the whole purpose of sitting Shiva,' I said gently. 'To realize what you've lost.'

'It certainly did that – even our truncated Shiva. But for now . . . I just want to come home.' He sounded weary. And oh, so sad.

'Listen, I'll hop in the car and come get you right now. No need to wait until tomorrow morning and take the train.'

'It's nearly nine.'

'And I'll get there at ten-thirty, big deal. Besides, traffic should be light driving into Chicago at this time of night.'

'I hate for you to have to do that. It'll be pretty late, driving back.'

'It's a three-hour round trip, so we can be back around midnight. Or, if we get hung up or want to stay over and drive back in the morning, we can do that. I don't work tomorrow.'

'That would be great.' I heard the relief in Pavlik's voice. 'I'm dead tired. I can't think of anything better than sleeping with you in my arms tonight, whether it's here on the daybed or up there with Frank.'

'Either way, we have about the same amount of space,' I said.

'Truer words never spoken.' A hesitation. 'Thank you.'

Ringing off, I turned to look at Mocha on the couch and Frank, who'd roused when I got off the phone with Pavlik. 'Now, what am I going to do with the two of you?'

FIFTEEN

I t was an uneasy truce.

Yes, between Frank and Mocha, but more so with Sarah and Courtney. And it was my fault.

'It's really up to you,' I told Sarah on the phone. 'I can leave the dogs alone overnight, but Mocha will have to be in the crate and they'll both have to be let out and fed first thing in the morning.'

'Let me get this straight. My choice – in doing this favor for you – is to come back to your house right now and stay overnight to referee your crazy dogs or do it at the crack of dawn to feed and water them?'

'Or you can let me stay instead of you,' I heard Courtney protest in the background. 'It's just for one night. Not even one night. It's practically bedtime now.'

I didn't know what fifteen-year-old went to bed at nine p.m., but I had to give her props for the argument.

'If you come to my house,' I told Sarah, 'you'll be leaving Courtney there. What's the difference?'

'The difference is her brother will be here.'

I heard an 'eeeeeyuuuh,' as only a teenage girl can say it. 'I'm so much more mature than Sam is. He was banging up cars when he was my age, remember?'

Nobody was likely to forget.

'Listen,' I said. 'I don't want to cause problems. I'll see if Helen next door is back from vacation. Maybe she can come over in the—'

'No,' Sarah said. 'Courtney is right. She's more mature than Sam, and I know I can trust her completely.' There was an unspoken 'or else' at the end of the sentence.

'Yes!' The word was in the background and then Courtney was on Sarah's phone. 'If you leave before I get dropped off, write down your Wi-Fi password.'

God forbid that she would have a night on her own and not

have Wi-Fi. But Eric was the same way. And Sarah. 'It's next to my computer, with that password, too. As far as the dog food and—'

'Oh, I'll find that,' she said, having taken care of the important stuff. 'No worries. Have fun.' She rang off.

I called back, and Sarah answered. 'What?'

'You're all right with this?'

'I said I was, didn't I?'

'We may not be home until noon or even later, with the Chicago rush hour to deal with in the morning. It goes both ways, you know. In and out of the city. Plus, I don't think it's right to just breeze in, collect Pavlik and breeze out. I want to spend at least a little time with his dad.'

'Hello? Is this Maggy Thorsen I'm speaking to? The one who went to great pains – and inconvenience to me, yet again – to engineer an excuse not to stay with the folks.'

'It is,' I said. 'And I'm sorry. Both for inconveniencing you and pre-judging them.'

'Good. Now go get Pavlik. Just be sure to leave the door unlocked and the lights on.'

'Will do.'

'And Maggy?'

'Yes?'

'Lock your bottom left desk drawer.'

'Done.' I rang off.

Frank was eying Mocha on the couch as I came back into the living room after talking to Sarah.

'Be nice,' I warned.

Frank threw me a dirty look.

'Not you. I was talking to Mocha.'

Reassured, Frank put a tentative paw on the couch. Like I said, he didn't often climb up there. Not because I forbade it – I mean, get serious, the dog sleeps in my bed – but because he doesn't fit on the couch very well. Body parts dangle.

Mocha growled.

'I said be nice. It's Frank's couch, if he chooses to lay on it, and you need to share. You're just a visitor in this strange land.'

Mocha stood up, circled and lay back down again.

Frank lifted a second paw.

'Grrr.'

Provoked, Frank sprang on the couch with one . . . well, I wouldn't call it a leap, necessarily. More like a thud.

He lay down.

Scrabbling and a little sputtering marked Mocha's progress as she tunneled her way back up to the surface of Mount Sheepdog, looking astonished.

Still, she managed another growl, this one a little oxygen-deprived.

Frank settled his big ol' head on the arm of the couch and went to sleep.

Meanwhile, Mocha's eyes were wide with alarm at her unexpected bedfellow. It occurred to me that I'd probably looked about the same that morning I woke up with the nippy little chihuahua nose to nose with me as a kid.

'You'll survive the night,' I said. 'I promise.'

'When I left, she was asleep with her head on his back. Can you believe that?'

'Sounds kind of uncomfortable, given their respective sizes.'

Not quite as uncomfortable as the two of us on the daybed in what had been Pavlik's boyhood room.

Len Pavlik had greeted me with a hug and asked that I take off my shoes, so the neighbors downstairs wouldn't complain about the noise. Then he offered up chocolate cake and his room to us. 'I'm afraid we don't have a couch, but I'm sure you'd rather be together anyway.'

My parents would have insisted on separate rooms and beds. But then I'd been in my teens the last time that situation had presented itself.

Anyway, we'd declined his kind offer of both the cake and his queen-size bed. By morning we might regret the bed, at least, but for now things were just fine. I snuggled up under Pavlik's arm. 'I'm glad we're not driving home tonight.'

'Me, too,' Pavlik said, pulling me even closer. 'And you said Courtney was staying over? What made Sarah change her mind?'

'The prospect of having to do it herself, I think. And—'
My phone buzzed a text message.

I leaned off the bed to pick it up from the floor and nearly
fell. Pavlik righted me. 'The phone? Really?'

'It's just because Sarah hadn't dropped off Courtney when
I left and . . .' I was looking at the screen. 'Yup, she's there
now, but can't get the Wi-Fi to work.'

I tapped in: *It's small F on Frank. And don't forget the
exclamation mark.*

'You're giving her the guest Wi-Fi I set up for you,
right?'

I looked up from my phone. 'Well, no. I can never remember
that.'

Pavlik sat up. 'It's GuestofFrank. How hard is that?'

I shrugged. 'I just figured—'

'These aren't the old days, when the whole neighborhood
poached off somebody's signal and it didn't make a difference.
Anybody who gets on your network has access to everything
that's connected in your house. You might as well leave your
front door unlocked.'

Oops. Did that, too. 'So what if they can turn on my vacuum
cleaner or program my DVR? That's not such a terrible thing.'

'Maggy.'

I sat up, too. 'You're serious about this. You're upset
because I gave Courtney my Wi-Fi?'

'Mike Hallonquist and I have spent countless hours with
Cybercrimes on this. It's not just your vacuum or DVR. It's
your computer. Right this second, somebody could be selling
all your information – your passwords, your social security
number, your charge card numbers – on the dark web.'

Pavlik must be tired to make such a big deal of this, so I
decided to let it slide. 'You're right. Next time I'll use the
guest password.'

Pavlik slid back down under the covers. 'Good. Thank you
for humoring me.'

'You're welcome,' I said, lying down, too. 'If it's important
to you, I'll do it.'

'It should be important to you, too.'

'It is.'

'You say that, but I don't think you—' Pavlik caught himself. 'OK, good.'

I laid my head on his chest.

There was just the sound of our breathing and then Pavlik said, 'It's after eleven o'clock. Shouldn't Courtney be in bed? Tomorrow's a school day.'

'It's summer.' I kissed him on the cheek. 'So, did Angles give you a time of death on Mitchell Walker?'

All I got was an exaggerated snore in response.

'You fake fell-asleep last night,' I said as we drove home the next morning.

'Well, I *genuine* didn't-want-to-be-interrogated.'

Fair enough. 'No matter,' I said. 'I was thinking, though.'

Pavlik didn't look surprised.

'Rigor starts in about two hours and is full-on by twelve, right? Arial and I heard what I thought were gunshots at about seven-fifteen. Sarah and I came back to the house at about noon and Marian discovered the body a few minutes later.'

'So nearly five hours after the shots.'

'Exactly. When Marian pulled the body into her arms, thinking it was her husband, both Sarah and I noticed pretty advanced rigor in the upper body.'

'Also noted by the pathologist.' I'd succeeded in getting Pavlik's participation.

'But I thought rigor started in the small muscles, like in the face, at around two to six hours. Wouldn't it have taken longer for the large muscle groups, like the shoulders and legs?'

'Usually. But there can be unusual circumstances that affect rigor.'

Of course, everybody knew that. Like dying in a freezer, for example. Or the Sahara. The prior slowing rigor, the latter speeding it up. 'The room didn't seem unusually warm or cold.'

'It's not just the physical location of the body that affects rigor, but also the body temp itself.'

'Body temperature before death? Like somebody with a fever might go into rigor faster?'

Pavlik took one hand off the steering wheel in half a 'who knows?' gesture. 'I'm not an expert, but that's what I've been told. Even physical activity before death, like running away from an assailant.'

'Because it raises body temp?'

'Yes, it has to do with adenosine triphosphate.'

ATP. That I'd heard of, too. 'The loss of ATP is what causes the muscles to stiffen, right?'

'Right. When you die, your muscles are robbed of oxygen and nutrients, and ATP is converted into ADP, adenosine *di*phosphate, instead. That's what causes the stiffening. But intense exercise also depletes the ATP in the muscles used.'

'Meaning those muscles would go into rigor faster?'

'Exactly. In our fleeing example, the legs might be first.'

'Even though they're large muscle groups.' I was thinking about our victim. 'If Walker's shoulders and arms were in early rigor, maybe it means he fought off his attacker.'

'If it was a prolonged or intense fight, it's possible. But there was no sign of it in the room.' Pavlik slapped at his own leg. 'Are you sure you de-flead this car?'

'Positive,' I said. 'I sprayed it and the living room.'

He did a double-take in my direction. ''Didn't you tell me the chihuahua wasn't in the house that night?'

'Just preventative spraying,' I fibbed. 'I mean, in case one hopped in from the porch.'

'And she's flea-free now?'

I'd filled Pavlik in on Mocha's status as a house guest. 'Yup. All clear.' Or so I hoped.

The sheriff didn't press it. 'We have to make some decisions about where we're going to live long term.'

'I know.'

'Also, when we're going to get married. My dad was asking.'

'He's OK with a Lutheran now?'

'He was always OK with you, I think. At least, once he met you.' A pause. 'Dad is thinking about selling their condo.'

That surprised me. According to Pavlik, his parents had been in the Randolph high-rise since it was built in the sixties, when Lake Shore Drive ran on the other side of the building. The road might have been diverted, but the only changes the Pavliks had made was turning their son's room into an office with the daybed we'd slept on. At the thought of the daybed,

I stretched my shoulders and did a little head circle. 'Is that why there's no couch in the living room?'

'Sold it to the neighbor down the hall.'

'Already?'

'Two chairs and a rug, too. Now it's just a big empty room and the neighbors downstairs are complaining.'

'Which is why I had to take off my shoes.'

'Exactly. They're not too crazy about the TV volume, either.' It sounded as if Pavlik had found that out first-hand.

'Don't you think your dad should take some time? They say you should wait at least a year to make any big life decisions after somebody dies.'

'Passes.' Pavlik was staring straight ahead.

'What?'

'My dad doesn't say my mom died. He says she *passed*.'

'A lot of people do.' I put my hand on his arm. 'I suppose it's a gentler way to look at it for them. Passing on to a better place.'

His jawline was hard as he continued to watch the road. 'My dad and I are cops. We know people die. Even the ones we love.'

I felt sick. Here I'd been leading the discussion in the direction of Walker's body, time of death and rigor mortis, when Pavlik's own mother had died at nearly the same time, if under very different circumstances. 'Oh, God. I'm really sorry.'

He glanced over at me. 'We're all sorry Mom died. But it is what it is.'

'No . . . well, yes. Of course I am. But I meant I'm sorry I brought up death and . . . all.' What should I say? I'm sorry that everything that is happening to Walker's body as we speak is also happening to your mom's? It was an awful thought, and if it wasn't already in Pavlik's head, I didn't want to put it there.

But while I might not know what was in his head, he seemed to know where mine was going. 'I'm OK, Maggy. You learn to wall off your private life from what you see on the job in my line of work.' He put his hand on mine.

I squeezed it. 'Still, it—'

'Angles called this morning while you were in the shower.'

I knew it was a deliberate change of subject, so I went with it. 'Did she have anything new?'

'Beyond your big wad of dog hair?'

Hadn't I mentioned the poo to Pavlik? Maybe not, given everything that had been going on. And I'd only turned it over to Angles the night before.

'I know it may be nothing, since I cut it off her Friday morning at about two a.m., which was before the murder. Or at least I think it was before the murder.'

'Hence your asking about time of death.'

'Exactly.'

'It's not an exact science, but it looks like Walker's time of death could match the timeline on the shots you thought you heard.'

'Friday morning. I mean, at seven-ish, not midnight or one a.m.' There went that theory. Or a whole slew of theories.

'Yes,' Pavlik flicked on his turn signal to merge on to the southern bypass around Milwaukee toward Brookhills.

'So I wasted your department's time with the poop sample.' Not to mention spending an hour in the backyard on my hands and knees with Sarah, who would never let me forget it. I was beyond deflated.

'Actually, you didn't.'

I sat up straight. 'I didn't?'

'No. Turns out you were right. There was blood mixed with the poo.'

I was usually happy about being right. But in this case, I'd make an exception. 'But how can that be? You just told me Walker was killed around seven on Friday morning and that's probably also when Mocha was shot.'

'The dog was shot? Angles didn't tell me that.' Pavlik stepped on the gas to shoot ahead of a tractor trailer that was moving into our lane.

'See? He didn't even see us in this car.'

Pavlik glanced over at me. 'Stop avoiding the subject. Does Angles know the dog was shot or not?'

'Not. But Sarah just found the wound last night after Detective Angles left.'

'You don't have a phone?'

As I opened my mouth, he waved me off. 'Don't answer that. Did she take the dog to the vet? Was a bullet extracted?'

'No bullet,' I said, feeling as if I'd failed yet another evidence test. 'It's really just a scratch – a crease, Sarah called it. I'm not even sure it was from a bullet, but she seems to think so.'

'Sarah. The real estate agent/coffeehouse owner who knows just enough about guns to be dangerous – and presumably even less about gunshot wounds.'

Except for the one she had, which I wasn't going to go into. If Sarah hadn't told me after all this time, I could only assume it was something she didn't want broadcast. 'Maybe Sarah is just willing it to be a gunshot wound because she thinks it explains the blood on Arial's face.'

'And it doesn't?'

'No, because I wiped the blood off Arial's cheek before we heard the shots.' I turned sideways on the passenger seat to face Pavlik. 'You know what I think?'

'What?'

'Something else violent happened during the night. For all we know, Arial was attacked by Walker.' I was warming to my idea, which was a variation of the intruder theory Sarah and I had discussed.

'And she killed him in self-defense a few hours later? You were with Arial when the shots were fired.'

'I'm thinking more *Arial*-defense than self-defense – by George Satterwite when he got home. I saw him in the garage just before we heard the shots and we know George and Arial were in touch about Mocha. Maybe she—'

'How do we know that?'

Another thing I hadn't mentioned. 'I texted George in the middle of the night when I found Mocha. He thanked me and said he'd have Arial call me in the morning. Maybe when he got hold of her, she told him about Walker hurting her.'

'So when George arrived home, he found Walker there and they got into it?'

'Exactly. Both George and Arial are missing, and Marian Satterwite thinks they were having an affair.'

Pavlik looked dubious.

'It makes sense,' I insisted. 'Whether Marian is right or not, George could have confronted Walker and the gun went off.'

'If it was accidental, why not call the police?'

'Because there were no witnesses. You didn't see the scene, but it was pretty horrific. Part of Walker's head was blown away. Maybe George realized it looked more like an execution than self-defense and thought running away was their only chance.'

'Pausing to drop off the dog at your place on Saturday night, nearly thirty-six hours later?'

'It's not like they're professionals. Maybe they decided Mocha made them too identifiable. Man, woman and dog fugitives. Or they just couldn't take her where they were going.'

'Which would be where?'

'No clue, but it all fits, doesn't it? George's car is missing, along with Arial's overnight bag and purse, and probably George's luggage from his trip to Minneapolis, right?'

Pavlik nodded.

'You said yourself that money had been withdrawn from the Satterwites' accounts. They'd use that to finance their escape.'

'There's one problem.'

Pavlik was going to lift his leg on my theory. 'What's that?'

'The blood on the chihuahua the night before.'

Bitten in the butt by my own poop wad. 'Like I said, there was an altercation before George got home and Walker hit Arial.'

Pavlik pulled on to the Brookhills off-ramp. 'You didn't see any sign of injury on Arial – just the blood?'

I cocked my head. 'Blood on a woman's face isn't enough?'

Pavlik held up his hand in a placating gesture. 'I just wanted to make sure.'

'So you agree it makes sense?'

'I would, except for one thing.'

We'd pulled up to the stop sign at the end of the ramp. The same ramp where I'd first caught sight of Mocha. 'What's that?'

He put the car into park and swiveled to face me. 'The blood you found on Mocha belongs to George Satterwite.'

SIXTEEN

Oddly enough, the speed of the results surprised me nearly as much as the fact that it was George Satterwite's blood.

'How can you know that? I gave Angles the specimen' – suddenly the poop wad had been elevated – 'last night.'

'And she took it straight to the lab.' A car pulled up behind us and sounded its horn. Pavlik raised his hand in apology and put the car in gear.

'But Angles sat down and had pizza with us,' I said. 'I didn't get the impression she thought it was pressing or even important.'

'I told you she was a good investigator,' he said, turning the car toward home.

Angles hadn't touched her wine. That should have tipped me off immediately. 'So she was chatting us up. Hoping we'd say what?'

Pavlik shrugged. 'You'd be surprised what people reveal when they're put at ease.'

By an expert, apparently. I had to give Angles props. I also would have to think back to what we'd said to her. 'She came over to see if the neighbors had spotted anybody dropping off Mocha. I was the one who asked her to stop by the house. She didn't even know why.'

'Again, that's why she's so good. She adapted and took advantage of the opportunity when it was presented.'

Yeah, yeah, yeah. Angles was terrific. 'But how did she get DNA results overnight? That has to be a record.'

'We don't have DNA back yet, but the lab typed the blood and it matches George Satterwite.'

I felt my brow crease. 'And thousands of other people, probably? And what about Arial? Do we even know what her blood type is?' Geez, what was wrong with me? Was I so enamored with my theory that I would prefer it to be Arial's blood instead of George's?

'No. But it's unlikely she'd also be Type AB, PGM-two.'

'George Satterwite has a rare blood type? I thought that only happened in books.'

'It does,' Pavlik said. 'Roll with it.'

Fine. 'So how rare is this AB, PGN?'

'PG*M* – phosphoglucomutase. Less than two tenths of a percent of the population.'

Rare enough, for our purposes. 'Assuming DNA bears it out, that means George Satterwite was home before Mocha ran away Thursday night into Friday.'

'Right.'

'So when I texted George's cell phone around two-thirty on Friday morning he was already home. But Marian said she got a message from George saying he'd been delayed and wouldn't be back until Friday. Unless she lied.'

'No, we confirmed that text message. It was sent to both her and Arial, letting them know.'

'Then George lied and came home early. Maybe Marian is right that George and Arial were involved. He wanted to surprise the girl with a romantic rendezvous and found her, instead, with Walker.'

'Or George Satterwite laid a trap that the other two walked into.'

I got a shiver up my spine. 'That's ugly, but then so is the whole thing. Satterwite had a fight with Walker or even Arial, which is what sent Mocha running into the night?'

'If there was a violent confrontation between Satterwite and Walker, there was no sign of it. No disruption in the room and no defensive wounds on Walker's body. No bruising at all, except on each of his shins, according to the medical examiner.'

'The shins of both legs, as if somebody made him kneel on something hard before shooting him? The house has marble floors.'

'Possible.' Pavlik turned the car into the driveway and pulled up next to the house. 'Or he fell down.'

Even more possible. As I got out of the car, I could hear

Mocha yapping. 'I suppose the blood could have been on Mocha for a while like the fleas were. Even—'

'Are you kidding me?' Sarah was standing on the porch. 'You saw that house. And Mrs Clean. No dirty butts allowed.' As she said it, she was toeing what looked suspiciously like a butt of her own off the porch.

'You quit smoking, remember?' I said, bending down to pick it up.

'I did,' she said. 'That must be Courtney's. Wait until I see—'

'It's hers,' Courtney said, breezing out the screen door with Mocha in her arms. 'She thinks I don't know she sneaks out to smoke.'

'I do not,' Sarah said sullenly.

'Shame on you,' I said, leaning over to toss the butt in the trash can next to the porch. 'Not only the sneak-smoking but blaming it on poor Courtney.'

'You should vape, Mom,' Courtney said.

Sarah's mouth dropped open.

'What?' Courtney demanded. 'You think smoking is better?'

'You called me Mom,' Sarah said. 'It's the first time anybody has. Ever.' She was bright pink with pleasure or maybe confusion.

'Sorry, not sorry.' Courtney gave her a kiss on the cheek. 'Don't make a scene.'

'Vaping could be a gateway back to cigarettes, Sarah.' Pavlik, ever practical, had come up behind us with our bags from the car. 'I don't think I'd take the chance if I'd already success-fully kicked the habit.'

I stepped sideways to let him pass by to the bedroom.

'Tell him I'm sorry about his mom, OK?' Sarah said after him. 'You know how I am.'

'Yeah, totally unfeeling.'

'She's such a softie,' Courtney said, rolling her eyes.

'OK, you two,' Sarah said uncomfortably. 'I just came here for Courtney, not to be abused.'

For sneak-smoking. And having feelings. 'Who's minding the store?'

'Amy's back today. Did you forget?'

That's right – it was Monday. Since Thursday we'd met the parents and lost one of those parents, found a dog, returned a dog and found it again. Discovered a body. Two people had gone missing. Bank accounts had been breached. An affair hinted at. Not to forget the Shabbat and semi-Shiva.

'How'd it go, Courtney?' Pavlik had come back out. 'You must have tired the dogs out. Frank is sound asleep.'

The sheriff sounded disappointed. The sheepdog usually went crazy when I came home, even more so when Pavlik did.

'It was great,' Courtney said. 'We just took them both to the dog park.'

'We?' I raised my eyebrows at Sarah. 'You went back to the dog park?'

She sighed. 'Courtney had to fill in for somebody's shift, so I bit the bullet and took her.'

I punched my partner in the arm. 'Courtney's right. You *are* a softie.'

She punched me back. Hard. 'Let's go, Court. Hand over the fleabag.'

I went to take Mocha, but the little dog was all eyes for Pavlik. 'I think she wants you.'

The bushy little tail wagged.

'She seems to like men more than women,' Courtney said, giving her over to Pavlik.

'Go figure,' Sarah said sourly. 'I guess men don't stuff her in their purses.'

'Who would do that to you?' Pavlik said, holding Mocha up in front of his face. She licked his nose.

I walked Sarah and Courtney to Sarah's Firebird. 'Please don't tell me you loaded Frank in here.'

'Nah, we took your Escape.'

'Help yourself,' I said.

'I did.'

'I know. And it's fine with me. Did I sound like it wasn't fine with me?'

Sarah cocked her head. 'Not sure. It might have been a little snarky.'

'It was not.'

'Stop.' Courtney held out her hand for the keys. 'I'll drive.'

'Sure you will,' Sarah snapped.

Courtney caught my eye as Sarah climbed into the driver's seat. 'Now *that* was snarky.'

'Duly noted,' Sarah said. 'Now get in the car.'

'OK, Mom,' Courtney said, grinning. 'Coming, Mom. Be right there, Mom.'

She was still at it as they drove off.

I was standing there watching them disappear as Pavlik and Mocha joined me. 'Sarah's going to have her hands full with that one.'

'Already does,' I said, turning. 'And you seem to like your furry little handful there.'

Mocha was nestled with her head in the crook of his neck. 'She's pretty sweet, I have to say. In a totally different way than Muffin.'

'She is.'

'Not at all what I imagined,' Pavlik continued, 'when you mentioned a flea-bitten chihuahua.'

Mocha raised her head and looked at me with reproachful eyes.

I raised my hand. 'I swear I never said that. Just that you had fleas. And were a chihuahua.'

Satisfied, she snuggled back down and gave my fiancé an earful of tongue.

SEVENTEEN

'Honest to God, Pavlik is smitten.' It was the next morning and Sarah and I had retired to our office after the rush, so I could fill her in. 'Last night, I had to convince him that two people and two dogs in a queen-size bed was not a promising idea.'

'Frank is still sleeping with you? I thought you said that he's on the floor now.'

'Until the middle of the night when he decides he wants to be on the bed, too. And I imagine if we let Mocha on the bed, Frank would be right up there with her.'

'And where would you sleep?'

'Exactly. I'm surprised at how well they're getting along.'

'Pavlik and the fleabag?'

'No, in this case I was talking about Frank and the fleabag.'

'Oh yeah. I was surprised, too. According to Courtney, it's because Frank has asserted his alpha-ness. Or alph-ability.'

'He certainly didn't assert anything that first night. My poor sheepdog was terrified of the little thing, and I didn't blame him. She was all teeth, claws and snarls to him.'

'And fleas,' Sarah said. 'Don't forget the fleas.'

I shivered. 'How could I? I think they're gone, but that's another reason I didn't want her in our bed.'

'You said Pavlik's dog just died. Maybe the boy needs another one.'

'He has Frank.'

'Frank's your dog.'

'Who adores Pavlik. But it was Pavlik and Mocha who snuggled on the couch watching television all night.'

'You and Frank jealous?'

'Maybe,' I admitted with a grin. 'But it's more that I keep waiting for "Can we keep her, Mom? Can we?" from Pavlik.'

'Mom, huh?'

'Yes, like you,' I said with a smile. 'That was sweet of

Courtney, by the way. And totally spontaneous from what I could tell.'

'Nah. She probably wants something.'

I went to swat her but then remembered how hard she swatted back. 'Shame on you. You're the one who insisted the kids call you Sarah in the first place.'

'Because that's how they'd always known me. Or Aunt Sarah. Patricia and David had Sam and Courtney call adults Aunt this or Uncle that, even though we weren't related by blood.'

'I did that, too. It didn't seem right to have Eric call our friends by their first names, but Mr or Mrs seemed awkward, too.'

'Stupid. How did the kids know who's real family and who's not?'

'Actually, that came up because Ted has a brother, Bob, and one of our good friends was also named Bob. Eric called one Pretend Uncle Bob and the other just Uncle Bob.'

'Pretend Uncle Bob? You're kidding.'

'Well, not to his face. And as for what you're called, it's been almost three years and you're Courtney and Sam's mother for all intents and purposes. Courtney obviously thinks of you that way.' I put my hand on her arm. 'Enjoy it. You're loved.'

Her face reddened again, and I could have sworn there was a tear in the eyes that she sent skyward in an exaggerated eye roll. 'Fine. I'm loved.'

Too much sentimentality made Sarah a grumpy girl. A change of subject seemed in order. 'I showed Pavlik the wound on Mocha.'

'What did he think? Am I right that it's from a bullet?'

'He said it's very possible.' Actually, he'd just said 'possible,' without the 'very.' It was one of his favorite noncommittal words. But Sarah didn't need to know that. 'He also said that it's George Satterwite's blood we salvaged for Detective Angles.'

'You're kidding.' She seemed dumbfounded.

'I know. I was pretty certain they'd find nothing, too. Except the poop, of course.'

'But it's Satterwite's blood?'

'Seems so.' I explained about the rare blood type. 'They'll do DNA to confirm, of course, but that takes time.'

'The blood results were quick. The detective would just have turned them in yesterday, right?'

'Wrong. Pavlik said Angles took the sample right back to the lab from here Sunday night. She called him with the results yesterday morning as we were getting ready to leave Chicago.'

'And I'm just finding out about them twenty-four hours later?'

'He told me on our drive back, but I didn't want to talk about it yesterday in front of Courtney.'

'You don't have a phone?'

It seemed a popular question. 'I'm sorry.'

'You should be.' Something dangerously close to a pout. 'Now that Pavlik is back, you're bouncing your theories off him instead of me.'

'We weren't bouncing a whole lot of theories around yesterday once we got home.'

Sarah held up a hand. 'Spare me the details of your afternoon delight.'

'We weren't—'

But Sarah wasn't done torturing me. 'It is my niece that's missing, you know.'

I did know. And this latest information didn't put Arial in any better light as far as the investigation was concerned. 'Remember Angles' whole "Is that pepperoni?" and "Sure, I'll have a glass of wine" act? Apparently, it was just to get us talking.'

'About what?'

I shrugged. 'About Arial, I assume. I was trying to remember what we told her.'

Sarah went out into the store and came back with two cups of steaming coffee. She handed one to me and sat down at the desk with another. 'Let's see. First, we asked her about canvassing the neighbors to see if anybody had seen who dropped off the mutt.'

'Right. And nobody had seen anything.'

'Or so she said.'

Sarah was right. We couldn't assume that anything Angles

had told us was necessarily true. She'd been trolling for information from us, not delivering it. 'She spent a lot of time asking about you and Arial, as I recall. Your relationship, your family.'

'Because my sister told her I was the one Arial would go to for help.'

Which I thought was probably true. 'She also mentioned the supposed affair with George. I think she wanted to get your reaction.'

'She didn't get much there. We'd already heard the accusation from Marian Satterwite, so it wasn't a surprise coming from Angles.'

'Do you think it's true?'

'Honestly? I don't know. Growing up with Saint Ruth and Mother So Superior was tough. Arial missed having a dad and always sought male approval. Had crushes on her teachers, authority figures. You know the drill.'

'Then it's not out of the question?'

'That she fell for a much older, married guy? I'd like to say it is, but I'm not sure. Not that I was going to tell Angles that.'

'For the blood on Mocha to be George Satterwite's—'

'He had to return to Brookhills sometime Thursday or Thursday night. I get that.'

'Which means he was lying when he texted Arial and Marian that he wouldn't be back until Friday.'

'Question is, was the lie for Marian or Arial?'

I nodded. 'Marian assumes he was setting up a rendezvous with Arial, but Pavlik and I think he may have been setting a trap for Arial and Walker.'

'So you're sure she was doing both guys?'

'Sarah! She's your niece.'

'Fine. You're sure she was making sweet monkey love with both Walker and the married man? Better?'

'No, I—'

'Of course not. Couching things in euphemisms doesn't make them right.'

I supposed not. 'I'm just saying that if George Satterwite killed Walker, maybe it wasn't because he thought he was an intruder.'

Sarah rubbed her chin thoughtfully. 'No, but he could still use Castle law as a defense, assuming nobody knew about the affair.'

'Arial knew,' I said. 'Maybe she wouldn't go along with it.'

Sarah closed her eyes. 'So Satterwite took her. Or she's on the run from him.'

Yet it was George Satterwite's blood on Mocha. 'You're sure Arial hasn't contacted you?'

'I sure as hell wish she had.'

My phone buzzed, and I picked it up to read the message. 'Oh, no.'

'What? Is it Arial? Did they find—'

'No. Nothing like that.' I held my phone up, so she could see. 'Pavlik's dad just got an offer on his condo.'

'And that merits scaring the shit out of me?'

'Of course not. But Peggy, Pavlik's mom, has been dead for less than a week. His dad shouldn't be making big decisions so soon.'

'Maybe he just wants to be away from the memories the place holds for him. Can't blame him for that.'

'But from everything I've heard, they were good memories.'

'Sometimes those hurt the most,' Sarah said.

She was right. 'He was already emptying the condo when I was there. Couch, gone. Chairs, gone. Rug, gone. I have no idea about Pavlik's mom's clothes and all. I'm sure those things are painful to look at now, but I'm afraid he'll regret it.'

'Did you regret setting Ted's favorite chair on fire?'

'No, and I should have burned the recliner, too. That was his second favorite. But that was a divorce, not a death.'

Sarah looked a little shamefaced. 'I was just trying to lighten the mood. I kind of scared myself with that "good memories hurt" comment.'

'It *was* unusually sensitive.'

'Empathetic, even,' she said. 'Maybe it's being a mom.'

I didn't say anything, and she snapped her fingers to get my attention. 'Hey! That was funny. And even a little heart-warming. I don't get props for it?'

'I'm sorry,' I said, tuning back in. 'I was just thinking of the rug in Len's living room. Or the absence of the rug.'

'Len?'

'Pavlik's dad.'

'You're not going to call him Dad? I mean, what could it hurt? Yours is dead.' All of a sudden Sarah was the sensitivity police. Or insensitivity.

'*Anyway*, Pavlik says the neighbors downstairs are complaining because of the noise overhead.'

'Boo-hoo for the neighbors. The guy's wife is dead. Cut him a break.'

'But don't you see? A rug cuts down on noise.' I turned to her. 'The theater room had all those heavy curtains and big speakers and acoustical this and that, but a hard marble floor and no rug.'

Sarah closed her eyes, like she was picturing the room. 'The chairs had been moved to the side. Maybe the rug was out being cleaned.'

'Or maybe,' I said, 'the rug was used to clean up.'

Sarah just stared at me.

'As in to clean up a body,' I said.

'Whose? Not this Walker guy. He was still—' She stopped. 'You mean George Satterwite?'

I was nodding. 'What if George Satterwite was killed in that room Thursday night and the body – and all the blood that Mocha walked in – was disposed of along with that rug?'

'You got all that from "absence of rug"?'

'Don't you see? That explains everything, including the lack of bloody paw prints in the room. The prints were there on the rug before it was rolled up and carted away with the body.'

'By who? Arial? She's all of a hundred pounds. She couldn't have carried the body of a full-grown man. In a rug, no less.'

'I didn't say it was Arial.'

'Then, like I said, who? And, meanwhile, what was my niece doing all night?' Sarah put down her cup hard enough to make the coffee splash out and on to our pile of receipts. 'Waiting around for another body to drop, like she was waiting for a bus or something?'

'I . . . well, I don't know.'

'No, you don't. So don't go around acting like you do.'

'It's just a theory.' A damn good theory in my book.

My phone buzzed again, and I checked the message.

'What's the emergency now?' Sarah said sarcastically. 'Len sold his car?'

'No,' I said, reading the message.

'Then what?'

I held it up again. 'They just found George Satterwite's body.'

EIGHTEEN

'Any sign of Arial?'

I was busy texting. 'Sorry. I'll find out. I was just checking if George's body was wrapped in a rug.'

'Because your theory is more important than my niece?'

'Yes . . . no. I mean, I honestly wasn't thinking about Arial at all.' Other than maybe being the murderer, that is.

'Well, think about her.'

I shot off another text.

My phone rang.

'I thought it would be easier for you to question me by voice,' Pavlik said dryly.

'Hey, you're the one who texted me in the first place.' I was honestly surprised he'd told me about the discovery so quickly, but I wasn't going to look a gift text in the mouth.

'How did you know about the rug?'

'Mocha's vanishing paw prints. They started just inside the door and led down the hall. But there was no point of origin.'

'Which was the body on the rug.'

'Yup. It was your dad's living room that made me think of it. How echoey it was with the furniture and rug gone. I wondered why the Satterwites wouldn't have a rug in the theater, with all their soundproofing.'

Apparently bored, Sarah disappeared into the front of the store with our cups.

'They would have,' Pavlik said. 'It was one of the first things Angles noticed.'

My thunder stolen. But the detective seemed to know quite a bit about the equipment, so it wasn't surprising. I lowered my voice and turned away from the doorway to the shop. 'Is Arial a person of interest?'

'She's been a person of interest.'

I could hear Sarah setting down the pot after presumably pouring us refills. 'But not a suspect, I mean.'

'Two men are dead and she's missing. It's not a leap.'

Suspect. 'For all we know, she could be injured or dead herself.'

'Then who dropped off the dog?'

'We don't know anybody did.'

'Mocha is cute, but I don't think she has GPS.'

'No, but—' Sarah came back into the room with the two steaming mugs of coffee. 'Where was the body found?'

'I assume Sarah has come back into hearing range?'

'Yes. I mean where, besides wrapped in the rug?' I nodded a 'See?' toward Sarah, who rolled her eyes.

'OK, I'll play. In the back of the Navigator, which was parked at the airport.'

'At the airport,' I said for Sarah's benefit. 'Nobody noticed it?'

'It was tucked in a dark corner in long-term parking.'

'Long-term parking. Had he been shot, too?' This was like a homicidal game of Twenty Questions.

'Yes, and before you ask, we don't have time of death yet.'

Sarah was signaling me to ask about her niece. 'And you said no sign of Arial?'

'Nope. Though if Sarah has an idea where she might be—'

'Sorry, but Sarah is the one who asked. She's worried.'

'I don't blame her.' He rang off.

'What did he say?' Sarah asked, sliding me a coffee.

'That he didn't blame you for being worried and you should let him know if you hear from her. He'll do the same.'

Sarah nodded and sat down. 'She's a suspect, isn't she?'

I started to shake my head, but my partner was no fool. And I was no liar. Unless there was a really good reason. 'She is. But the good news is they don't think she's injured.'

'Or dead.' Sarah circled her finger in the air as if it was a party noisemaker. 'Yippee.'

'That *is* a yippee,' I said. 'Alive is a definite yippee.'

'Murder suspect, not so much,' Sarah said. 'They think she's alive because of the mutt?'

I nodded. 'Who else would have dropped Mocha off?'

'I don't know. Marian, maybe?'

'Why? She came by Uncommon Grounds looking for her. And, besides, she doesn't know where I live.'

'That's a problem.' Sarah pulled the computer keyboard toward her and typed 'Maggy Thorsen Brookhills' into the Google search window. My address on Poplar Creek Road popped up. 'Look at that. Problem solved.'

Point irritably taken. 'So Marian could have dropped Mocha off at my house. But why?'

'I don't know. To throw us off? Make it seem like George and Arial had Mocha when they didn't?'

'But to what end?'

'Like I said,' Sarah said irritably, 'I don't know.'

All right. 'Hey, while we're on the computer, let's pull up that neighborhood message board again and see if we can get in. There was that item about a peeping Tom. For all we know, that was Thursday night.'

I leaned over her shoulder and typed in the URL.

She punched enter and turned. 'Can I have my personal space back?'

'Certainly.' I straightened. 'We're looking for the Pinehurst neighborhood.'

'I know, but we still need a password to get in.'

'Let's see if we can join.'

'OK.' She clicked 'Join.' 'We need an address in the neighborhood.'

'We can't use the Satterwites, since they are already registered. Use a house number a couple of digits off.'

'I don't know the Satterwites' address.'

'I think it's 429 Pine Avenue. See if it will take four thirty.'

Sarah typed in the number and hit enter. 'I'm in.'

'Great.' I leaned forward to look at the postings. 'The post about Mocha being lost is still here, without any replies other than a couple of "Oh, no" type comments.'

'She still is lost, as far as Marian Satterwite knows.'

Though not Arial, presumably. Not that she'd post about it from whatever lam she was on anyway. 'Click on firecrackers or fireworks, whichever it was. George was shot. Walker was shot. I want to see if anybody heard gunfire.'

'Besides you?'

'Yes.' It was my assumption that there'd only been one murder that made me doubt myself. Now that we had two dead bodies and knew the blood on Mocha was George Satterwite's, odds were that what I'd heard the next morning were the shots that killed Walker.

'Posts with complaints about firecrackers about the time you heard them. The first one was from Arial.'

'That's interesting,' I said. 'Maybe she was trying to plant the idea they were firecrackers before anybody could leap to the conclusion they were gunshots?' The *correct* conclusion.

'Or she honestly believed it.'

'*After* she'd gone back into the house?' I pointed to the time of the post. 'Seven-twenty.'

Sarah shook her head. 'Arial is smart. It ticks me off to think she's applying her horsepower to cover up a murder. Especially one committed by somebody else. What's the name of the neighbor in the house behind them again?'

'Ryan Lyle.'

'Got it. Here he is Friday morning saying he's calling the police. Firecrackers and also something about . . . infrasonic sound?'

'That's what he thinks the Satterwites are bombarding him with from their theater.'

'He couldn't just say noise?'

'This is sound he can't hear.'

'Silent sound. There's an oxymoron for you.'

'Apparently it's a real thing. There are tests. Even an app.'

She was scrolling down the page. 'Here's Becky Lyle saying her husband should take a chill pill.'

'Does she actually say that?' I squinted over her shoulder.

'Not in so many words, but close. About one o'clock in the afternoon the discussion turns to the shooting – lots of specu-lation that the firecrackers were shots. Now all of a sudden everybody is claiming they heard them.'

'Herd mentality.'

'Is that "ea" or "e"?'

'E, but cute.'

'Here's somebody who says they saw the Navigator leave.'

I craned my neck. 'What time?'

'He says it was around quarter to eight, which would fit.

Didn't see who was driving but thought there was just the one person in it.'

'What about the peeping Tom?'

Sarah scrolled back up and then down again. 'Here it is. Jane somebody saw . . .' She stopped.

'What? Where?'

She leaned into the screen. 'The figure of a man creeping around in backyards. Thursday night.'

This was promising. 'Where does she live?'

'Four-three-one Pine, it says.' Sarah turned to me. 'That would be right next door to the Satterwites.'

And across from our fictitious 430. 'Click on it and scroll down to the comments.'

Sarah obeyed. 'After the murder, the discussion lights up. Jane comments again. Now she says the guy had a gun in his hand and he was looking in windows.'

'At the Satterwites?'

'Yeah, but not just them. Her house and the Lyles, too.'

I was reading the comment. '"*Just think, it could have been me dead.*" She says she's calling the police to report it.'

'Wow.' Sarah sat back. 'That's a relief.'

'You mean because there's another potential suspect?'

'Damn square. With both Satterwite and Walker dead, Arial was the only one left standing to hold the bag.'

And she might still be. The man Jane spotted could be somebody we'd already included in the body count. 'I hate to say it, but how do we know the peeping Tom wasn't Walker?'

'The dead guy?'

'He wasn't dead Thursday night.'

Deflated, Sarah chewed on that. 'You mean Walker was the one lurking outside with the gun.' She brightened. 'He was waiting to kill Satterwite, which clears Arial.'

Maybe. 'But who killed Walker? We still don't know if either Arial or George Satterwite knew him. Who is this guy?'

'His picture was in this morning's paper,' Sarah said, nodding to the folded newspaper on the desk. 'I didn't realize he was just – what? Twenty-nine?'

I nodded.

'Closer to Arial's age than the Satterwites.'

'Yes.' I didn't comment beyond that but continued to scan the posts on the screen. 'I wish we had a time of death on George. There's nothing here about firecrackers or fireworks before Friday morning, though.'

'Maybe the killer used a silencer.'

I raised my head. 'Or maybe the room was the silencer.'

'What?'

'On Friday when I heard the shots, the front door of the house was open. And now we know the rug was gone, and when we went in with Marian, the double doors to the theater room were wide open, too. If all those things weren't true on Thursday, the sound of the shots might have been contained inside.'

'Or at least muffled,' Sarah said.

'Ryan Lyle didn't say anything about firecrackers bothering Harry the day before and God knows he doesn't hesitate to complain.'

'Harry?'

'Becky and Ryan Lyle's big German shepherd. You may have seen him at the dog park. Becky runs it.'

'Oh, right. Frank and the Kraut got on just fine.'

The front door of Uncommon Grounds swung open hard, crashing against the condiment cart. 'Mom? Sarah?'

If it had been a male voice, it could have been Eric calling out to Sarah and me. As it was, though, Eric was at school in Minneapolis, and the voice was female. And, apparently, still a little confused about what she should call her guardian.

Courtney rounded the corner. 'You're never going to guess what I just realized.'

'That the door will break if you swing it so hard?' Sarah guessed.

'That, too.'

Sarah sniffed. 'You smell like dog.'

'Oh, sorry.' She lifted one heel. 'I was working at the park. Do you have something I can use to wipe this off?'

My life had been consumed by dog poop. I handed her a napkin.

'So what did you realize?' Sarah asked as the girl balanced on one foot as she swiped at the bottom of the other shoe.

'You know your dead guy?'

'We don't think of him that way—' I started.

'Yes, we do,' Sarah said. 'And now we have two.'

Courtney's eyes got big. 'Somebody else is dead?'

'George Satterwite.'

'Mocha's dad?'

'Yes,' I said. 'Did you know him?'

She nodded up down, up down. 'He's really nice. Or he *was*, I guess now. And he has this great movie theater in the house. I watched movies there a couple times with Arial and hung out.'

'When was this?' From Sarah's expression, she didn't like the fact she'd known nothing about it.

'Oh, a couple of weeks ago. It's no big deal.'

'What did you do there?'

'I told you.' Courtney's bottom lip had popped out in a pout. 'We just hung out. Watched movies, played video games.'

'Just you and Arial?'

Courtney's face lit up with anticipation again. 'No, that's what I've been trying to tell you. Doug came over a couple of times, too.'

'Doug?' Sarah cocked her head. 'I don't think I know—'

'Isn't that the guy from the dog park?' I asked.

Courtney was nodding as I turned to address Sarah. 'I heard about him from Clare Twohig and Becky. He's a volunteer there. Does a lot of work for the park.'

'Oh, right. The guy who pried the Pekingese out of Frank's butt-crack,' Sarah said, perking up. 'If Doug and Arial were dating, maybe he knows where she is. Can you get hold of him, Courtney?'

Courtney was shaking her head back and forth. 'That's just the point.'

'Becky said Doug hadn't been there for a couple days,' I told Sarah.

'That's right,' the girl said. 'That's who I subbed for yesterday, Sarah. Remember?'

Apparently, in the heat of the moment, 'Mom' had flown out the door again.

'Vaguely,' Sarah said. 'You think he and Arial are off together somewhere?'

I could tell the thought that Arial wasn't alone lifted my partner's spirits. But Courtney dashed them just as quickly. 'No, that's what I'm trying to tell you.'

She picked up the newspaper from the desk and waved it in our faces. 'My Doug is your Mitchell.'

I grabbed for the paper. '*My*—'

'Mitchell Walker,' she said, flipping it so we could see the picture on the front page. 'The murder victim.'

NINETEEN

Courtney was somewhere between excitement and tears with the revelation that her friend Doug from the dog park was the now deceased Mitchell Walker.

I sat her down in the desk chair. 'I'm sorry about your friend.'

'Did you know him well?' Sarah asked, bringing her a bottle of water. 'He was a lot older than you.'

'He was mostly Arial's friend, like I said, but we'd talk at the park. He said I was great with dogs.' She threw Sarah a reproachful look.

'I never said you weren't,' Sarah said. 'Just that I'm not letting you stay over at strangers' homes to sit. Who knows what can happen?' I knew she was thinking of Arial.

'You knew him as Doug,' I said to Courtney. 'Did you know his last name?'

'Walker.' Her face said 'duh.'

'Maybe Douglas is his middle name,' Sarah said.

I picked up the paper. 'It's Arthur, according to this. Mitchell Arthur Walker.'

Courtney laughed now. 'Doug didn't like either of his names. He used Doug because he thought it was funny.'

I didn't get the joke. 'What's funny?'

'Doug Walker, Dog Walker – get it?'

'Clever.'

'No, it's not,' Sarah snapped. 'It's stupid.'

'Back in olden times, people were named for what they did all the time,' Courtney said. 'Like Baker or Fisher.'

'Or Harper? Must be a stringed instrument in your DNA.' If Sarah was trying to shut down Courtney – and any information she might have – she was doing an admirable job of it.

'Courtney's right,' I said to encourage the girl. 'Families

also took their surnames from where they lived. Kingston was
King's Town. In Norway, it might be the name of your father.
Thorsen means son of Thor.'

'You're related to Thor?' Courtney asked, wide-eyed.

'Thor, a farmer in rural Norway,' I said. 'Not Thor, king of
the Norse Gods.'

'Still,' Courtney said.

'Fascinating,' from Sarah.

'Now we know what Walker's connection was to Arial,' I said,
as the front door of Uncommon Grounds closed behind
Courtney.

'Fat lot of good it does us,' Sarah said sourly. 'Maybe Arial
and "Doug" were friends, maybe they were dating. Courtney'
– finger quotes – '"isn't sure."'

'It's no surprise she shut down. You were questioning her
like she was a suspect.' I put our cups in the dirty dish tray
and hoisted it on to my hip. 'I'm surprised you didn't pull out
the bright lights and rubber hoses.'

'You kidding? Kids her age wouldn't know what they were
for. She'd probably think they were for growing pot in the
basement.'

Sarah was showing her age. 'I doubt very much that Courtney
knows anything about growing marijuana,' I said, setting the
tray in the service window. 'Basement or otherwise.'

'You are so naive.'

Maybe I was. Eric hadn't dabbled in drugs, thank the Lord.
But then he had the whole gay and coming-out thing to occupy
him. 'I'm just saying that you made her feel defensive.'

'Forgive me for being concerned. Courtney is fifteen and
she was hanging out watching movies and playing video games
with a twenty-nine-year-old guy who got himself murdered.
In that very same house.'

By Sarah's niece, or so investigators believed.

'Let's think about this,' I said. 'We know that Walker spent
time at the house with Arial—'

'And Courtney,' Sarah said, in case I hadn't gotten the point.
'Who says she thinks George Satterwite might have met Doug
Walker, too. Maybe. But not when she was there.'

'Courtney wasn't at the Satterwite house Thursday night, though. Right?'

'Of course not,' Sarah said. 'She was home with Sam, remember? I was dog-sitting for you.'

I did remember. Sarah had said they were on their devices and she was irritated she couldn't find my Netflix password. I just wasn't sure that meant Courtney was there the entire night. In fact, we didn't even know when George Satterwite had died. I was just assuming it was around eleven p.m. when Arial said Mocha had disappeared.

Another time of death to try to pin down.

'Let's assume that Arial had Walker over for a movie, thinking neither Marian nor George would be home that night,' I said. 'Marian was stuck in Chicago after a long international flight, and George had texted both her and Arial that he was staying an extra day in Minneapolis and would be back Friday morning.'

'If Walker wasn't some intruder, who was lurking in the backyard?'

Our peeping Tom. 'George maybe? Spying on the other two?'

'But the Navigator was in the garage. If Satterwite didn't want to be heard, wouldn't he park it on the street?'

True. 'Maybe he did, and the guy I saw in the garage on Friday morning had moved it inside to load the body.'

'So Walker loaded Satterwite and the rug into the Navigator. Makes sense. We know Arial couldn't have done that.'

At least not alone. In fact, it would have been a struggle for Walker, too. They don't call it 'dead weight' for nothing. 'I wonder if that's how he got bruises on his shins.'

'Who?'

'Walker. Pavlik said the only injuries on him—'

'Other than having half his head blown off.'

'Yes, other than that, were bruises on his shins. I thought maybe somebody shoved him down and made him beg for his life.'

'No rubber hoses this time?'

'No.' She was right, though. The 'beg for his life' was kind of a cliché. 'Anyway, maybe he got the bruises as he wrestled the body into the back of the vehicle. That couldn't have been easy, and he'd have had to climb up into the Navigator and pull the rug and Satterwite in.'

A light bulb went on. 'Which might explain why Walker was in early rigor. He'd been using the large muscle groups in his shoulders and legs.'

'I don't get it.'

'Exertion causes body temperature to rise in those muscles and Pavlik says that can jump-start rigor mortis.'

'Ahh, got you. Would have been easier without the rug,' Sarah pointed out.

'And messier,' I said. 'They were probably committed by that point.'

'They?'

Oops.

'You're assuming Arial was an accomplice?' Sarah continued.

I lifted my shoulders and dropped them. 'I'm sorry, Sarah, but Arial must have been sucked into this in some way. I just don't see how else it could have played out. Think about it. She invites Walker over and Satterwite walks in on them.'

'Doing what?'

I held up what was meant to be a let's-not-get-ahead-of-ourselves hand. 'For all we know, they were innocently watching a movie and Satterwite is a nut job and went off on them.'

'If Arial and Satterwite were having an affair, like Marian thinks, that would make some sense,' Sarah said grudgingly. 'They got into it and Walker killed Satterwite in self-defense.'

'Then who killed Walker?'

'Not Arial, if that's what you're thinking,' Sarah said. 'You said yourself that she was with you when you heard the shots. So instead of looking for ways to break *her* alibi, let's find people who don't have one.'

I cocked my head. 'I wish Marian's alibi wasn't so airtight. The affair gives her motive.'

'If there was an affair,' Sarah said stubbornly.

'If there was,' I stipulated. 'But even so, where does Walker fit? The two people she *should* have killed were George and Arial.'

'Somebody have divorce issues, much?'

She was talking about me. 'I don't mean Marian should have killed George and Arial. Just that Walker's death doesn't fit the scenario.'

'Nothing explains Walker. Have you noticed?'

'So maybe we should concentrate on people who had a beef with George Satterwite, like Ryan Lyle.'

'Didn't you say that just after you and Arial heard the shots, Lyle came up the walk from his house, complaining about the noise?'

'Yes. Which would have been great cover, if he'd just come from the theater's back door after killing Satterwite. But it was Walker who was dead in there.'

'Mistaken identity?'

'It was broad daylight. Even with the acoustical curtains drawn, that would be a stretch.'

'Then maybe Lyle was planting the idea of kids with fire-crackers as a precaution. Just in case somebody heard him shoot Satterwite the night before.'

'Except it was Arial who brought up firecrackers. Ryan was just looking for the source of the noise.'

'The guy sure has a bug up his butt about noise, audible and not.'

'He does,' I admitted. 'And I can imagine him getting out of his bed to go over and complain. I can't see him taking a gun, though.'

'I can,' Sarah said. 'But maybe that's just me.'

It was. 'Thing is, Arial said she was the one watching the movie.'

'With George?'

'If so, what was Arial doing while Lyle killed her supposed lover? And, again, how does Walker fit in? And what about the text, come to think about it?'

'You and your texts. Between that and doggy doo—'

'One particular text. The one I got from George Satterwite's phone a little bit before three a.m. on Friday morning, saying he'd have Arial call me. Assuming George was already dead, somebody else had to text me from the dead man's phone.'

'And by somebody else you mean Arial. But it could have

just as easily been Walker. Who knows what the guy was in to? Just because he was Arial's friend doesn't mean he was a good guy. Like I said, she has daddy issues.'

At twenty-nine, Walker wasn't all that much older, but maybe that didn't matter. 'Pavlik said Walker got into trouble as a kid. Shoplifting and such.'

'Once a thief, always a thief. Maybe that was why he was hanging out with Arial and Courtney there. He was casing the house.'

'And was in the act of robbing the Satterwites when George walked in?' We'd circled back to the intruder theory. 'I didn't see any sign of a burglary, though, and Marian didn't say anything was missing, except . . .' I stopped.

'Except what?'

'The money from the Satterwites' bank accounts. Marian thought George had withdrawn it to finance his escape.'

'With Arial.'

I nodded. 'But George didn't leave the house alive. Who withdrew the money?'

Sarah's face was wooden. 'Arial again, right?'

I rubbed my forehead. 'I'm afraid so.'

'How? She'd need the account numbers and that's something you can't Google.'

'But Arial's been living in their house for days and weeks at a time. Who doesn't occasionally leave a checkbook or credit or debit card and PIN lying around their office or kitchen?'

'That would be careless.'

'Yes, but we're all that way in our own homes. We don't expect somebody to be looking.' I thought of leaving the doors unlocked and handing out my passwords willy-nilly. Then there was the bottom left drawer. 'I need to let Pavlik know.'

'About what?'

I had my phone out. 'About Mitchell being Doug the Dog Walker, of course.'

'And maybe Arial's boyfriend.' She put her hand on my arm. 'Please don't.'

Sarah didn't say 'please' very often. And she was my best friend, God help me.

But then there was Pavlik, who was even more than that. 'I can't lie to him.'

'Just don't call, then. You won't be lying.'

'I will by omission. Besides, it's very possible he already knows Doug and Mitchell are the same person and that the dog park is the connection between him and Arial.'

'If that's true, he didn't feel it necessary to tell you, did he?'

The implication was that I wasn't honor-bound to tell him. 'Pavlik tells me what he wants me to know.'

'And you're fine with that.' Now she was trying to make me feel bad about not feeling bad.

I wasn't going to let her. 'I understand that his job makes it necessary. And hard as it is sometimes, I try to be a big girl and understand that.'

'*You're* a big girl? You kept the man dangling for weeks before you told him you'd marry him. How mature is that?'

Where was this coming from all of a sudden? 'Plenty mature. I'd been through one divorce and that was one too many. You don't just say yes to something because somebody asks.'

'You do if you love him.' She rolled her eyes. 'But you can't even tell him that.'

I knew this was Sarah deflecting the conversation from the more painful – for her, at least – subject of Arial. And, of course, I was going right along with it. 'I tell him all the time.'

Well, not all the time. But lots. And definitely more than I did.

'Like when?'

'Every time we say goodbye, for one.'

She snorted. 'I've heard you on the phone to him. "Love you. Miss you." You're incapable of even putting an "I" in front of it.'

'Since when is "*I* love you" different than "Love you"? Pavlik and I are on the phone together – just the two of us, except for your eavesdropping. He knows the "I" is implied.'

'Yet you can't say it. "Love you" is a throwaway line. Something you say before you hang up with your mom or favorite aunt. It's not a commitment.'

I threw up my hands. 'I've committed! I'm marrying the

man. If it's good enough for him, why isn't it good enough for you?'

'Are you sure it's good enough for him?'

'What's with all this touchy-feely from a woman who can't even let herself be happy her daughter – yes, Courtney *is* your daughter – calls you Mom?'

'Sure,' Sarah said, with a hurt expression on her face. 'When they go low, go lower, huh?'

Damn, but she was good at manipulation. 'You're the one who went low in the first place.'

'I'm just trying to help you. Your interpersonal skills suck.'

'*My* interpersonal skills?' Here we went again.

I took a deep breath. 'I am going to tell Pavlik – whom *I* love – that Mitchell Walker is Doug Walker and that Arial knew him. I won't say anything about them dating.'

'We don't know they were anyway.'

'Correct.'

I'd started around to the back of the service counter, but Sarah put out a hand to stop me. 'Help me find her before they do. Please.'

TWENTY

There was that 'please' again.

Unfortunately, the other problematic word in Sarah's plea was the 'they.' Meaning Pavlik and his investigators. She wanted me to help her find Arial before the authorities did.

And while I would help her as best I could, I wouldn't go behind Pavlik's back. At least not very far behind his back.

'Anybody home?' I called when I opened the door of the house I now shared with the sheriff, Frank and our temporary house guest, Mocha.

But no sign of anybody, despite Pavlik texting me half an hour earlier that he was heading home.

'Hello?'

'In the office,' Pavlik called back.

I stuck my head in. 'Whole gang is here, huh?'

Frank and Mocha were lying on the rug, Frank's head resting on the little dog's back. 'Is Mocha all right? She looks kind of squished.'

'Frank thinks she's a pillow.'

'You realize we're going to have to give her back at some point, right?'

'Right. Damn!' Pavlik hit 'enter' three times and turned. 'Your internet is screwed up.'

'How come it's only "my" internet when it misbehaves?' I bent down to peer over his shoulder. 'What is it doing now?'

'Nothing. That's the problem. I can't connect.'

'It was fine the other day.' I punched random keys.

'Was that before or after you gave the world your password?'

'I'm sure letting Courtney use my Wi-Fi didn't crash the internet.'

'Says you,' Pavlik sniffed, shutting down the computer.

'Bad day?' I sat on the edge of the desk.

'Not as bad as Marian Satterwite's.'

I didn't envy this part of Pavlik's job. 'Did you break the news to her?'

'Angles did. I thought it might be easier coming from somebody she already knew. Or at least met.'

'Then you haven't met Marian?'

'Hadn't, until she came in to identify her husband's body. It's never easy.'

'Where was he shot? On his body, I mean.'

Pavlik looked up, surprised. 'Chest, close up. Why?'

I waggled my head. 'I actually asked because of Marian having to identify the body and how awful that would be if George was shot in the head like Walker.'

'And now?'

'Now I'm interested because of what it may mean. Walker shot in the head, Satterwite in the chest. Does that mean two different shooters?' Which would fit my multiple theories.

'Not necessarily. This isn't somebody like a hit man or serial killer on television, who has a signature method.'

'Just your ordinary person or persons who shoot somebody.'

'Unfortunately, it happens.'

'George was shot close up, you said. Contact wound?'

'No, but there was stippling.'

The speckled pattern from discharged gunpowder on the body would mean the muzzle of the gun had been a few inches to maybe a couple feet away. 'That close and directly in front of him, since it was his chest. Could there have been a struggle for the gun?'

'Entirely possible. There was gunpowder residue on Satterwite's hand, which would support it.'

That was a twist. 'Because it's obviously not a suicide.'

'Hard to roll yourself in a rug and drive to the airport.'

It was. I nodded toward the computer. 'Somebody posted on the Pinehurst neighborhood message board that they saw the Navigator drive away.'

'We saw that. Angles talked to him, but he couldn't tell us any more. In fact, he couldn't swear it was the Satterwite's Navigator in the first place.'

'There's more than one burgundy velvet metallic Navigator in the neighborhood?'

Pavlik smiled. 'The guy wasn't sure it was a Navigator, much less burgundy whatever. Only that it was a dark SUV of some type.'

'He seemed a lot more certain on the message board.'

'They usually do.'

The internet giveth, the internet taketh away.

'If you saw that post, did you also see the one about the peeping Tom?'

'Yup. That one's been a little tougher to pin down. It could have been Walker.'

'That's what we thought, too.'

'We, being you and Sarah?'

'Of course. We were also wondering about the neighbor, Ryan Lyle.' I explained about Lyle's complaints on Friday morning.

'I know Angles interviewed all the neighbors. I'll find out how forthcoming Lyle was about his relationship with Satterwite.' He made a note. 'Any other thoughts?'

'I don't suppose that somebody could have disposed of the body trying to cover up a suicide?'

'That somebody being the widow? Satterwite didn't have life insurance with a suicide exclusion, if that's what you're thinking.'

It was an oldie but a goodie. 'That would only work if Arial had found George's body and worked it out with Marian anyway.'

'And there are better ways of disposing of a body than putting it in the victim's own car and parking it at an airport.'

Touché. 'It also doesn't explain Walker's murder. In fact, *nothing* seems to explain his murder. Could he have been robbing the place? Was anything missing?'

'A couple of charge cards, but nothing else.'

Arial could have stolen the cards and used them to get cash. I took a deep breath. 'Courtney came blasting into Uncommon Grounds with some information on Walker. You may already have it. But I thought, if not . . .'

Pavlik pushed back the desk chair and crossed his legs at the ankles. 'Are you going to tell me?'

'She saw his photo in the paper this morning and recognized him. Not as Mitchell Walker, but as Doug Walker, a volunteer at the dog park.'

Pavlik blinked. 'That I didn't know.' He sat up and pulled a tablet of yellow lined paper toward him to make a note.

'Arial knew him, too.' I felt like a traitor, but I knew I had to tell him. Besides, he'd find out anyway with what little I'd already given him. 'Courtney said she's gone over to the Satterwite house and watched movies with Arial and Walker when the Satterwites were out of town.'

'That means he was familiar with the house. Is that why you asked if anything was missing?'

'Yes. I assume there's no question George Satterwite was killed first?'

Pavlik shook his head.

'That means the man I saw in the garage with the Navigator had to be Walker, just before he was killed himself.'

'Loading up the body.'

'Which would explain the rigor in the large muscles.'

I could see I wasn't telling Pavlik anything he didn't already know. 'Curious thing about Satterwite. He sent the text to his wife and Arial – the one saying he wasn't coming home – at about four-thirty in the afternoon, when he was already on his way.'

I assumed they tracked the phone by the cell towers along the five- to six-hour drive from Minneapolis to Brookhills. 'Does that mean we know what time he got there?'

'Between nine and ten.'

'Arial said Mocha ran away around eleven, so that would jibe with some kind of altercation after he arrived home.'

'Assuming Arial Kingston was telling you the truth.'

There was that, wasn't there? 'George obviously had this planned but didn't want Arial or Marian to tip to the fact he was coming home early. Why?'

'Marian Satterwite thinks he sent the text because he didn't want her to know he was going to be there alone with Arial.'

'Then including Arial on the text was a red herring, meant to mislead Marian?'

'It's possible,' Pavlik said. 'When George sent the text,

Marian was still in the air. Her Milwaukee flight was canceled about two-thirty, so he could have known she was going to be stuck in Chicago and the coast would be clear.'

'We're sure Marian spent Thursday night in Chicago?'

Pavlik grinned. 'Yes, *we* are sure. The Milwaukee flight was the last one for the evening, and it's not unusual for it to be canceled. Marian Satterwite is a gold member or whatever, so the airline put her up for the night and booked her on the ten thirty-five plane the next morning.'

'Nice to have pull. They usually load me on a bus.' Probably the last thing Marian would have tolerated after a long international flight. 'What time did she land here on Friday morning?'

'A little after eleven, which tallies with her arrival at the house around noon when you saw her. We even found the cab driver who delivered her.'

Tight, but without having to wait for luggage, it was definitely doable. And Sarah and I had seen the taxi.

I still didn't like the woman. Or quite trust her. Marian's visit to Uncommon Grounds was supposedly in search of Mocha, but it was obvious from the first that she didn't care about the little dog. Then there was her theatrical revelation about the affair. At first, I'd suspected she'd come to find out what Sarah and I knew about Arial's whereabouts. But maybe the visit was meant to plant information, not elicit it. 'Does Marian seem a little too eager to have us all believe that Arial and her husband were having this affair?'

Pavlik uncrossed and then recrossed his ankles. 'Angles is convinced Marian Satterwite is telling the truth about the affair between her husband and Arial.'

That wasn't good. 'Could she be wrong? Detective Angles, I mean?'

'She could. I talked to Mrs Satterwite today, though, and came to the same conclusion.' He held up his hand. 'And, yes, I could be wrong, too. Or Marian could herself be mistaken about the affair. But there's some evidence to support her claim.'

This was not going well for Sarah's niece. 'What kind of evidence?'

'Gifts – like a purse and jewelry – that were purchased by George Satterwite—'

'But not given to Marian.' Shades of the philandering husband in the movie *Love Actually*. 'Early Christmas shopping?'

'It's July.'

I opened my mouth.

'Before you ask, Marian's birthday was two weeks ago.'

'And no purse or jewelry from George, apparently. Then we're back to the question of why George told Marian he wasn't going to be home and showed up when he expected her to be there.' I hesitated. 'Maybe suspicion was a two-way street in the Satterwite household. Could George have believed there was something going on between Marian and Arial?'

'Maybe,' Pavlik said. 'But there's no evidence he was right. And if your aim is – as I think it is – to get Arial off the hook, that's not going to do it.'

'I know. But as the proud mother of a gay son, I don't like to overlook the possibility of same-sex relationships when I'm looking for homicide motives.'

'Commendable,' Pavlik said.

'Thank you.' I chewed on my lip, thinking about Ryan Lyle again. 'A guy then.'

'Again, no indication.'

Dang. 'Have ballistics come back? Do we know if the same gun was used in both murders?'

Pavlik smiled.

'What?' I asked. 'You keep smiling when I ask questions.'

'Only when you say "do *we* know" this or that.'

I think I blushed. 'Like I'm part of your department, you mean?'

'More like we're Nick and Nora Charles.'

Now I smiled. 'Sorry about that.'

He sat forward and took my hand and turned it palm up. 'I'm not. Just as long as you realize that I can't share everything with you.'

I cocked my head. 'I understand that completely. In fact, I'm a little surprised how much you're telling me on this case. Especially since I'm personally involved.'

'Which seems true of most of my cases these days.'

'But with Sarah's niece involved . . .'

'What?'

'I'm just wondering if you're keeping me in the loop so I'll let you know if Arial gets in contact with Sarah.'

He traced his fingers on my palm. 'Maybe. Plus, you have good ideas sometimes.'

'Thank you.' It's hard to get mad at somebody who's always honest with you. 'Now answer my question way back when. Could ballistics tell from the slugs whether the same gun was used in both shooting?'

'They could and it was.'

'Then whoever killed Mitchell must have taken the gun with him.' Or her. This seemed yet another road that led to Arial.

'Yes,' Pavlik said.

I looked up sharply. 'You know where the gun is?'

'We have it. I didn't tell you that?'

I pulled back my hand. 'No, you didn't. Where? Is it registered?'

Pavlik nodded. 'To George Satterwite.'

'But Marian said they didn't have a gun in the house.'

'Technically, that's true. We found the permit and empty holster in the glove compartment of the Navigator. She may not even have known her husband owned a gun.'

George Satterwite was shot with his own gun. 'Where'd you find it?'

'Rolled up in the rug with George Satterwite's body.'

TWENTY-ONE

'But how could the gun be rolled in the rug with George's body?' I asked Pavlik. 'Mitchell Walker had to be shot with it.'

'It means that the body hadn't been disposed of before Walker was shot.'

My head was hurting. 'I've been assuming that Walker put George in the Navigator, or at least helped. Arial certainly couldn't have done that alone.'

Pavlik's eyebrows went up. 'I'm surprised you're willing to concede that Sarah's niece is involved.'

'She almost has to be in some way. Even Sarah realizes that.'

'That's refreshing,' the sheriff said. 'Do you think Sarah would hide her, knowing that?'

'Honestly? Yes. But only if she genuinely believed that Arial was duped or drawn into this against her will and is running scared now.'

'For what it's worth, Angles has footage of the girl withdrawing money from ATMs on Friday afternoon.'

After I'd seen her at the Satterwite house and she'd subsequently disappeared. 'Using George's card or her own?'

'George and Marian Satterwite's. At the time, we assumed George was with her and had Arial go up to the machine to throw us off.'

I grimaced. 'George may very well have been with her, but—'

'Dead,' Pavlik finished for me.

Suddenly, Arial was sounding more like Thelma, with Louise dead in the back seat. 'Careless to use the ATM without a disguise of some type.'

'You're telling me. She's carrying the dog with her at one.'

Sheesh. 'That means you and Angles knew she had Mocha all this time?'

'And dropped her off at your place? Yup.'

'If you have all this, why haven't you picked her up?'

'Because all activity on the card stopped after Friday. No charge cards used, no money withdrawn. Arial Kingston has disappeared.'

'But how? I assume you still have her car and the Navigator was left at the airport. Has she rented a vehicle? Or bought a plane, train or bus ticket?'

'No rental car or plane ticket. She could have used cash to buy a train or bus ticket, of course. Or hitched a ride with somebody.'

I tried to take a step back and imagine the young woman on her own traveling cross-country to elude the police. She wasn't much older than Eric. 'You honestly think she killed these men?'

Pavlik took my hand again. 'I know she's Sarah's niece, but you said it yourself. At minimum, she was an accessory or accessory after the fact in the death of George Satterwite. Then maybe things just got out of hand.'

'And she blew off the top of Walker's head?'

'Honestly? Yes.'

'What if Walker killed Satterwite and forced Arial to help him?' And *then* she blew off the top of his head.

'Accessory after the fact, in the first crime. Like I said, it's possible. Maybe even self-defense in the Walker murder. But in order to know for sure, we have to find her.' He squeezed my hand. 'Will you please help me?'

First Sarah and now Pavlik.

'Are you asking me to snitch? Let you know if Arial contacts Sarah?'

'Maybe.'

'Well, she hasn't yet. Sarah asked me to help find her before you did.'

See? No secrets from anybody now.

That lasted all of about twelve hours, or until Sarah got me alone at Uncommon Grounds the next afternoon.

'What did Pavlik tell you?' She'd brought a sticky bun over to where I sat rolling silverware into napkins. 'Here.'

'I can't eat that here. I'll get it all over everything.'

'OK, I'll have it.' She sat across from me and pulled the plate toward her.

I had the feeling that had been the plan all along.

'So?' she asked, mouth full of sticky bun.

'So what?'

She swallowed. 'You know what. You were going to tell Pavlik about Mitchell Walker being Doug Walker. You didn't tell Pavlik about him and Arial maybe dating, though. Right?'

'I did not.' It honestly hadn't come up.

'What did he say about Walker? Or did he already know?'

'No.' I put a knife, fork and spoon in the napkin and rolled. Just like George and the gun being rolled into the rug.

'What?'

I looked up. 'What, what?'

'You just shivered.'

Oops. 'Sudden chill. Maybe I'm coming down with something.'

Sarah moved her chair back a smidge. 'So give. What's the working theory?'

I'd been thinking about how much of what Pavlik had told me I could share with Sarah. 'There seems to be consensus that George and Arial were having an affair.'

Sarah stopped shoveling sticky bun, mid-air. 'They're sure?'

'Not caught-in-the-act sure. But remember that Marian mentioned suspicious charges on their credit cards? They were for gifts George never gave her.'

'I knew there had to be something besides sheets.'

'Sheets?'

'Yeah, that Arial washed the sheets every visit.' She popped the bun in her mouth.

'Gotcha.'

She swallowed. 'What else?'

'Nothing else on the affair, but they've traced George Satterwite's credit cards.'

'And?'

I set another roll of silverware on top of my cutlery mountain. 'We were right that Arial is using George's cards. Or she was.'

Sarah set down her fork. 'Damn. They're sure?'

'This time, caught-in-the-act sure. They have her on the security camera at an ATM. With Mocha in one case.'

'Dumb.'

'I said "careless" – but yes. But then Arial isn't a hardened criminal.'

'She isn't yet,' Sarah said. 'Though if two murders don't make her one, I don't know what will.'

'She's a good kid.' Did I really know that?

'They're all good kids. Until they're not. Just like they're all good neighbors until the police find somebody's head in their freezer.'

We had personal experience with that one, but I didn't think we were talking about that case or Arial anymore. 'Something else wrong?'

'Besides my niece being the lead suspect in a double homicide? Not a thing.'

'Sarah?'

'It doesn't have anything to do with Arial. It's Sam. I found Tor on my computer, and I can't figure out what he's doing with it.'

'Tor's a video game?'

She reached over to my phone on the table. 'Would you like to Google it?'

I took the phone from her and returned it to its rightful place. 'Why don't you just humiliate me now with your superior knowledge? Save me the time.'

'Tor is privacy software.'

'What's wrong with that? Everybody shares way too much information online these days. It sounds like Sam is being respon—'

'You use it to get to the dark web.'

Now I sat up. 'Really?'

'Well, that's one of the uses.' She picked up a silverware roll off the pile.

'Now you've ruined these with your sticky fingers,' I said, taking the two rolls on either side of the one she'd picked up.

She went to lick her fingers, only to have the napkin stick to them, clattering silverware to the table. 'Anyway, Tor sends internet traffic through thousands of relays, so there's no way to track it. They call them onion routers.'

'For the many layers of an onion. I've read about that. Wasn't it developed by the US Navy?'

'Back in the nineties,' Sarah said. 'To keep intelligence data safe.'

'But now it's illegal?'

'No, not illegal. I mean, there are all sorts of good reasons to protect your data and search history. Journalists protecting sources and stuff.'

'And dissidents, too, right? So they can't be hunted down and persecuted?'

'Or killed,' Sarah said. 'And then there's the dark side. Criminals, thieves, pornography.'

'Have you asked Sam?'

'I don't know how.'

'How about "Why are you on Tor?"' Dodging subjects wasn't like Sarah.

'I don't mean I'm not going to ask him. I will. I actually deleted the program and have been hoping he'd bring it up himself.'

'Because that would mean he's not doing anything he thinks he has to hide from you?'

'Right. But then all this other stuff happened . . .' She waved her hand.

All this other stuff being Walker's death and Arial's disappearance, of course. 'You still haven't heard from Arial.'

'Are you going to ask me that every five minutes?'

'Of course not. But certainly once a day.'

'Well, I haven't. In fact, I was thinking of going over to the dog park. See what people know about Doug Walker and Arial.'

'Not a bad idea,' I said. 'You want me to go along?'

'Yes, and bring Frank. Going to a dog park without a dog is like going to the circus without a kid. People think you're creepy.'

TWENTY-TWO

When Amy came in at four, Sarah and I picked up Frank and Mocha and headed to the dog park.

'You sure we shouldn't leave fleabag here in the car?'

Said fleabag was sitting on Sarah's lap. My big lug was in the back.

'Of course not,' I said, pulling up in front of the dog park gate. 'Socialization is good for her.'

'But you kind of stole her,' Sarah said, climbing out.

'I didn't steal her. I just didn't give her back,' I said, coming around the car and opening the lift gate to let Frank out and snap the leash on him. 'I doubt we'll see Marian Satterwite here.'

'Like I said, only creepy people come without dogs.' Inside the second gate, she set down Mocha.

I let Frank through both gates and unhooked the leash. The two of them took off down the sidewalk, Mocha in the lead with her little legs churning, Frank at a gentle lope.

'Oh dear,' Becky said, hurrying up to us. 'Has somebody been bothering you?'

'Us? No,' I said, glancing around to see what could have given her that idea. 'We just arrived.'

'I overheard your friend say something about creepy people without dogs. I thought maybe our homeless friends might be causing concern.' She nodded toward a small knot of people on the hillside in the direction Frank and Mocha had disappeared.

'The dogs are up there,' I said, shading my eyes to see Mocha had reached the group and was getting pets from one of them. Frank was nowhere in sight. 'Maybe I should get them?'

'Oh, no. They'd never hurt them,' she said. 'And they typically stay very much to themselves and don't bother anybody. But with Doug gone now . . .' She looked as if she was going to cry.

'Courtney told us about Doug,' I said. 'I'm so sorry. You've met Sarah Kingston? She's Courtney's—'

'Mom,' Sarah said, sticking out her hand.

It beat 'the rather unpleasant woman,' which is the way Becky had described Sarah on their first meeting. And we purposely weren't leading with Sarah's connection to Arial, since the word was out that authorities were looking for her. We didn't want to spook anybody who might otherwise help us.

The two women shook hands, as I looked around for Frank. Still no sign.

'Courtney is such a wonderful girl,' Becky was saying. 'You should be very proud. She's been filling in for Doug.' She held up her hands. 'But don't worry, I'm limiting that to the park. Doug's liaison work with St Catherine's and the homeless requires a more mature person.'

'Somebody like me.' Clare Twohig had come up. She had a push broom in her hand. 'Much more mature.'

'Youngster,' Becky said, smiling. 'And I'm very grateful for your help.'

Clare's dog, Spike, the leggy, long-haired brindle, came bounding down the path and skidded to a stop. Cocking his head, he sniffed the air in front of me.

'Just coffee, I'm afraid,' I said.

He turned his nose toward Sarah.

'What?' she asked.

He nosed her jacket.

She held up her hands in surrender. 'OK, so I have a sticky bun in my pocket. You caught me.'

'You brought a sticky bun to a dog park?' I asked. 'Really?'

'I thought I might have to make friends.'

'Oh, you're going to make friends, all right,' Clare said, as Terra ran up to join Spike and sat in front of Sarah, batting her big brown eyes.

Clare laughed. 'The girl knows how to work it.'

Sarah gave her a scratch behind the ear. 'What a pretty girl. You want a treat?'

Terra stayed sitting as Sarah stuck her hand in her pocket. Spike, on the other hand, jumped up, one paw on each of her shoulders and planted a kiss like he had with me.

'Hey,' Sarah sputtered, as Frank came trotting up. I still didn't see Mocha but pretty much every other dog in the park was certainly descending on us. 'You're cute, but—'

'Sorry, Sarah,' Clare said. 'Spike, off!'

The dog obeyed.

'Tell them to sit, Sarah,' Becky instructed, as Harry joined the pack.

'Umm, sit,' Sarah said, swiping at her mouth with the back of her hand. The other one was still in her pocket.

The whole lot of them obeyed, Terra lifting her butt and replanting it to make the point. I counted nine dogs of various shapes and sizes. 'I hope that's a big sticky bun.'

'I'm not sure everyone would approve of sweets for their dogs,' Becky said. 'Let me get my treats.'

Retrieving them, she handed out the stash. One by one, the other dogs took off, leaving Spike, Terra and Frank still sitting patiently in front of us, as if they knew there was something more to be had.

'Oh, fine.' Sarah took out the bun and unwrapped it from the napkin. Or at least tried to.

'Damn paper is sticking to it.'

'That's why we don't wrap sticky buns in napkins,' I said. 'And put them in our pockets. To bring to the dog park.' I helped her pick off enough to give each of the dogs a bite.

Sarah balled up the remains of the napkin and stuck it back in her pocket. 'That's it. Scram.'

They scrammed, as I held up my sticky, paper-specked hands. 'Isn't there a water faucet around here?'

'There.' Becky pointed to a giant metal water bowl that had been chained down under a spigot.

'Coming?' I said to Sarah.

'No, I'm good. Dogs licked 'em.' She settled on a picnic bench with Clare and Becky.

This was the same woman who worried about a little drool on a coffee table. I rinsed my hands under the running water and dried them on my jeans.

Lydia had joined the group by the time I returned. Princess was nowhere in sight, though I'd yet to check under Frank's butt.

'We were shocked to hear about Doug,' Clare was saying as I sat down next to her. 'Is it true that you found him, Maggy?'

'Marian Satterwite did,' I said, wanting to keep the record straight. 'But Sarah and I were there.'

'Horrible,' Becky said. 'Doug was such a wonderful man. I would never have imagined something like that happening to him. And practically in my backyard.' She shivered.

'I could,' Lydia said. 'There was something off about him.'

Now we're getting somewhere, Sarah's expression said. 'Like what?'

Lydia cocked her head, thinking. 'He was just a little *too* friendly. To the kids, to the homeless who hung out here—'

'That's because he was helping,' Becky said. 'Shame on you, Lydia, for making it look like something . . . well, shameful.'

Lydia's face flamed. 'I didn't mean to imply that he's a pedophile or anything. It's just that here was a grown man – what, nearly thirty?'

'Twenty-nine,' I said.

'Right, and he hangs out at a dog park and homeless shelter. With no visible means of support.'

That was interesting. Nobody – including Pavlik and his people – had said what the man did for a living. 'Could he have been homeless himself?'

'Of course not,' Becky said, as Mocha trotted down the walk toward us. 'He was always clean and neat.'

'That doesn't necessarily mean anything,' Clare said. 'There's a guy at the homeless shelter who presses his jeans.'

I smiled.

'What?' Sarah asked.

'Just reminds me of somebody.'

Sarah didn't ask who. She had other things on her mind. 'My niece was friends with Doug. And Courtney said she hung out with them, too, sometimes. Do you honestly think he—'

Clare held up both hands, palms out. 'Don't listen to Lydia. Doug seemed fine to me.'

Mocha hopped up with her paws on my legs and I lifted

her on to my lap. 'Where have you been, baby? You missed the sticky bun.'

The chihuahua looked stricken.

'Is that Mocha?' Becky said, peering at her. 'I didn't notice when you came in, but isn't this the Satterwites' dog?'

I felt like a dognapper. Of course, Becky would be here and of course she'd recognize Mocha. Not only that, but Lydia would remember the dog she'd rescued. Busted. 'Yes. I—'

'Thank God you found her,' Becky said. 'She's been missing since what – Thursday? Does Marian know?'

'Well, no. I—'

'Good,' Lydia said. 'That woman doesn't deserve a dog.'

'Agreed,' Sarah said. 'Now about Doug Walker. Did he give you an address, Becky?'

'Just email,' she said. 'That's all anybody provides these days. And he does have a job. Programming or something he can do anywhere. He told me he preferred to spend his days outside and to work at night.'

'Like a vampire,' Lydia said, getting up stiffly. 'Well, I've had my say. I'll go now.'

'Bye,' I said to her back as she ambled away.

'Lydia's a little different,' Clare said. 'She didn't like Doug because he made her clean up after Princess.'

'Do you think the people at the rescue mission would know more about him?' I asked.

'St Catherine's?' Clare said. 'I can ask around tomorrow when I'm there. Or you can talk to Sister Anne yourself. What's your interest?' She flushed. 'I mean, besides having found his body.'

I glanced toward Sarah, who was talking to Becky. 'Sarah's niece, Arial, was staying at the Satterwite house with Mocha here when Doug was killed. And she's missing.'

'Arial is?'

'Yes. Well, actually both of them were missing for a while, but Arial still is.'

'Oh dear,' Clare said, as Terra came bounding up. 'I had no idea. Arial is wonderful.'

'Do you know her from here at the dog park?'

'And dog-sitting.' She took a stick the pup was offering her.

'She sat with these guys last time I went to London. I have her scheduled again for next week. I don't know what I'm going to do. You, by any chance, wouldn't—'

'I have all I can handle right now,' I told her. 'Maybe another time.'

'Sure. I guess I can try one of Arial's associates.'

That was interesting. 'She works for a company?'

'Not really a company. More a loose-knit association of pet-sitters. It's very smart, really. There's a central number and website. You tell them what you need, and a sitter comes out and meets with you and your animals. If you hit it off, you're all set. If not, they send somebody else.'

'I'll have to give them a try. Usually, Sarah comes over to stay with Frank, but she grouses. Last time, Courtney stayed overnight, but Sarah doesn't like her doing that either.'

Clare smiled. 'Sarah's so funny.'

That was one way of putting it. 'She is. Do you think I could get a list of the pet-sitters? Or the website? Maybe they could help us find Arial.'

'Of course.' She punched up something on her phone. 'I'll send you the URL for the website. Just click on the "Sitters" heading and you'll see the list.'

My cell dinged and I clicked on the link. 'Perfect. Remember when we had to write these things down? On paper even.'

'You're telling me,' she said, standing up. 'I was caught up in a hack and had to shut down everything, the whole nine yards. Hell, the whole hundred yards. I was lost without my computers and cash registers.'

Any business's nightmare. 'Was this recently? Pavlik said they just turned a big investigation over to Cybercrimes.'

'I wouldn't be surprised if this was part of it. That's why I had the IT guy in last week, beefing up my security at the shop and at home. My passwords and account numbers were being sold on the dark web. I was just glad they didn't get my social security number.'

The dark web again. 'Are you familiar with Tor?'

'Oh, sure. I use the browser all the time. Especially when I'm overseas.'

'Really?'

'Of course. That way you don't have to worry about security if you're using unsecured networks.'

'So there are legitimate reasons to have it on your computer?'

'Definitely,' she said. 'Why?'

'I just heard it could get you on the dark web.'

'I understand it can. But, believe me, I don't go there.'

Sadly, the same couldn't be said of Clare's personal information, I thought as she whistled for the dogs and waved goodbye.

'Fat lot of good you did, sitting there passing the time with Clare while I was pumping Becky for information,' Sarah grumbled, as we loaded the dogs into the Escape.

'Did you ask if her husband might have killed George Satterwite?'

'Please. Give me a little credit for tact. She mentioned that she hadn't been sleeping well, so I used the opportunity to ask about noise from the theater. Becky said they don't actually hear anything but Ryan is convinced his headaches are linked to the theater. He was gathering evidence to go to a lawyer, but now . . .' She shrugged.

'He doesn't have to. Interesting.'

'It doesn't really matter anyway,' Sarah said. 'Ryan Lyle's a dead-end.'

That surprised me, especially after our earlier conversation. 'How do you figure that?'

'Because we already have Walker for Satterwite's murder and I'm good with that.'

'Yes, but—'

'But nothing. Walker killed Satterwite. Nice and neat – let's leave it that way.'

It hadn't been nice *or* neat, but I took her point. 'So now you just want to know who killed Walker?'

'I couldn't care less who killed him. But I do care about Arial. Your firecracker alibi may not be enough to keep her out of jail.'

'I thought our mission was to *find* Arial.'

'And then get her off.'

I feared that second part wasn't going to be as easy as my partner made it seem.

We dropped the dogs off at my house and headed west into the countryside.

'You complain incessantly, but it's because of my conversation with Clare that we have any lead at all,' I pointed out as we drove.

'A nun.'

'A nun who might be able to give us more information on Mitchell "Doug" Walker.'

'For all the good that will do us.'

'Geez.' I stopped the car. 'Do you have a better idea?'

'No,' Sarah said. 'Why are we stopped in the middle of the street?'

'Because you're being yowly.'

A horn sounded behind me and I stepped on the gas, lifting a hand in apology.

'I'm always yowly,' Sarah said. 'Today that's a reason to get us killed?'

'The speed limit on this road is twenty-five miles an hour. I don't think we were in any real danger.'

'Never know. Could have been a farm tractor coming. Or a horse and carriage.' She looked side to side. 'It's pretty rural out here. How do the homeless get out here anyway?'

'I think I've seen a St Catherine's bus,' I said.

'Is that what that is? I thought it was for a senior center or something.'

I pulled into the parking lot, just as a woman in a dark suit came out of the door and down the steps, searching in her purse. She looked up and saw us getting out of the car. 'Can I help you?'

'We were looking for Sister Anne. Clare Twohig suggested we stop by.'

'I'm Sister Anne, but I'm afraid I'm just on my way out.'

'Would you mind if I gave you a call then or—'

'What do you know about Doug Walker?' Sarah blurted out.

Sister Anne backed up. 'I'm afraid we don't speak to reporters.'

'We're not reporters,' I said, holding up my hand in apology.

'This is Sarah Kingston and we're looking for her niece, Arial. We understand Doug was a friend of hers.'

The sister's face softened. 'He was, and I'm happy to help Arial. She's a lovely girl.' She checked her watch. 'I do have to go, though. Could you call or email me?'

'Of course.' I pulled out my phone and punched up contacts to add her. 'What's your email?'

'I'll put it in, if you like,' she said. 'Ours here are a little convoluted. Safety reasons, you know.'

I didn't know, but I handed over my phone.

She tapped in the email and then clicked out. As she started to hand me back the phone, she stopped. 'Oh, you have the girls' website. We're so proud of them.'

'The girls?' I glanced at my phone's screen and saw the website page Clare had sent me.

'They all stayed with us at one time or another, you know,' Sister Anne went on. 'Doug is the one who suggested pet-sitting as a way of getting back on their feet.' She turned to Sarah now. 'Arial helped recruit the girls and train them. You should be very proud.'

'Yes,' Sarah said.

'Beyond building self-esteem and giving the girls a way of earning money, it's a win-win. They have someplace to stay – besides here, of course – and their clients have responsible caregivers for their beloved pets.'

I would have expected Sarah to remark that if the girls were so responsible, they wouldn't be homeless in the first place. As it was, though, my opinionated partner was staying remarkably – and blessedly, as the sister would likely put it – quiet.

But that meant it was up to me to ask the uncomfortable question. 'Do the pet-owners know their sitters are homeless?' I was thinking about Mocha mingling with the homeless group at the dog park.

Sister Anne raised her eyebrows. 'Shame on you. God doesn't judge us by our pocketbooks.'

As she spoke, the rescue door opened and a man in tattered jeans came trotting down the stairs toward us. 'See you next time, Sister Anne.'

She reflexively put her hand to her nose to fend off the body odor wafting off him as he passed. 'Blessed day, Homer.'

Glancing back at me, she put her hand down. 'We do have showers and clean clothes for our residents. Some, like Homer there, just prefer not to partake.'

Again, no smart-ass remark from Sarah. My partner was standing back and letting me handle this one for some reason.

I held up the phone. 'Do any of these girls come back in between jobs? We'd love to find out if they've seen Arial.'

She peered at the list of names. 'I'm afraid not. Or I should say I'm overjoyed, really. They've been able to support themselves and move on from us here. That's what we pray for, after all.'

She dipped back into her bag and this time came up with the keys. 'I must go. Have a good evening.'

'You, too,' Sarah called after her. Then to me in a lower voice, 'I don't know why, but even as an adult, I'm intimidated by nuns.'

I didn't answer.

'Priests, not so much. Isn't that weird?'

'Uh-huh.'

'You're not listening to me.'

'No.'

'I guess you can't identify because you weren't raised Catholic.'

'No.' I turned to her. 'But thinking of all things sacred, do you believe in the holy grail? Because we may just have stumbled on it.'

TWENTY-THREE

'I didn't know Lutherans believed in the quest for the holy grail,' Sarah said. Apparently, nuns not only made her nervous, but chatty. 'Searching for those tiny plastic cups you guys use for communion wouldn't be much of a quest.'

'Sometimes there's a communal chalice,' I protested. 'If you don't mind the germs, I mean. But for the last time, I was speaking figuratively back there.'

'And a little overdramatically, don't you think? Must have been the religious setting.'

I took away her own wine and set it down on the coffee table. We were at her house and, yes, had ordered pizza. Again. 'Focus.'

Sarah rested her elbows on her knees, chin on her laced hands. 'Shoot.'

Sheesh. I shouldn't have let her open the wine before the pizza arrived. Apparently, she should have fed more of the sticky bun to herself and less to the dogs. 'Consider this: when Courtney Frank-sat for me, what's the first thing she asked for?'

Sarah blinked twice. 'Permission?'

Good answer, actually. 'Yes, from you. From me, she wanted the Wi-Fi access code. Pavlik scolded me for giving it to her.'

Sarah looked affronted. 'He doesn't trust Courtney?'

'It's not personal. He just says that people are too free with their personal information and it ends up on the dark web. I keep my passwords in a notebook in the top drawer of my desk.'

Sarah opened her mouth, but I pre-empted her. 'And, yes, I know what else I keep in my drawers. But my point is that people don't secure that kind of information in their own homes.'

'I don't write that stuff down.'

'How do you remember them?'

'Easy. I just use my birthday for all of them.'

Geez, how could somebody who knew what Tor was *not* know to set up strong passwords. 'Please tell me you're kidding.'

'Don't worry,' Sarah said. 'I switch it up. Sometimes I type it forwards, other times backwards, to confuse them.'

I didn't know about 'them,' but I was confused. 'How do you know which way you did it for each website, if you don't write it down?'

'For a while, I used forwards for websites that started with a vowel and backwards for consonants, but I thought that was too logical.'

I would beg to differ. 'What do you do now?'

'I do whatever I feel like when I register and then when I sign in, if one doesn't work, I just use the other. Before they block access, they always give you at least two chances.'

'Which is all a hacker would need, too.'

Sarah flipped open the pizza box. 'Hey, if they want my information, I figure they'll find a way of getting it.'

'That's a pretty pathetic way of looking at it,' I said. 'It's up to you to protect your information.' I was starting to identify with Pavlik's frustration on the subject.

But talking to Sarah about it right now wasn't going to get us anywhere. 'Anyway, back to what I was saying: people, except you, tend to write down their passwords.'

'Right.' She was inspecting the pizza, presumably for the biggest slice.

'So you understand what I'm saying.'

'Not a bit.'

'Pavlik said Walker sold papers he got off the internet to his friends when he was in school.'

'Stupid kids,' Sarah said, picking up her glass again and brandishing it. 'You don't have to pay to plagiarize.'

'You're right that pretty much anything you want is available online free.' I took the glass and handed her a slice of pizza. It was chicken pesto this time. Our version of walking on the wild side. 'What if Walker was putting the homeless "girls," as Sister Anne called them, into houses as pet-sitters in order to steal passwords and personal information to sell on the dark web? There's been a rash of identity thefts in the area that the sheriff's department just turned over to the state cybercrimes unit. Maybe Walker was behind it.'

'Seems kind of low-tech to actually have to go into houses.' Suddenly, Sarah was paying attention.

'But think of it. Notebooks full of passwords, account numbers from checkbooks, charge cards. Birthdays, social security numbers – we keep it all in our homes. Think of the access somebody has when they're staying in our homes alone.'

'Some of the owners must have security cameras. They'd see.'

'See what? It's not like the girls are carting out television sets or rifling dresser drawers for jewelry. So what if the dog-sitter is sitting at the computer? They were given permission to use it. Or looking for a piece of paper in a desk drawer? You'd have to know you'd been robbed to even look at the footage that closely. And, like you said, most people would assume their information was stolen online, not from right inside their homes and under their dogs' noses.'

'I said that?' Sarah asked.

'Sort of.'

'But how does Arial fit into this? She's not homeless.'

'But she is a friend of Doug's and a dog-sitter. Sister Anne says she even recruited other girls for him.'

Sarah sat back. 'We're right back where we started, but now Arial is not only a murderer but a cyber thief. Thanks, friend.'

'I'm sorry.' I didn't know what else to say. 'It should make you feel better about Sam, though.'

'What does Sam have to do with this?'

'Nothing – which is what I mean. You found Tor on the computer and assumed Sam had downloaded it and was using it for . . . well, I don't know what.'

'Searching for porn was my first thought.'

Please. 'You don't have to use Tor to do that. It's all over the web.'

'They make you pay for it these days. Whole damn internet has been monetized.'

Well, boo-hoo-hoo. 'Anyway, you said that Arial stays at your house between jobs. Maybe she downloaded it, not Sam.'

'Possible,' Sarah said, considering. 'If you're sure of all this, why aren't you at home right now, telling Pavlik?'

Good question. 'I guess I wanted to talk it through with you first. See if it all hung together before . . .'

'Before adding another charge to my niece's rap sheet and sending the cops to confiscate my computer.'

'Well, yeah.'

Sarah stood and picked up her glass. 'How's this? You go home to your honey.'

'What'll you do?' I asked, standing, too. 'Will Courtney and Sam be home soon?'

'Couple of hours. But don't you worry. I've got my friends here.' She held up the wine glass and pointed to the pizza. 'We'll be just fine.'

I'd been summarily kicked out of the Kingston/Harper abode. I wasn't worried about leaving Sarah alone with the wine. She really wasn't that much of a drinker. The pizza, though, was a goner.

Back home, Pavlik just listened as I laid out my theory. We were sitting on the couch, Frank with his head on my feet, Mocha on Pavlik's lap.

'What do you think?' I asked when I was finished.

'It's plausible,' he said. 'I'll have Hallonquist go through the list of cyber victims.'

'See if they have dogs?'

'Silly as that may sound, yes. And used a dog-sitter, of course.'

Mike Hallonquist probably wouldn't be thrilled to have the cases dropped back in his lap. 'I thought the identify thefts had been turned over to the state.'

'They have, but this local angle will be much easier for Hallonquist to run down. He's met these people. May even know off the top of his head whether they have dogs.'

'Or cats or any other pets, don't forget. According to the website, they've expanded beyond dogs.'

'I didn't recognize any of the names on the list, except Arial. You?'

'No. Though who knows if they're using their real names.

Personally, I find Kitty Belle and Tippy Greenfield highly suspect.' And maybe absolute genius if they were moonlighting as adult film stars.

'Doug/Dog Walker was equally cheesy.'

'Somebody had too much time on his hands,' I agreed. 'Which reminds me. Did Walker have a job?'

'Freelance IT work – jibes nicely with your theory.'

It did, and it also reminded me of something. 'Clare Twohig might have been part of your hack.'

'The antique store owner?'

'Uh-huh. And she told me she used Arial as a dog-sitter.'

'I'll let Hallonquist know.' Pavlik had his phone out. 'Can you send me the link to the sitter website?'

'Of course.' I forwarded it. 'I'm not sure if there are email addresses for the individual sitters or you have to contact them through the website.' And, presumably, either Arial or Doug.

'We'll sort it out.' Pavlik finished his text and set down his phone. 'Good work.'

'Sarah didn't think so. This all just gets Arial into more hot water. Sister Anne said Arial recruited the girls for Walker.'

'He's a cyber-pimp.'

'Is that a thing?'

'If not, it is now.'

I wiggled my toes, causing Frank to groan at the disruption. Mocha hopped off Pavlik's lap and lay down next to the sheepdog. 'How does this fit into the murders? Maybe George Satterwite caught on to what they were doing?'

'It would explain why he came home unexpectedly. Awkward crime to prove on your own, though. It's not like you can catch people in the act of looting your physical possessions.'

'What about Castle doctrine?'

Pavlik peered at me. 'Are you asking if it would pertain?'

'I guess I am. Could George Satterwite shoot Doug Walker because Walker was in his house, stealing information?'

'If Walker was trespassing, he could.'

'But assuming Satterwite confronted Walker, why was it Satterwite who ended up dead?' Or, at least, ended up dead first. 'They struggled for the gun?'

'There was no powder residue on Walker's hands.'

I closed my eyes and opened them. 'Maybe he wore gloves. Or peed on his hands.'

'Either one is possible, though using urine to eliminate GSR isn't proven.'

And was pretty disgusting anyway. But I was entertaining even darker thoughts. 'If Walker didn't shoot Satterwite, then . . .'

'Arial,' Pavlik confirmed.

'George Satterwite was shot from close range, you said. Maybe Arial grabbed the gun and shot George, trying to protect Walker.'

'Who, in turn, was shot a few hours later.'

Hard to imagine two accidents. Self-defense for the second murder? 'Arial had blood on her cheek before Walker was killed. Maybe he hit her.'

'And after you left for work, she went back in and shot him? Are you discounting the shots you heard?'

I lifted my shoulders and dropped them. 'Arial is our only suspect, so maybe I was wrong. And what about Ryan Lyle?'

'What about him?'

'There's a back door to the theater room. It's behind big heavy curtains, but somebody could have come in that way.'

'Angles spoke to Lyle and you're right that he has a grudge. He even admitted lurking outside the Satterwite house on Thursday night with his cell phone testing for sound.'

The app. The peeping Tom had a cell phone, not a gun. I sat up straight. 'What time? Wouldn't the app capture the gunshots, even if they were muffled by the acoustical treatment of the theater?'

'Excellent deduction,' Pavlik said appreciatively. 'We're having the data further analyzed, but it appears that the app registered one shot at eleven-ten.'

An app measuring noiseless noise determines time of death. 'How does that compare with the medical examiner's finding?'

'Time of death tallies.'

'Ryan didn't see anything though?'

'No, he didn't even realize what he'd captured until Angles asked to see it.'

'So where does that leave us?' I said, laying my hand on

Pavlik's thigh. 'We know George Satterwite was killed at eleven-ten p.m. If I heard gunshots at seven-fifteen the next morning and Arial was outside with me and George was already dead, there's no—'

I stopped.

'What are you thinking?'

'I'm thinking your jeans look perfectly pressed.'

Pavlik blinked. 'Thank you, I think. But what does that have to do with anything?'

'It has to do with everything.'

TWENTY-FOUR

Sarah would have cited me for excess drama. Pavlik just waited.

'You despise wrinkles,' I said. 'Right?'

'Right.' The sheriff's patience, though epic, was running out.

'Would you put on a white linen suit to take a puddle jumper from Chicago to Milwaukee?'

'I wouldn't put on a white linen suit for pretty much any reason. But I assume you're referring to Marian Satterwite. May I assume she was wearing a white linen suit when she came home on Friday?'

'Yup.' I stood up, this time dislodging both Frank and Mocha. 'Sarah accuses me of being dramatic, but I don't hold a candle to Marian standing there in the theater in that blood-streaked suit.'

Pavlik, who hadn't been here for the main act, was trying to follow. 'This was when she thought it was her husband's body.'

'Or so we're to believe. She cradled him in her arms and then, realizing it wasn't George, stood up and let his head hit the marble floor.'

'And it's the linen suit you're questioning?'

'Exactly.'

'She'd been on a long trip. The suit was the last clean clothes she had with her.'

'Which begs the next question: who packs a white linen suit in their carry-on luggage? It would have been a wrinkled mess. And hers wasn't.'

'Then she ironed it.'

'*You* would have. But her?' I tried to picture Marian Satterwite in the Red Roof Inn, ironing an expensive suit. 'I just don't see it.'

'Let's take a step back here. We know that her flight *was*

canceled, she *did* check into that hotel and she *was* on the ten thirty-five flight the next morning.'

'You're sure of that.'

'Absolutely. It's not like you can slip somebody your ticket these days and have them take your place. Or not show up, but still be on the plane manifest.'

I chewed my lip. 'I know she did it.'

'Are you sure you just don't want to believe Arial did it?'

'What about the shots we heard?'

Pavlik shrugged, as his phone rang. 'Like you said, you must have been wrong.'

'I—'

'Just this one time.' He dug his phone out of his pocket. 'Hello?'

'Dad,' he mouthed to me.

I held up a hand to indicate that I understood and scribbled him a note before picking up Mocha and tiptoeing out of the room. Frank followed me.

When I got to the hall, I put Mocha down. 'Road trip, anyone?'

It was nearly eleven at night, so I wasn't surprised I had to ring three times before Marian Satterwite came to the door.

'Maggy?' she said, squinting. 'What—'

'Surprise! Look what I found.' I held up a squirming Mocha.

'Oh, how nice.' She looked anything but pleased.

Mocha was even more unhappy. I'd left Frank in the car.

'And that's not all,' I said, edging toward the door. 'They found Arial.'

'Really!' She backed up to let me into the foyer. 'Where?'

'You're not going to believe it.' I strolled down the hall toward the theater as I spoke. 'She was right under our noses.'

'She's not here, if that's what you're thinking.' Marian Satterwite hadn't moved.

I set Mocha down in the theater room and turned. 'Now, why would I think that?'

'I . . . well, I don't know.' She joined me. 'You barged right into the house, for one thing.'

'I'm sorry. Just had to see this room again. Want to go out, Mocha?' I went to the back door and pushed aside the heavy curtains to open it. Mocha just looked at me. 'Maybe not.' I closed the door and let the curtains fall.

'Had the crime-scene cleaners in, I see,' I said, returning to the center of the room. 'Are you going to replace the rug?'

Marian cocked her head. 'That's a little insensitive, isn't it?'

'Because your husband's body was rolled in it? I suppose. But I'm wondering why you didn't remark on the rug being gone when we found Walker's body.'

'I assumed George had sent it out to be cleaned. Mocha has . . . accidents.'

The little dog stopped and glanced at her, before squatting on the marble floor and letting loose.

'Retaliation pee,' I said. 'She really doesn't like you.'

'Well, I don't like her either,' Marian said, snagging the coat that still hung over the theater chair before the puddle could spread in that direction.

'Cashmere,' I said. 'I'm sure you have paper towels or something that will absorb better.'

Marian didn't move. 'Why are you here?'

'I told you. To bring back Mocha and tell you about Arial.'

'So you said. But you haven't told me where they took Arial into custody.'

'Why are you assuming she's alive?'

She couldn't quite conceal the relief on her face, quickly replaced by concern. 'Oh dear. She's been killed, too.'

'No. Just wondering why you haven't asked if she's OK.' I tapped the tweeter thing on the top of the speaker. 'The last two people she was with are both dead, after all. Murdered.'

'By her.'

'That's what somebody would like us to believe.'

'Like who?'

'Like you.'

She backed up a half step before she caught herself and faced me. 'You've lost your mind.'

'No, but I think maybe you have, or maybe you're just

insanely jealous. You honestly believed Arial and your husband were having an affair.'

'I saw the charge card bills. The gifts he bought her.'

'Actually, those were gifts she bought herself. Arial is a little thief, but not a murderer. And she doesn't fool around with married men, either.'

'You mean—'

'I mean that she was helping herself to your charge cards, but not to your husband. But she must have told you that when you drove up here, believing George had set up a rendezvous, and found them in each other's arms.'

'No, I—'

'Oh, that's right. You were busy dropping your coat on a chair and picking up the gun he'd brought with him.'

'It was George's gun?' That surprised her.

'Oh, yes,' I said. 'Properly registered and usually kept in the Navigator's glove compartment. Maybe he bought it because of all the driving he did, but, regardless, George brought it into the house that night to confront Arial. He only set it down when she fell apart on him.'

'Fell apart about what?'

'I just told you. Arial is an identity thief. She and Walker had been stealing charge card numbers, financial institution information and passwords from households all over south-eastern Wisconsin.'

'But then why was she—'

'In his arms? He was comforting her. Maybe your husband was a pushover or maybe Arial is just a good actress and played on his sympathies. Or maybe – just maybe – she genuinely wanted out of the scheme Walker had cooked up, and hoped you and your husband would help her.'

'She didn't tell me any of this.'

I smiled what I hoped was a humorless smile. 'Oh, but she did. She confessed it all, and you used it to keep her quiet. You knew she couldn't go to the police about what you'd done without incriminating herself.'

'Shooting George was an accident. He grabbed for the gun and—'

'It went off. Yada, yada, yada.' I picked up Mocha. 'Poor

little Mocha here, she must have been scared to death. She loved your husband.'

'I loved my husband.'

'Yet you admit you killed him.'

'I—' The realization that she was being played dawned on her. 'You didn't find Arial at all, did you?'

'Why do you say that? Because you gave her your debit card and told her to withdraw enough money on Friday to be long gone by the time your husband's body was discovered? You knew everyone would assume she'd killed George.' I cocked my head. 'Unfortunately for you, she didn't go far enough.'

She made a move toward me. 'How—'

'How far did she go? Or how did I know?' I waved my hand. 'It doesn't matter which. I can answer both. How far was just down the road. Arial was staying with the homeless who sleep in the dog park. She'd made friends in the group, recruiting pet-sitters. They all hoped they'd be next to land a plum job and were happy to help and keep her safe. Besides, nobody ever really looks at the homeless, and she was careful to keep her sweatshirt hood up and stay away from people who might recognize her.'

'But how?' she asked again.

'Mocha here,' I said, scratching the little girl behind one ear. 'Ran right up to the homeless group in the park, when she tends to be standoffish with strangers. She didn't even come back for treats. It didn't register at the time, but once I gave it some thought . . .' I shrugged, and Mocha licked my nose. 'That park and Doug Walker were the center of everything,' I continued. 'Which reminds me: why did you shoot Walker?'

'I didn't. Arial called him to help us with George's body. She said he'd keep it quiet.'

I shook my head. 'Not likely. It was Walker who had the upper hand in that relationship. He really was like a cyber-pimp. He recruited Arial and then used her to recruit other girls. Girls who had no homes and were happy to do his dirty work, while he took most of the profit. Arial couldn't have controlled him – he controlled her.'

'Which must be why she cracked and killed him.'

'You lying bitch.' Arial pushed aside the curtain over the door and stepped in. 'Marian killed him. She waited until he had loaded George's body in the Navigator and helped us clean up, then she shot him in the head.'

'You really should have closed the door first,' I told Marian. 'Arial and I heard the shots, as did your neighbors.'

I turned to Arial. 'Quick thinking, though, planting the idea it was firecrackers.'

The girl didn't seem to know what to say, except, 'Thank you.'

Marian sure did, though. 'You said it yourself, Maggy. The man was a pimp. He was going to blackmail us and he would never have stopped. Right, Arial?'

She didn't answer.

'Arial and I had it all set up,' Marian said. 'She agreed to keep her mouth shut and disappear. But the two of us alone couldn't take care of everything.'

'"Everything" being disposing of your husband's body. Don't you feel any remorse? The man wasn't even cheating on you. He saw the purchases Arial had made on his charge cards about the same time you did. But you came to two entirely different conclusions. You were willing to believe that your husband was cheating on you. He, on the other hand, suspected that his charge card had been stolen and he believed he knew by whom. When George texted that he was delayed, Marian, he knew you would be stuck in Chicago. It didn't matter to him whether you were home or not. He intended to arrive unannounced and confront Arial with his suspicions. He knew that she was young and that he could rattle her.'

'He wanted to give me a chance to tell the police myself.' Arial was close to tears.

I could see why George Satterwite wanted to help her. I was ready to cry myself. I shook it off. 'How did you get the blood on your face?'

'Doug was in the garage with George's body. He told me to get the gun, so he could roll it into the rug. I'd just picked it up when I heard you pull up the driveway. I must have touched my face.'

'What did you do with the gun?'

Arial swiped at her cheek as if the blood was still there. 'I left it on a chair and came out to greet you. She must have—'

'He came in and threatened me,' Marian said.

'And you picked up the gun.'

'He came toward me and tried to take it.'

'To put in the *rug*.' Arial was still defending the man.

As far as I was concerned, nobody here deserved defending. Except for Mocha. 'You're better off with none of these people,' I told her.

'I swear the gun just went off,' Marian said.

'Twice,' I said dryly. 'How did Mocha get shot?'

'Oh, I don't know,' Marian said irritably. 'What does it matter?'

'She said it was a ricochet,' Arial said.

'George or Doug?' I like to get my facts straight.

'George,' Arial said. 'Mocha was so upset, and in pain.'

'She ran off,' I said.

Arial hung her head.

'Will you please suck it up?' Marian snapped at her. 'There are two of us. We can take care of her and—'

'I don't think so.' Sarah stepped out from behind the curtain, her beloved gun in hand. Sans purse.

'Arial was where I said she would be?' I asked.

'Right there in the dog park.' She held up her cell phone. 'And, before you ask, I've got every word recorded and Pavlik is on his way. He's not very happy with you.'

'I'm sure.'

'You're sure right.' My fiancé had used the front door. 'You couldn't have told me what you had in mind?'

'You were talking to your dad and I didn't want to interrupt.' Or be deterred.

'Next time, interrupt.'

'I will.'

'Good. Thank you.'

'You're welcome. I know it's important to you.'

'It should be—' He interrupted himself. 'You're playing me again.'

'Maybe.' I smiled. 'But guess what the good news is?'

'What?'

I held up Mocha. 'You get to keep the dog.'

TWENTY-FIVE

'I still don't understand,' Sarah said. 'How did Marian get up here to Brookhills? Her flight was canceled.'

Arial Kingston and Marian Satterwite had been taken into custody. Arial wouldn't do as much time as Marian, but she'd do some unless she could somehow cut a deal.

As for the five of us – Sarah, Pavlik, Frank, Mocha and me – we were sitting in our living room. Pavlik and me on the couch, Sarah on a chair, Mocha on Frank. Frank on the floor. It was three a.m.

'She rented a junker,' Pavlik said. 'You know, at one of those off-brand places near O'Hare Airport. She picked it up at eight-thirty Thursday night, checked into the hotel, messed up the room and then drove up to Brookhills. The rental company said the car was returned the next morning around nine.'

'If Marian left her house right after I did on Friday morning,' I said, 'she had just enough time to get back to O'Hare, return the car, change clothes and walk on to the ten-thirty-five flight, as if she'd spent the night in Chicago.'

'She just left Arial there at the house with Walker's brains spread out on the floor and drove back to Chicago?' Sarah asked.

'This one they didn't have to clean up,' I said. 'And to be fair, Arial hopped into the other car and drove away with George's body. Nobody is exactly a schoolgirl in this.'

'I suppose not,' Sarah said. 'But how did you know?'

'The murderer wore white,' Pavlik said. In answer to Sarah's unspoken 'huh?' he added, 'I know. I don't get it either.'

'Sure you do,' I said. 'I've already told you that a woman wouldn't take a white linen suit on a long trip to Sydney, especially if she was carrying on her luggage.'

'But I thought we'd agreed that even if it was wrinkled, she could have ironed it.'

'Marian Satterwite iron?' Sarah said. 'Please.'

'See?' I told Pavlik. 'But also, there were the black clothes in the dirty clothes hamper in the Satterwite laundry room. Arial wouldn't have left her own wash in there and, from what Sarah had said, I knew she already would have washed whatever the Satterwites had left behind.'

'She is her mother's clean freak,' Sarah said. 'You think the clothes were from Marian's carry-on?'

'Wait,' Pavlik said. 'You can surmise that from miscellaneous black clothes in the hamper?'

'If you travel a lot, it's easiest to pack mostly black,' I said. 'Goes with everything, looks chic.'

'I'll take your word for it,' Pavlik said, shaking his head. 'And why did Marian find it necessary to unpack during her quick trip home to kill her husband?'

'She had to have room to take her suit.'

'But white linen? Please,' Sarah said. 'What a drama queen.'

'I thought so, too,' I told her. 'And you know how I love my drama.'

'Amen. So that was it? The suit and the wash?'

'And the coat.'

'What coat?' Pavlik asked.

'In the theater room. There was a cashmere coat draped over one of the chairs.'

'So?'

'So, it's July. Nobody wears a wool coat in July in Wisconsin. It hits fifty degrees, we're pulling out the Coppertone.'

'Whose was it, then?' Sarah asked.

'Again, Marian's.'

'But wait,' Pavlik said, putting an arm around me. 'You just said nobody would wear a wool coat in July.'

'Not here in Wisconsin. But on her trip, she would have. And for the very same reason she *wouldn't* have taken a white linen suit on the trip.'

'And what's that?' Pavlik asked.

'She went to Sydney, remember?'

'So?' This from Sarah.

'So Australia is in the southern hemisphere. It's winter there.'

*   *   *

Sarah had gone home about four a.m., and Pavlik and I were still cuddled on the couch. The kids were cuddled on the floor.

'I'm really impressed,' he said into the top of my head. 'That was some great detecting.'

Take *that*, Cindy Angles. 'Thank you. That means a lot coming from you, Jake.'

He kissed the top of my head. 'It scares me when you call me Jake. Makes me think it's a preamble to something serious. Like another shoe is going to drop.'

'The other shoe to using your first name would be using your last name.'

'It would.' He pulled me close. 'Are you taking mine or keeping yours?'

'I'll probably keep Thorsen, because it's Eric's, too. Do you mind?'

'Uh-uh.'

We were quiet for a while. 'What will happen to Arial?'

'Honestly? She's in big trouble.'

'Not as big as Marian Satterwite.'

'No, thankfully. But she will be prosecuted along with the other sitters from St Catherine's.'

'You'll turn it over to Cybercrimes?'

'It's their case. Which is just fine with me, and Hallonquist is delighted. And since we already put Sarah's cousin in jail—'

'Ronny's more of a *pseudo*-cousin,' I said.

'OK, pseudo-cousin. I don't want to do the same for her niece. Especially when I feel sorry for the girl.'

'Arial hasn't had it easy, from what Sarah said. Families.' I sat up and turned to face him. 'Is your dad all right?'

'You mean the call?'

'Uh-huh.' It had been after ten, which violated an unwritten rule about late calls in the Pavlik family.

'He's fine. Just wanted to tell me he's decided the offer on the condo is too low. He's pulling it off the market.'

'But he sold his couch.'

'And rug. And chairs. And God knows what else. He'll get new ones.'

'I don't know your dad well, obviously. But it sounds like

he's trying to deal with your mom's death in the best way he can. He just doesn't quite know how.'

Pavlik pulled me close and rested his chin on the top of my head. 'I don't think it ever entered his mind that she'd die before him and he'd have to go on alone. I've honestly never seen two people so much in love as my mom and dad. Susan used to say they set the bar too high for us.'

I drew in a deep, steadying breath, trying to ignore the twinge I always felt at Susan's name. Silly, sophomoric twinge, but there nonetheless. I'd have to get over that. Pavlik and Susan shared a child together, as did Ted and I. We'd all be in each other's lives for a very long time.

And that was OK.

I snuggled in. 'I think there's a lot to be said for shooting high.'